Praise for Dell Shannon's
ROOT OF ALL EVIL

"One of Shannon's best."—*Observer*

"A Luis Mendoza novel means superlative suspense."
—*Los Angeles Times*

"Another racy, well built story of Lieutenant Mendoza. . . .
Very good value, consistently gripping."
—*Daily Telegraph*

"Lieutenant Mendoza, an old favorite, is back again and in
form."—*Spectator*

**Other *Mystery Scene* books available
from Carroll & Graf:**

DELL SHANNON
ROOT OF ALL EVIL

Carroll & Graf Publishers, Inc.
New York

Copyright © 1964 by William Morrow and Company, Inc.

All rights reserved

Published by arrangement with the author's estate.

First Carroll & Graf edition 1993

Carroll & Graf Publishers, Inc.
260 Fifth Avenue
New York, NY 10001

ISBN 0-88184-978-2

Manufactured in the United States of America

How pleasant it is to have money,
heigh-ho!
How pleasant it is to have money.
—Arthur Hugh Clough, *Dipsychus*

One

Master John Luis Mendoza and Miss Teresa Ann Mendoza yelled. Collectively and loudly they howled into the night, and their joint volume was astonishing.

After a long moment, Alison sat up and said sleepily, "Damn." She slid her legs over the side of the bed and groped for her slippers. Mendoza mumbled something indistinctly profane.

"All right, I'm *coming*," said Alison crossly, fumbling for her robe.

"—Senseless," said Mendoza.

The collective howls redoubled from the next room. "I'm beginning to think you're right," said Alison, yawning. She felt her way over to the door and put on the hall light. He heard her soothing voice reassuring the twins.

He shut his eyes again and tried to close his ears, but it was hopeless. After three minutes he got up, switched on the bedside lamp, put on his robe, and joined Alison. "It is simply not common sense," he said. "At this age, they don't know or care who comes running when they yell. We've got enough money, God knows, to hire a nursemaid. Let *her* stay up all night—in the back bedroom. With the door shut." He took Miss Teresa Ann from Alison and looked down at her screwed-up small face without, at the moment, much affection. Miss Teresa Ann had a good deal of curly black hair and a pair of large brown eyes framed in long black lashes, but right now the eyes were squeezed tight shut, the rosebud mouth was open, and she was emitting regular bellows. Resignedly Mendoza walked up and down joggling her.

"Ridiculous," he said. "If anybody had told me a couple of years ago I'd be walking the floor with a baby at 2:30 A.M. just like any ordinary domesticated male—!"

Alison passed him, going the opposite direction, joggling Master John Luis. "Not exactly your forte," she agreed with somewhat malicious amusement.

"And all so unnecessary! But no, you remember all those tear-jerking Victorian novels about the poor little rich child whose mama and daddy left her to the servants— *Caray*, how can one five-month-old infant make such a racket? Do they *all* do this?"

"Most of them," said Alison. They had to raise their voices over the formidable noise. She sat down in the nursery chair and joggled Master John automatically, shutting her eyes. "I'm beginning to think you have something, Luis."

"Of course I've got something. My God, I can sympathize with Art now—'like a time-bomb,' he said. How right he was. How the hell do people stand it who can't afford—"

"Surprising what you can get used to," said Alison through a yawn, joggling Master John grimly.

"Well, I'm too old to change my habits," said Mendoza.

8

"I'm used to sleeping at night. I've got a job to do all day. Right now, specifically, this burglar-rapist." He peered down at Miss Teresa's red face. "Though from one point of view, I can sympathize with him—slaughtering females." He yawned too. "*Te estás engañando a tí misma*—you're just fooling yourself. At five months, they don't know whether it's Mama or a nice kind hired nurse. Later on you can be the loving parent. When they've learned to sleep at night."

"Think I agree with you," said Alison, nodding sleepily over the yelling Master John. "But the back bedroom isn't decorated for a nursery."

"*¡Eso basta!*" said Mendoza. "So, get the painters back— put up the pretty circus animals on the walls! And make this a nice neutral spare room. But the first thing to do is to acquire the nursemaid, *¿es verdad?*" He joggled Miss Teresa violently.

"Yes," said Alison. "You're perfectly right. I'll go looking tomorrow, if I've got the strength."

"Today. It's nearly three o'clock. Where the hell do *they* get the strength?"

"Babies," said Alison sleepily, "have a lot of energy. If they're healthy babies."

"These two must be the damnedest healthiest babies in Los Angeles County," said Mendoza bitterly. "If anybody had told me I'd be— Do you think it'd be any good singing lullabies?"

"We've tried that," Alison reminded him. "They don't seem to be very musical— I think I sing reasonably well, but it just makes them yell harder. Maybe I don't know the right lullabies." She shifted Master John to the opposite arm.

9

"There must be hundreds of nice experienced nurse-maids available."

"Well, I couldn't say. I'll go and look."

"Today," said Mendoza. "This is undermining my morale, *cara*. I used to think I was a fairly tough fellow, when I was getting eight hours of sleep every night. But with these two time-bombs going off regular at 2:30 A.M., I'm feeling my age."

"I will," said Alison meekly. "I promise. Of course we don't want just anybody, but a good employment agency ought to—"

"I'll tell you one thing," said Mendoza. "It's very damned lucky we haven't any near neighbors, or they'd be complaining to the police. A nice thing, veteran officer like me getting reported for disturbing the peace." Miss Teresa let out a particularly rousing bellow, and he looked at her small person even more bitterly. "I amend the statement," he said. "The damnedest healthiest babies in the state of California!"

As usual, the twins drifted off into beautiful quiet slumber at 5 A.M. Mendoza was prodded awake by a sleepy and sympathetic Alison at eight o'clock; by the time he'd shaved and dressed and had two cups of coffee he felt slightly more human.

"You go and look for that nursemaid," he admonished her.

"I said I promised. I back down," said Alison. "You're quite right, it's senseless when we can afford to pay somebody else."

When he came into the office at a quarter to nine, Hackett surveyed him and grinned. "I told you so, didn't

I? You live through it, but you wonder how." He spoke from the mature viewpoint of a parent whose offspring had achieved its first birthday and was creating different kinds of disturbances than sleepless nights.

Mendoza sat down at his desk. "You needn't sound so damn smug. I've got Alison to back down—she's going to hire a nurse. Senseless damn thing, these sentimental notions— After all, as I pointed out, what about me? Valuable public servant, nerves all shot to hell. And why in God's name I ever got involved in all these domesticities in the first place— If anybody had told me a few years ago I'd be—"

Hackett laughed. "We mostly get caught up with sooner or later. . . . We've got a possible ident on that Garey Street corpse. Fellow called in just a few minutes ago— he's coming down. One James Ellis, sounds very ordinary and level."

"Oh? That'd be a step forward."

"I thought you could see him. I want to go over what we've got on this rapist with Palliser."

"All right," said Mendoza, yawning. The rapist was being a tough one; that kind of thing always was. The burglar-killer had, so far as they knew now, entered seven houses—very crudely, in broad daylight—and finding women at home, had assaulted four (raping two of them), and in the course of assault killed the other three, burglarizing five of the houses afterward. The four survivors had been seriously beaten and mauled, but had been able to give the police a good description: it added up to the same man, but that didn't help much in pointing out the right fellow. A Negro, said the survivors, medium dark, a big fellow over six feet and broad, with a pock-marked

11

complexion. They all said, shabby work clothes, dark pants, a tan shirt; one woman said, a tan billed cap. One of those women and two of the neighbors of others had seen him get away, and said he was driving a battered, middle-aged, light-blue pickup truck, a Ford or Chevvy. The fourth, woman, one of those he'd raped, was under psychiatric treatment and not very coherent or helpful.

And that might sound as if they had quite a lot on him; but it wasn't too much, actually. Los Angeles County had a very large Negro population; a certain proportion of it, of course—larger than you might expect—was made up of professional people, educated people, a good many of whom had very respectable incomes and lived in upper-class residential areas. But there was a larger proportion left over. A lot of men both white and black wore tan shirts and dark pants. And there were a lot of middle-aged, light-blue pickup trucks around.

Right now they were going through the list, gleaned from the D.M.V. records in Sacramento, of all such trucks registered in L.A. County. No guarantee that the right one was on the list, no guarantee that the right one was registered in L.A. County. But it was quite a list and was taking time and manpower to go through. If it didn't turn up anything interesting, then they'd ask Sacramento for wider coverage and start over again. Meanwhile hoping that Lover Boy wouldn't get the urge again before they got a line on him.

That was the kind very tough to crack.

Mendoza yawned and thought about the Garey Street corpse. He was interested in the Garey Street corpse because it looked like an offbeat sort of thing.

It had turned up on Monday morning; this was Wednes-

12

day. A very shocked and upset Father Michael Aloysius O'Callaghan had reported that it had been found by some kids at the far end of the playground of a big parochial school. A homicide crew had gone down to look at it, and at the first casual glance it had looked like a fairly run-of-the-mill thing. The body of a young woman, between, say, twenty and twenty-four, a middling good-looking young woman when she'd been alive, blonde; no handbag, no observable exterior injuries, and no clues on the scene at all.

Hackett had said then, grimly, "Another dope party, probably. Or third-rail stuff. Girl passes out on them and they ditch the body the handiest place." Mendoza had agreed. That wasn't the classiest section of town, Garey Street. That kind of thing had happened before: a party of young people experimenting with heroin, or homemade liquor, one of them getting a little too much, the others dumping the corpse in a panic.

The only reservation in his mind was because of the place she was dumped. The parochial school was a large one and, like the public schools, had a twenty-five-foot-high chain-link fence around its playground. The several gates were, of course, locked overnight. It wouldn't have been the easiest job in the world to hoist a body over that fence; and there were all sorts of other places where the body could have been abandoned without any trouble at all: dark alleys, side streets, empty lots.

Still, it had looked fairly run-of-the-mill, until Dr. Bainbridge sent up the autopsy report. The middling good-looking young blonde hadn't died of an overdose of heroin or straight alcohol. She had died from an overdose of codeine; and Bainbridge had pinpointed it as a rather

13

common opiate prescription, even named the firm which manufactured it.

Which aroused Mendoza's curiosity in the blonde. A lot of people committed suicide by taking sleeping-tablets, but suicides didn't confuse things by removing their bodies to unexpected places. This had been, in all probability, a deliberately planned murder; and contrary to all the fiction, a big-city homicide bureau didn't run into that sort of thing very often.

"This Ellis seem very positive?" he asked Hackett now.

"Kind of cautious," said Hackett. "Said when he and his wife saw the cut in the paper this morning they both thought it could be—but of course a corpse doesn't always look very much the way it did alive. They were coming right down." He looked at his watch. "I've got a date with Palliser, see you later." He went out, and a minute later Sergeant Lake put his head in the door and said a Mr. and Mrs. Ellis were here.

James Ellis was a stocky, short man in the fifties, very neatly and conventionally dressed: thinning gray hair, honest blue eyes, a square jaw. Mrs. Ellis was his counterpart: a plain middle-aged woman, just now looking distressed but also very conventional, obviously in her best clothes—printed silk dress, navy-blue coat and hat. Ellis was a bank teller: a very respectable fellow.

He was now sitting in Mendoza's office, still looking a bit pale and shaken even twenty minutes after his visit to the morgue, and taking long breaths, mopping his forehead agitatedly.

"Just a terrible thing," he said. "A terrible tragedy. Poor little Val."

14

Mrs. Ellis was crying gently. "We did try to help, Jamie, you know that. I'll never believe she was really *bad*. It was just it all came at a bad time for her—she couldn't— Only twenty-three, it doesn't seem hardly fair. Poor child."

"Valerie Ellis," Mendoza prompted gently. "What can you tell me about her, Mr. Ellis? She was your niece, you said."

"Yes, sir, that's right. I just can't figure who'd have done such an awful thing to her. But I've got to say we didn't know just so much about—well, how she was living, who she went around with—lately. Now, Mabel, don't you carry on. You know we *tried*. But she—" He mopped his forehead again, looked at Mendoza earnestly. "It was like she turned against everybody she knew, when it happened, see. Of course we told her right off, come and live with us —only relations left, and she was only nineteen then—and our own two both off and married, you see. It wasn't right, a young girl like that on her own. But she wouldn't. I'm bound to say she talked kind of wild—"

"Oh, but, Jamie, she wouldn't have done anything wrong! Fred's girl—"

"Well, I dunno," said Ellis slowly. "Kids that age, they go off the rails sometimes, get into bad company. It was a damn shame, but in a kind of way all Fred's own fault. I told him often enough—"

"Mr. Ellis. If you'd just give me what information you have, in order? I realize you're upset, but—"

"Oh, sure—sure. I'm sorry, sir, I see you don't know what I'm talking about." Ellis tucked his crumpled handkerchief away, brought out a second immaculate folded one, and blew his nose. "Damn shame," he said. "Little Val. She was an awful cute youngster . . . I dunno whether

15

you'll be interested in all this, Lieutenant, you just say if you're not. First off, I guess you want to know where she was living. Far as we know, up to last week anyway, it was a place on Mariposa Street in Hollywood." He added the address. "We'd offered to take her in, way I say, and maybe we should've checked up on her more—her only relatives, and she was so young. But it was—"

"We *should* have," said his wife. "Just because she was maybe a little bit wild, all the more reason—" She wept gently.

"Well, maybe so, but it was—difficult," said Ellis. "I'll tell you how it was, Lieutenant." His steady blue eyes were troubled. "See, Fred—my brother—he was a go-getter. Not like me," and he smiled briefly. "He was a money-maker—top salesman with DeMarco and Spann last fifteen years, big engineering firm, maybe you know. He made a pretty high income, ever since little Val'd be old enough to remember—*and* he spent it. Time and again I told him, Fred, you ought to sock some away, just in case—you know? Buy some stock, bonds, invest in real estate. Sensible thing to do. But Fred, he couldn't see it—he never did." Ellis shook his head disapprovingly. "They lived right up to the hilt of what he made—house in Bel-Air, two Caddys, a maid— He wasn't ever a snob, not Fred, nor Amy either, they used to invite us to their parties and all, but— Well, you see what I mean. Excuse me, I get to talking— you want to hear all this? I don't know——" He was an earnest, unhappy, conventional little man.

"Everything you can tell me," said Mendoza.

"Time and again I tried to tell him, it's just not sense to run charges, the interest— And he never would take out insurance either, it was like he was superstitious about it,

16

it'd be bad luck. Excuse me, you don't want to hear—
Poor little Val. Maybe we *should* have tried harder, I
dunno, even when she acted rude and— But what's done's
done. Mabel, don't take on so . . . It was four years back
Fred and Amy got killed, in a car accident. The other fellow's fault, it was, drunk driver—but that didn't help
Fred or Amy. These damn drunks. Fred only just turned
forty-nine—tragedy, it was. Well, just as I could've predicted, there wasn't anything left, see. A lot of debts—the
house wasn't paid off—car was a wreck, of course—no
insurance. Time everything was settled, the equity he had
in the house just about paid off the debts, and little Val
didn't get anything. She was nineteen, just in her first
term up at Berkeley—just joined some swanky sorority
up there. And she'd always had, well, everything—you
know what I mean. Clothes, her own car since she got out
of high school, anything she wanted. And she—kind of—
went to pieces, I'd guess you could say, when she was left
like that." He cast a side glance at his wife, unhappy.

"I suppose it was only natural," she said. "A girl that
age, and they'd spoiled her. Having to quit college, find a
job and earn her living." She wiped her eyes. "We couldn't
have afforded to pay her college fees, you see, but we told
her she should come right to us for a home—only right
thing to do. But she wouldn't. She—"

"She was resentful?" Mendoza filled in as she hesitated.
"Bitter at being left with nothing, when she'd been, you
might say, brought up in luxury?"

"Yes, it was like that," said Ellis. "She said some pretty
sharp things about taking charity. Well, she was some
spoiled, way Mabel says. She went off on her own, and—
well, we tried to keep in touch with her, we'd ask her over

17

for dinner now and then, like that. But then again, you know, Lieutenant, *as* I said to Mabel at the time, it doesn't do any harm to young people to be on their own, have to support themselves, learn the value of money. Just the opposite. I thought maybe she'd straighten out, start to get some sense, being all on her own like that . . . She worked at Robinson's first, as a sales clerk. I said to her, she ought to take a business course, nights, get to be a secretary. But she didn't—" He stopped, looking miserable.

"What other jobs did she hold, do you know?" Mendoza was taking notes. "Know any of her current friends?"

"No, sir, I'm afraid we don't. We hadn't seen her just so often this last year. I do recall her mentioning a Paul, but not what his last name was or what he did, anything like that. She worked at The Broadway after Robinson's, and then since about six months ago she was working as a hostess at a restaurant—The Black Cat out on La Cienega. But I don't know—" He broke off nervously.

"She was still working there, as far as you know?"

"Well," said Ellis, "that's just it. I—I suppose we've got to tell you. Damn it, Fred's girl—little Val—"

"I'll never believe she was *bad*," said Mrs. Ellis. "Maybe she got into the wrong company, but— Of course we've got to tell them, Jamie."

"Yes. Well, thing is," said Ellis, "the way I say, we tried to keep in touch with Val. Asked her to dinner once in a while and so on. Sometimes she'd come, but the last— oh, couple of years or so, more often she'd make some excuse. She always acted kind of bored when she did come, didn't stay long. Well—middle-aged people, and she was young." He blinked apologetically. "Thing is—she never

18

said, about quitting her job at the restaurant, but then we hadn't seen her for a few months. It was about a week ago, wasn't it, hon, you stopped off at her place—"

Mabel Ellis nodded solemnly. "We've been worried about it ever since, you can see, Lieutenant. It was a week ago Tuesday—yesterday. I happened to be passing, and I thought I'd leave her a note, ask her to come to dinner on Sunday. Alice and Jimmy were both coming, with the kids, and I thought— Well, it was about three o'clock, naturally I didn't expect she'd be home. But she was. She—acted queer. She wanted to get rid of me, I could tell—as if she was expecting somebody she didn't want me to meet. And when I asked her about her job, if she'd quit, she said— she said, sounding sort of wild and—well, *queer*—she said, oh, she wasn't a sucker to slave at an eight-hour job . . . She wouldn't say any more—she sounded— But I can't believe she was really *bad*," said Mrs. Ellis tearfully. "Such a pretty little girl she was— Oh, Jamie, she wasn't really *bad*, was she?"

Two

Mendoza collected Dwyer and drove up to Mariposa Street in Hollywood. It was a quarter past ten; he trusted that Alison was just setting forth on her quest for a nursemaid. That jolly domestic, Bertha, was due at ten and could keep an eye on the peacefully slumbering twins, and feed the cats . . . Of all the damned senseless things, putting up with that pair when they could afford to pay somebody else—

The apartment house on Mariposa was an old one, and not very big; all of forty years old, about twelve units in two stories. It was scabrous yellow stucco outside, dark and smelling of dust inside. Six apartments downstairs, six up. Locked mailboxes set into the left-hand wall, and the first door to the right bore a brass plate with *Manageress* on it. "'S hope she's not out marketing," said Mendoza, yawning as he pressed the bell.

She was not. She opened the door almost at once and faced them, a scraggly middle-aged woman, black hair turning gray, pinned back in a plain bun: old-fashioned rimless glasses, sharp blue eyes. "Yay-ess?" Borderline southern.

Mendoza explained, produced identification. The woman took a step back. "Murdered!" she exclaimed "Well, don't that beat all!" She sounded curiously pleased. "Guess that shows I wasn't woolgatherin' after all, about that young woman. I was figurin' on askin' her to get out. Some funny goings-on."

"Oh? We'd like to hear anything you can tell us, but also we want to see her apartment."

"Sure you do. Tell you the truth, I been kinda curious myself, 'n' I figured it was my right—bein' responsible for the place, so to speak—an' I slipped in to look it over, t'other night. Just to see. I reckon you'll be pretty int'rested in some things, gennelmen." Her sharp little eyes almost sparkled; she was avidly interested. "Yessir, I was goin' to tell her to get out. I don't want no immorality on the premises. Mr. Bennington upstairs is bad enough, but there's plenty o' men like one big spree regular o' Saturday nights, 'n' it just makes him want to sing and like that. All the same—" She had moved to an ancient desk beside the door, rummaged for a bunch of keys; she came out to them, selecting a key. "That's *her* door right across there. See, bein' right opposite, I could sort of check up on her. She allus was kind of a queer one."

"How long had she lived here?" asked Mendoza.

"Roundabout a year and a half. I don't interfere with tenants so long as they behave themselves, but I allus did wonder about Miss Ellis. Not having no regular job, see. It was funny—young single girl. I'm bound to say, I kept an eye out for *men*, but I can't tell you I ever saw anything like that. Says to me, she's a commercial artist, see, works at home. Well"—the woman uttered a high whinnying laugh—"time I looked around in here, I sure didn't see no artist's paints. There was a few goings-on—"

"Let's hear about that," said Mendoza. It was an apartment typical of its age and kind: a fairly good-sized living-room, with very tired furniture sitting around haphazardly: an old round-armed couch, chair to match, in faded green frieze; a couple of straight chairs, a 1920 version of a lady's writing-table; a shabby flowered rug. Through a door at the left he glimpsed a corner of white-tiled kitchen drain-board; the door on the other side of the room would lead to the bedroom, with the bath off that.

"Well! Guess I oughta say, by the way, my name's Montague. Miz Montague. If she really was murdered, I reckon 'twas something to do with it, that fella on Sunday night, so I better tell you 'bout that first. See—"

"Sunday night?" The autopsy report put the time of death between noon and midnight on Sunday.

Mrs. Montague nodded portentously. "I'd seen her— the Ellis girl—go out about ten that morning, see. I'd been figurin' on it, 'n' I said to myself, I'll catch her when she comes back, tell her to get out. It bein' near enough the end o' the month. So I was kinda listening for her to come back, see what I mean. And roundabout eight-thirty that night, I hear somebody come in the front door 'n' go to this here door, so I just steps out—and it wasn't Miss Ellis atall, 'twas a man. Stranger to me . . . Well, I don't know as I *would* know him again, hall's awful dark, you know, 'n' I just had a glimpse at him. But he had a key —that I saw. Hangin' on a bunch. And it was the right key, because he'd got the door open."

"Very interesting." So it was. The murderer? He'd pre-sumably had Valerie Ellis's handbag, and contents.

"Well, I started to ask him what he thought he was do-ing and where's Miss Ellis, but I never had a chance. Way he acted, I guess I scared him out of a year's growth—had

22

his back to me, see, he'd just got the door open when I spoke. I hadn't hardly said three words before he took off like a scalded cat. I guess now, afraid I'd seen him good and could say what he looked like, maybe. Anyway, he bolted straight out the front door—and he dropped the keys. These are them, not mine. You reckon, Miss Ellis's keys?"

"Very possible." Mendoza was pleased. That was luck. X coming to look through her apartment, find out whether there was anything incriminating on him there, and being prevented. X a nervous type, to bolt like that? How he must have cursed himself for dropping those keys . . . So if there was any lead, it would probably still be here. He stared absently at the glistening new TV in one corner. Quite a large screen. "Go on talking," he said to the woman, "I'm listening." He walked over and switched the TV on, keeping the volume down.

"Well! You understand, Miss Ellis bein' how she was, I wasn't too surprised . . . Why didn't I do anything about it? I didn't know then she was murdered. When I said go-ings-on, well, nothing I could really put a finger on, just funny. Her not having a regular job and all. Commercial artist, my foot. Nor I didn't like the looks o' some o' the people come to see her. Couple o' men, and that other girl —Maureen, I heard Miss Ellis call her—by the looks of her, no better 'n she should be, all tarted up." Dwyer had vanished into the bedroom. Mendoza stared at the TV, and Mrs. Montague uttered a ladylike snort. "For all she was supposed to be workin' at home, Miss Ellis went out most days, stayed out—but no regular times, see. She was out most evenings unless she had people in. I could hear her coming and going, you know. And then she'd go away."

23

"Go away?" It was a color TV, a very expensive model. Say around seven hundred bucks, thought Mendoza. He switched it off.

"Sure. She'd go out one day 'n' I wouldn't see hide nor hair of her for maybe two days or so. That happened a lot of times. Nothing regular about it, no, sir."

"You don't say. Ever ask her about it?"

"That I did. Only natural I would, wasn't it? But she flared up, called me an old snoop and told me to mind my own business." Mrs. Montague snorted again. "Real snippy little thing, she was . . . I guess one o' those men came was a regular boy friend, I couldn't say for sure. A lot of times, these two come to see her together. Which was one of the funny things. I wouldn't know their names, but once I just happened to be goin' out when they come, 'n' I heard her say, Hello, Paul. One of 'em"—she stared at Mendoza reflectively—"matter o' fact, looks a little bit like you, sir. T'other one's bigger 'n' kind of blond. And then there was another girl besides that Maureen— Maureen came a lot—the other one's a real platinum blonde, looks about the same kind as that Maureen though. Sometimes there'd be parties and a lot of noise when they got to drinking. I had to go 'n' knock on the door a couple of times. Well, like I say, it all looked kinda funny, and after that strange fella came on Sunday night I thought 'twas my right have a look around. And after *that* I figured all the more, I'd get her out—"

She'd have said it all over again, but Mendoza eased her out. She gave him a malicious smile on the threshold and said, "I reckon you'll be awful int'rested in a couple of things here."

"I just reckon we will be, Lieutenant," said Dwyer from the bedroom door, as the outer door closed. "However she

24

was earning a living, it was a damn good one. Come in here."

In the bedroom the furniture was as shabby and aged as that in the living-room; the kind of furniture you always got in these places—cheap veneer double bed with a sagging mattress, an old painted bureau with the paint chipped; a straight painted chair, a worn carpet too small for the room. Dwyer hooked the stem of his cold pipe round the closet door, which had swung to again on sagging hinges, and pulled it open. "As you might put it, Lieutenant, *considerar*."

"Are you taking night courses too? Yes, I do see what you mean." In this shabby room, the closet was packed with clothes. Not—he lifted down the nearest hanger—the kind of clothes a former sales clerk could afford. (And, *de paso*, apparently she'd lied to the Ellises about that hostess job, at least: she hadn't worked regularly, so far as Mrs. Montague knew, for about a year and a half.) The label on this evening gown, a frothy affair of blue chiffon, was that of Robinson's most expensive Little Shoppe. He recognized it, having once (somewhat staggered but ashamed to show it) paid forty-nine fifty (plus tax) for a simple little house robe for Alison at the same place.

There were suits, daytime dresses, a jumble of shoes. In the wide drawers of the old bureau, piles of expensive lingerie. On the vanity table, in the bathroom, a miscellaneous assortment of expensive cosmetics, lotions, creams, bath salts.

"You figure maybe," said Dwyer gravely, "she had one of these fairy godmothers? Quite a trick, without a regular pay check. Or should I say a fairy godfather?"

"Could be," said Mendoza. "Could be . . . The boys from Prints ought to be here soon. Interesting to see what

25

they pick up. But—" He considered, conjuring up the dead girl's face. Alive and animate, she'd have been a good-looker—not pretty. In a Scandinavian sort of way—high cheekbones, a wide mouth, winging brows. Tawny blond, not bleached. He visualized that face alive, and saw that it was a reckless face. "Wild," James Ellis and his wife had said.

He said absently, "Isn't it the truth, *dineros son calidad*—money talks." She had grown up with money—money thrown around. "Anything she wanted," the Ellises said. And "spoiled." Then, all of a sudden, no money—on her own—working as a sales clerk. Seeing other women—women without her youth or looks—buying all the pretty things she couldn't have any more. Four years ago. Look up the record, but apparently she hadn't turned crooked—as without much doubt she had, some way—until about a year and a half ago. Was that a valid deduction? Had she ever held that job at The Black Cat?

He wandered back to the living-room. Ill-gotten gains spent on the ephemeral things. She hadn't been interested in her surroundings: not very domestic. Maybe that would have come next, the classy apartment.

"You have an idea?" asked Dwyer, watching him.

"A small one," said Mendoza meditatively. "People who get themselves murdered, generally speaking their inward characters have something to do with it . . . All those clothes jumbled together. All that underwear just tossed in the drawers, not folded. No trees in the shoes—"

"I don't get you," said Dwyer.

Mendoza contemplated the garish lithograph hanging on the long wall, and with an effort refrained from reaching to straighten it. Himself, he was the kind rendered acutely unhappy by the wrinkle in the rug, the coat

26

sprawled over a chair instead of hung up tidily; he'd have been more likely to draw to an inside straight than to neglect putting trees in his shoes or hanging up his suits properly . . . "She was grabbing," he said absently. "Greedy for all the things she'd once had and lost. Buying everything in sight—once she could. Once she had them, not taking care of them. Just liking the satisfaction of having them. She was careless—impulsive. A year and a half . . . Yes, maybe the classy apartment would have come next. And—damnation, I should have asked the Montague woman about garages—probably are some in back, this old a place— I wonder what Valerie was driving? And where the hell are Marx and Horder? I want to have a thorough look here, and I can't until— You go and look for the garage, Bert, find out which was hers and if her car is there. If not, see if the Montague woman knows what she was driving."

He went out to the Ferrari at the curb and used the phone in it to call his office. "They'll be there," said Sergeant Lake soothingly. "I think they just left, Lieutenant."

He walked around the building—driveway down the left side—to find Dwyer, with the bunch of borrowed keys, struggling with the padlock on the first of a row of ramshackle old frame garages across the rear of the lot. "I suppose there could be a chance that there was a print left on one of those," he said mildly.

"All accounts, they've had a lot of handling," said Dwyer defensively. "Montague says—sharp old biddy, isn't she?—the Ellis girl had a '59 Dodge convertible, two-door, white. Damn this thing." But the key turned finally and the old double doors swung open. They looked at the white Dodge convertible.

"Naturally," said Mendoza, "the padlock being fastened.

27

And we're both experienced enough to know better, damn it—all the fault of those damned twins, I'm not operating on all cylinders. X's prints just might have been on that padlock. Because, considering the fact that the body was dumped away from here, I think she died somewhere else. That he brought the car home to tidy it out of the way . . . What else can we say? Did he know which garage was hers, or just have the luck to pick the right one? I think X was nervous— I also think he's a very cautious man. Or—wait a minute—yes. Yes. If he'd brought her home, put an empty pill bottle beside her, ten to one we'd have put it down as suicide or accidental death. Was that what he was starting to do Sunday night when Mrs. Montague caught him? It could be. And then, having dropped the keys, he couldn't come back for another try. He probably had heard from Valerie about her snoopy landlady . . . Mmh, yes, I do wonder if he left any prints around."

"They're mostly smart enough these days to wear gloves," said Dwyer glumly.

"Nevertheless, we'll print the car." Mendoza went back to the apartment and wandered through all the rooms, waiting for Marx and Horder.

Again he pulled open the closet door, contemplated the jumble of expensive clothes crushed together. Shoes haphazard on the floor, not paired, half lying on their sides. There was a cheap fiber suitcase resting half on the shoes. He looked around, hooked the chair over to prop the door open, and pulled the suitcase out. It was not latched; he lifted the lid with his fountain pen. "*¡Qué interesante!*" he murmured to himself.

"Something?" asked Dwyer behind him.

"Something." Mendoza moved aside; Dwyer looked and said he'd be damned.

"Just loose like that—made-up reefers—my God, must be hundreds of 'em. So, no fairy godfather? I will be damned. But, Lieutenant, it's not often a woman takes to—you think maybe the boy friend?"

"Could be," said Mendoza. He yawned again; he wondered what success Alison was meeting in her hunt for a nice kind nursemaid.

Marx and Horder arrived. Mendoza stood around some more while they went to work printing every surface. They hooked open drawers and lifted out printable objects with tongs or tweezers. They wouldn't be hurried.

In the kitchen, a very basic supply of staples: a few cans, the refrigerator nearly empty. She hadn't done much cooking at home. In the first of the two cupboards, along with a scattering of a few staple items (breakfast cereal, crackers, packaged soups), a half-empty fifth of a popular brand of Scotch, a full bottle of vodka, and a bottle of wine.

Mendoza looked at the bottle of wine twice. A very moderate drinker himself, he wasn't familiar with the liquor trade; but there was something rather unusual-looking about that bottle of wine. When Marx had thoroughly dusted it and lifted what prints were on it, he inspected it closer.

A black-and-white label looking old-fashioned, if that was the word for it. *Rutherford and Miles*, and a dignified-sounding London address. Below that in large ornate lettering, *Madeira*, and below that, *Malvasias*—in parentheses, *malmsey. Alcoholic content 20%.* The wine was a dark amber-red color, looking thick.

Mendoza straightened and stared at the cupboard door. *Malmsey.* There had been some British duke—a long time back—"drowned in a butt of malmsey." Unusual, you could say, if this was the same stuff. He'd heard of a wine called Madeira, but it was vaguely associated in his mind with bygone times—seventeenth, eighteenth century? Evidently it was still produced. But it couldn't be a very popular wine? Something not much called for, maybe. Maybe a lead? Valerie Ellis had kept it on hand—for the boy friend?

"O.K., I guess we've covered everything, Lieutenant," said Horder. "It's all yours. Found an address book in the desk, here it is. You want the car printed? O.K."

"Thanks very much, boys." Mendoza pounced on the address book eagerly.

Looking through it, he sighed. It was going to be quite a job to locate all these names. These damned untidy females with the disorganized minds! Valerie Ellis had written a wild scrawl of a hand, scarcely legible; and in only a few places had she put down addresses—mostly just phone numbers. The scribbles were in a variety of mediums, pencil, ballpoint pens in blue, green, and red, a broad-nibbed fountain pen. Moreover, she hadn't listed names alphabetically. On the same page as *Paul Manton*, *NO-1-6494*, was *Gloria*, *CR-3-2894*, and an illegible scrawl which might be either *Frank* or *Fred*.

The little book was very full. Somebody—Sergeant Lake—would be contacting the telephone company to get matching addresses for all these numbers.

Here was *Maureen*, and a Hollywood number. *Ricardo*. *Bob*. Then, *Glessner*, and a dash, and *meet Rikki's 5 p.m., get $5000*. Well, well.

Paul Manton.

She had used this little book, evidently, as a current reminder, half desk diary. Some of the notations—no telling how recent any of them were—were extremely interesting. There was that one about Glessner, and later on,

Hoess—meet 8:30 *Cat, no double talk.* And, later on, *Monteux, Cat,* 8 *p.m.*, $$$. Altogether, fourteen similar notations.

Somebody—presumably Valerie Ellis—had been collecting under-the-counter money from other somebodies, for something. Did that say? Or had she been working the racket—whatever the racket was—with somebody else?

The reefers? But the one amount mentioned, five thousand bucks, was too high for a reefer-peddling business. Current price, about two bits apiece, here. Of course reefer peddlers frequently graduated into pushing the big H.

Some other racket, the reefers on the side? Obligingly storing the reefers for the boy friend?

And that *Paul Manton* rang a very faint bell in his mind. "Paul Manton," he said. "Does it hit you any way, Bert? I seem to remember the name, but I can't connect it with anything."

"New one to me. We can ask Records."

"Yes." Mendoza was still leafing through the address book, pausing to decipher hasty scrawls. "I think we will. Just in case."

Here was an intriguing one. *Wilanowski, s.o.b.!!!!* Did that say, maybe, that Wilanowski had failed to pay up? For what? Mendoza grinned at the exclamation points, bitten deep into the page. He turned that page and paused again.

Call P., R.'s bar 8 *p.m. Marion,* and a phone number. *Meet Vardas* 8, *Cat*, $$. Psychological point—so interested in money, she couldn't resist adding that symbol. But, *caray*, the untidy, disorganized way she'd jotted all this down, she'd have had to consult every page to find what she was looking for—

There were nine pages blank at the end of the little book.

31

He studied the last filled-in page. *Imarosa, 10 p.m. R's $$$. Call P. home.* In a different ink, *Maureen, new no., 015-4965.* And far below that, scrawled with a blue ball-point, in letters twice as large as she normally wrote, the legend *Farlow, 1566 Willoughby, Hlywd!!!!!!!!*

Well. Quite a little to puzzle over there. Quite a little of interest.

Mendoza found himself yawning again. He wondered what Hackett and Palliser were getting on Lover Boy the rapist. Lover Boy concentrating on obviously wealthy areas: West Hollywood, two of the victims in Beverly Hills, so that force was in on it too. He'd taken some nice loot in most of the places . . . Sooner or later the D.M.V. list ought to yield results.

He glanced at his watch; it was a bit after noon. Have lunch somewhere, start Lake on getting addresses for all these numbers. What the hell kind of racket had it been that Valerie Ellis was running?

The Black Cat restaurant on La Cienega. By the address book, maybe used for some of the pay-offs? But the personnel there might be quite innocent. Look, of course.

He yawned again. He said, "O.K., Bert, you get back downtown, you and Jimmy can get busy matching up these phone numbers with addresses. But copy them down, will you? I want to study this little book more thoroughly. Oh, and check with the Ellises for all her former addresses, will you? I'll poke around here a little more . . ."

Three

"Well, I don't know, I suppose she's all right," said Alison in a slightly dissatisfied tone. "She's got scads of references praising her to the skies—she certainly seems experienced."

"So what more do you want? What's her name?"

"Jane Freeman. Miss. I suppose she'll be fine, it's just that she rather reeks of antiseptic, if you know what I mean. She's coming tomorrow. I'll get Bertha to help me move the cribs and so on. I thought the Freeman can have the room next to the back—"

"Yes, fine," said Mendoza absently. He was leafing through Valerie Ellis's address book again, and thinking about several puzzles—small and large—that he wished he knew the answers to. He raised his eyes and stared abstractedly at Master John Luis, who was prone on a blanket on the floor making vigorous swimming motions in the direction of Sheba, curled under the coffee table.

Ramifications, he thought. Going to be a tough one to unravel, all right. Some very unlikely and mystifying little things had come to light, besides the reefers . . .

33

There was also Lover Boy. Mendoza sighed. Lover Boy was important not only for the obvious reasons but because the irresponsible section of the press and a committee of muddleheaded citizens were using him as an excuse for another campaign against the incompetent police. Over a period of nearly three months this dangerous and brutal criminal has—et cetera, leading to: obviously the police are not trying hard enough, or are simply incompetent. The average citizen just didn't realize how tough one like that could be. They hadn't got the word about the light-blue truck until a week ago, from his last but one victim, the next confirming that. They were working that as hard as they knew how . . .

They'd had an hour's excitement this afternoon, when the patient routine check of light-blue trucks had turned up one registered to an address down on Washington Boulevard, one of the Negro sections. The owner was the proprietor of a garage, and seemed like a very upright citizen; nothing against him, no record. But he employed two mechanics, both of whom sometimes drove the truck. Dave Roberts and Jerry Byrd. He said indignantly, did Mr. John Wilkinson, that Dave and Jerry were good respectable boys, they wouldn't do anything like that . . . But it presented a little problem, which Hackett had laid before Mendoza when he came in from more poking around in Valerie's apartment.

"We don't want to jump the gun, Luis. You see what I mean. There they are, we've got to check. Neither of 'em has any record, they're both regular churchgoers and so on. But—" He didn't have to explain the problem to Mendoza. "How'll we handle it?"

On their rough physical descriptions—size and age—

either could have been Lover Boy. But Hackett didn't think either of them was, because neither of them was pock-marked. Also, they had good records, and both were educated boys, high-school graduates. He didn't think Lover Boy was that type, and Mendoza agreed with him. However, a good many white people didn't trouble to distinguish one Negro from another; and a woman who has been forcibly and brutally assaulted might easily make an unconscious mistake.

Mendoza said after thought, "Let Mrs. Gunnarson look at them." Mrs. Gunnarson was the older of the two women who had managed to get away from him. She'd have a little less emotional involvement, and also she was a stable, sensible woman of forty.

And of course she had looked and said, "No, it wasn't either of these young men. He was badly pock-marked, and bigger than either of them."

Hackett had thanked her with emphatic sincerity. With these Black Muslims kicking up all the trouble they could, the last thing they needed was a wrongful identification of an innocent Negro. Shaken, Dave and Jerry had gone back to work with a little story to tell. Hackett and Mendoza and every other man on the force could hope, a little story which would include the fact that the police had leaned over backward to be fair to them. But of course it wasn't the Daves and Jerrys they needed to convince of that: the Daves and Jerrys were already honest citizens. It was the distrustful ones, the insecure ones, the ones on the border-line . . .

Mendoza jumped and opened his eyes at sudden uproar. Master John, doggedly propelling himself with churning motions across the floor, had reached Sheba and started chewing her tail. Sheba shrieked, spat, and fled. Master John roared. El Señor, who had been brooding darkly to himself on top of the credenza, jumped to his self-appointed job and began washing Master John's tearful face.

"No, Señor!" said Alison. "Heavens, you'll have all the skin off—" She made a dive for the baby. El Señor gave her a cold look and stalked out of the room. The whole episode amused Miss Teresa highly; she crowed with delight. "That cat!" said Alison. "It's very nice of him to want to help, but he doesn't realize how rough his tongue is."

"After tomorrow—" said Mendoza.

"Yes. I only wish I liked her better," said Alison. "Oh, well, we'll see how she works out. And I'd better get these two into bed and to sleep."

"For exactly five hours and a half," said Mendoza, looking at his watch. He watched her out, leaned back and shut his eyes, and meditated on what else had turned up today on Valerie Ellis.

Aunt and Uncle Ellis had been nice trusting relatives, never suspecting anything about Valerie, all right. It turned out that she'd held that job at Robinson's just five months, and then been fired for shoplifting. Naturally, no reference given. The store hadn't prosecuted because it was a first offense and it had got most of the loot back.

She'd never worked at The Broadway at all. Nor as a hostess at The Black Cat. So, call it three and a half years she'd been on the bent somehow, alone or with ditto pals. In this racket or that . . . They knew her at The Black Cat. She came in fairly often, sometimes alone, more often with men. Different men, but the same one several times also. Looking interestedly at Mendoza, the head bar-

36

man had said, "That one looks a little bit like you, sir. About your size too."

Well, he was not unique, reflected Mendoza. Especially in Los Angeles, there were probably some hundreds of men walking around who were about five-ten, slim and dark, with narrow black mustaches.

They now had about three quarters of the list of matching addresses. She'd known a lot of people. And probably they'd find that a large number of them had been purely casual acquaintances. Or, of course, would say so. Anybody who'd been in a racket with her—if anyone had been —wasn't going to speak up about it.

As he looked at the first few full names and addresses Sergeant Lake had laid in front of him, Mendoza had suddenly remembered who Paul Manton was and why the name was familiar. So he hadn't asked Records about him.

A small two-paragraph story on the third page of the *Times* a couple of days ago. An amateur flier, in his own small Cessna, making a successful if dangerous emergency landing along a section of freeway mercifully free of cars . . . He got Jimmy to call the *Times* to check it. Paul Manton, all right, and he was described as a mechanic employed by InterState Airways, Inc.

So he'd been a friend of Valerie's. It didn't say much, yet. Not until they knew more about him—and everybody else mentioned in that little book.

Requestioned, Mrs. Montague had said that Valerie had been away from Wednesday to Friday, getting home on Friday evening. Mrs. Montague had been keeping tabs on Valerie, lately at least; she said Valerie had come in about eight in the evening, and there was a man with her.

No, she hadn't seen his face; as with the Sunday evening stranger, he'd had his back to her.

As the names and addresses turned up, automatically they were relayed to Records. So far, not one had any pedigree . . .

After he'd advised Hackett about Dave and Jerry, Mendoza had driven up to Willoughby Street in Hollywood. That last entry in the book, with its row of triumphant exclamation points, interested him.

Willoughby Street was a street of older, dignified homes: very solid wealth. The address Valerie had scribbled down turned out to be a handsome French Provincial house, very neatly maintained, fresh-painted gray and white; ivy in the parking, trim beds of ivy geraniums. Mendoza pressed the bell and presently faced an equally neat, pleasant-faced woman of middle age.

"Mrs. Farlow?"

"Who shall I say it is, sir?"

He gave her his name; she looked surprised and curious, but just asked him to wait. A few moments later she came back and ushered him into a cavernous dim living-room. Another woman was standing by the hearth.

"Lieutenant—Mendoza?" she said in a warm contralto voice. "I'm Mrs. Farlow. I must say I'm curious as to what the police want with me! But do sit down, won't you?"

She was in her late forties, he thought, and not looking it: blond by request, but a subtle job, not obvious. Poise and manner: she spent money on herself and the result was worth it. She'd kept a very good figure. The china-blue eyes were perhaps a little small, the arch of the rather long nose a little too high, the mouth a trifle narrow; but a nice-looking woman, with pride in herself and her home.

Mendoza sat down. "I believe you knew a Miss Valerie Ellis, Mrs. Farlow?"

She was in the act of lighting a cigarette; she had sat down on a long, low, gray-upholstered couch opposite the large gray-upholstered chair he had chosen. She looked at him over the lighter flame. She said, with an upward inflection, "Knew? I—we do know a Valerie Ellis, yes, why?"

Mendoza told her, watching her. She reacted with apparently genuine astonishment and horror. "My God, I saw that in the paper about a body found, but I never— How horrible! Who on earth could have—"

"Did you know her well, Mrs. Farlow?" This was an atmosphere far removed from either Mariposa Street or that of pro crooks.

"I—no," she said slowly. "My God, what a horrible thing to happen. Poor Valerie. What did you—? Why, no, it was rather odd actually, it was only a few days ago I ran across her again. I hadn't seen her for, oh, it must be all of six years—more. She was just a high-school kid then. So I'm afraid I can't help you much, Lieutenant—I wouldn't know who her friends were now, or what she'd been doing. Excuse me, but how did you know I knew her? Because, as I say—"

"Your name was in her address book," said Mendoza, not mentioning those very interesting exclamation points.

"Oh," said Mrs. Farlow, enlightened. "Well, that was the only time I'd seen her in a good six years—last Saturday—so I couldn't tell you anything useful, I'm afraid."

"Mind telling me how you happened to know her, how you happened to run across her again?"

"Why, of course, but I don't see how it'd help— Well, perhaps you know that she used to live down in Bel-Air.

Before the Ellises were killed in that awful accident— I saw the newspaper stories about it, we'd moved by then, but you see, they'd been neighbors of ours there. Two houses down, on Bellaggio Road. That was in 1958, Valerie'd have been—oh, sixteen, seventeen, I suppose. We knew her as you would a girl that age, living in the same block. No, we didn't know the Ellises well, actually we only lived there about a year."

"I see. When did you move?"

"Sometime that year—March, I think. And I never laid eyes on the girl again until last Saturday." She spoke a little impatiently now. "It was just one of those coincidences —you know how things happen. She'd been calling on the people next door. I just happened to be coming home when she came out, and she—we recognized each other. We said hello, and so on, and that was about all there was to it. I never knew her well."

Mendoza studied her. If it was an act, it was a damn good one: sounded very genuine. Then why the row of exclamation points after her name?

Well, no clue as to what Valerie's racket had been. There was money here, obviously; and Valerie had liked money. Maybe she'd figured Mrs. Farlow as a mark, having an in with her because Mrs. Farlow had known her as an innocent child?

"Did you ask her in?"

"No, actually I was rather tired and—well, as I say, I'd never known her well, it was just a—chance encounter." Now she sounded a little bored. "I did say I'd been sorry to hear about her parents, I think, and she thanked me— we only talked a few minutes, and then she went off and I came in."

"I see." He was silent a moment; it all sounded very likely and genuine. "Did she—"

The front door banged and a boy's voice announced, "I'm home! Anybody here?" He poked his head round the door, a nice-looking boy about nine or ten, well grown for his age.

"Hi, Johnny. I'll be with you in a minute," said Mrs. Farlow. "Mrs. Bennett's been making fresh cookies, maybe she'll let you have some."

"Oh, boy!"

"And—Johnny! You've still got that extra piano practice to make up, don't forget!"

"O.K., Aunt Grace, I will." He vanished down the hall.

She smiled at Mendoza. "Kids," she said. "Sometimes it seems like more trouble than— But Johnny's a good boy."

"He sounds it." He returned her smile. "Did Miss Ellis say why she'd been calling on the people next door? Which house, by the way? 1568, thanks. Do you know them?"

"Not at all. They haven't been here too long. I suppose she just knew them. No, I couldn't tell you the name, it's a foreign-sounding one, Polish or something. They only came here about six months ago. I think he's a professor of some kind. No, Valerie didn't say anything about them . . . I'm afraid I'm no help to you at all."

Those exclamation points. But very probably that was the answer: Valerie had seen Mrs. Farlow as an easy mark for some racket, had been feeling triumphant at running across her again, a woman who'd automatically believe in her honesty. A woman who didn't know that she'd been left penniless after her parents' death.

The people next door—

That house was Mediterranean, with a little balcony above the front door, a red tile roof. It was a man who opened the door, a grave-faced dignified man in the fifties, with strong aquiline features. Mendoza produced identification, asked his question, and the man listened gravely.

"You had best come in, sir. My name is Dvorzhak, Jan Dvorzhak. I do not think we can be of much aid, but we shall see. Anya!" He spoke heavily accented English.

A quick high young voice answered him from somewhere upstairs, in another tongue, and high heels clattered on the stairs. But before the owner of the voice appeared, another woman materialized from the shadows at the far end of the hall—a dumpy little woman in dowdy black clothes, skirt too long. She asked him a question in the same tongue, sounding frightened.

He said in English, "It is nothing, Marya—nothing. Do not be foolish, you know that the police here are not as the police *there*. The gentleman wants only a little information . . . Ah, Anya. Now—you have said, it is Lieutenant? What is all this asking about Miss Ellis? You will please tell us why you ask?"

Mendoza told them why. The older woman chattered in a frightened high voice, in her own language—Polish, Russian? Dvorzhak soothed her in English. "But what a terrible thing to happen! Now, Marya, be quiet, this is nothing to do with us. Come, control your nerves, my dear. You must forgive my wife, sir, you comprehend we are not safe here a long time, she is—nervous."

"Yes. You knew Miss Ellis well?"

"But how horrible!" said the girl called Anya. "What a dreadful thing to happen! You are—quite sure—it was

Valerie? Oh—" She might be twenty; she was slim, dark-haired, fair-skinned, with feathery-lashed dark eyes. Apart from her accent, she was more Americanized than her parents, dressed smartly.

"We're quite sure—is it Miss Dvorzhak?"

"Yes, yes," she said impatiently. "I can hardly believe it—such a way to die. Who would—? Yes, she is a—an acquaintance of mine, sir. An acquaintance only, I have only a little while ago met her. How do you know?"

He explained about Mrs. Farlow briefly. "Oh—" said Anya, a finger to her lip. "I did not know—" Her mother babbled again and was soothed.

"Where did you meet Miss Ellis and when?"

"Oh, one talks to everyone here, sir. It was a few weeks ago, I am in a shop—a very nice little shop on Wilshire Boulevard, I am shopping for a dress, and Valerie was there also. We began talking—she was pleasant, we liked one another, so then we went to lunch together. This is how I met her, but I did not know her well, not at all. Last Saturday afternoon—we had exchanged our addresses, you see—she said she was driving past near here and stopped to see me, a few minutes only. That was how it was."

Of course the name hadn't been in Valerie's address book.

"I see," said Mendoza. "So you didn't know any of her friends—anything about her private life?"

"But nothing, I am sorry." She flung her hands wide in expressive gesture. Her father stood watching gravely. "How should I? I have only met her twice, three times. She seemed a nice person, I am so very sorry to hear of this dreadful thing, but—"

And, a very small something—that the name hadn't

43

been in the book. Possibly Valerie hadn't had the book with her, had copied down the address on a scrap of paper and omitted recopying it. Nothing said Anya Dvorzhak wasn't telling gospel truth. And as for Valerie deliberately (could you say?) making up to her—well, she might have guessed, money, when Anya chose the "nice little shop" on Wilshire, and maybe pick her as an easy mark too . . . What the hell had her racket been?

And then, just as he got back to the office at five-forty, the bombshell had exploded.

They'd nearly reached the end of the D.M.V. list on the trucks, and he was listening to Hackett and agreeing tiredly that they'd better ask Sacramento for lists on Orange and Ventura counties, when a shaken-looking Sergeant Lake looked in and said, "It's the FBI, Lieutenant—" and a tall excited man pushed past him.

"What the hell is all this?" he demanded of Mendoza. "Where—what the hell—"

"Just what I might ask you. Credentials, please?"

"For God's sake!" said the other man, and produced them as if absent-mindedly. "Sorry, but we're all on the jump over this one. You wired some prints to Washington about eleven this morning—" Mendoza nodded; it was second nature: prints not in their own files, they asked Washington, and the Feds were so quick off the mark. "So I get a wire fifteen minutes ago chasing me over here. Where the hell did you pick up the prints and when?"

"I couldn't say until you tell me which prints they were."

"Oh, Lord—sorry—but this one's really got us worried." The Federal man mopped his brow. "They're Osgar Thorwald's prints—that's why, friend. I—"

44

"That Thorwald?" asked Hackett incredulously.

"That Thorwald," said the Fed. "The Thorwald that passed top secrets on to Moscow six years back and got clean away from us. At least we knew—we thought we knew—he was somewhere behind the Iron Curtain, all nice and cozy. We don't want him back in our midst, but my God, if he is we'd like to know where. Where'd you pick up the prints?"

"*¡Porvida!*" said Mendoza blankly. "*¿Como dice? Esto es otro cantar*—what the hell is this? The only prints we sent—"

When they came to sort it out, Thorwald's prints had come off that bottle of Madeira wine in Valerie's kitchen cupboard.

The Federal agent said sadly that it figured. "One of Thorwald's foibles—he never drinks anything but Madeira. It was the way we picked him up, before he got away from us—not many places carry it."

So now the Feds were buzzing around, going over that apartment for themselves and demanding hourly bulletins about Valerie. Damned annoying. Talk about surprises. Just try to link any of that up. It didn't make sense.

Tomorrow, see a lot of the other people she'd known. Ask questions. Poke around.

Osgar Thorwald, for God's sake . . .

Talk about an anonymous one like Lover Boy being tough. Once in a long while you got a complex business like this that was twice as tough. He tried to take his mind off it; he needed all the sleep he could get. Must get to sleep. As long as he'd be allowed . . .

"Hmm?" he said sleepily.

45

"I just said, I wish she didn't look so—so *starched*," said Alison in the darkness, snuggling closer.

"Probably a very efficient nurse. Just think, tomorrow night we can sleep all night."

"You *are* feeling your age," said Alison wickedly.

"*¡Zorra roja!* Lawful wives have no business being so impudent. Come here . . ."

Some two hours later, Master John Luis commenced to yell. His sister joined him.

Alison stirred. Sleepily she sat up. She said, "Damn." She groped for her slippers. As she fumbled her way into her robe, she added crossly, "I don't *care* how starched and stiff the woman is. As long as she'll deal with them. Little monsters. All *right*, I'm coming!"

Mendoza tried to close his ears. It was no use. He sat up, switched on the light, lit a cigarette, and thought exasperatedly about Valerie Ellis.

Sooner or later routine would lead them to Lover Boy; but Valerie Ellis . . .

Four

And he wondered overnight whether the Feds would take over the case because of the political angle. Well, a funny twist, but he didn't think this murder had been political.

They fell on him like ravening bloodhounds when he came into the office, screaming for the address book. They hadn't known about the book until he'd left last night. They chased one of their minions off to have it photostated, every page of it; everybody mentioned in it would get a thorough screening.

They'd flown a man in from Washington who'd been on the Thorwald case before—a big genial fellow, Waltham. They crowded into Mendoza's office, listened raptly to him repeat what they'd heard last night, for Waltham's benefit—the very little they knew about this case so far. They'd taken the key to Valerie's apartment last night, and evidently spent most of the night going over it, but hadn't come up with anything Mendoza's crew hadn't already come across. As he could have told them.

"I don't know what organizations she belonged to, if any," he said patiently to that question. "Nothing else political shows at all. And it doesn't smell that way to me. Naturally you're welcome to all we've got, the other prints and so on. Are you taking over?"

"Well, I tell you, it's like this," said Waltham in his quiet voice. "We can't tell one way or the other whether the Ellis murder is political. I agree it doesn't look that way —not the professional taking-off. We're naturally interested in Thorwald, and in her because there was evidently a link there. But we do know that Thorwald himself was on the run from the Reds."

"Oh? Thieves falling out?"

Waltham grinned. "Something like that. The news was that he gave them the slip and got as far as East Berlin. That was about seven months ago. No trace of him since. Well, now we know he got here. It's easy enough to get in illegally if you can't legally, and he may have a forged passport or something. But—"

"Excuse me, sir," said one of the other agents, "but could that be a double bluff? The word spread that he's in bad with them, so he can—"

Waltham shook his head. "We don't think so, and neither does the C.I.A. where we got the tip. It looks pretty straight. So you can see that tells us Thorwald himself may not be—er—political any more. Just a stateless citizen making tracks for home, to go to ground. So whatever his connection was with the Ellis girl, it could be a private thing entirely."

"Yes," said Mendoza thoughtfully. "And what the hell was the connection?"

"Well, you don't know much about her yet, do you? Just that she had some racket. Could be plain and simple hustling? Thorwald was always a man for the ladies."

"No. For about ninety-nine per cent sure. She had a suspicious landlady who'd have spotted that. The landlady says a man came home with her Friday night but he didn't stay long. She didn't get a good look at him—just his back —as per the Sunday night intruder. She heard him leave about an hour later. But she doesn't think she'd ever seen him before. Which says nothing, of course."

"Well," said Waltham, "I think we'll handle it like this, Lieutenant. We'll take over the Thorwald investigation, and leave you to sort out the murder. Something may show up to prove the two are unconnected—or vice versa, of course—let's just keep both possibilities in mind, shall we? Tally"—he looked at one of his colleagues—"let's really get press coverage on it. The scare headlines—appeal for public help, all the trimmings. O.K.? Run big cuts of our Osgar—of course, no guarantee he still looks like that, after six years, but—" He shrugged. "I want every place in L.A. County that sells liquor alerted for any customer asking for Madeira wine. Though he may be smart enough to lay off that. Although he evidently bought a bottle on—" He broke off, and said, "My God, but how do we know? The day, I mean. He could have left his prints on that bottle months ago, damn it. Look—Adler, you set it up on the liquor retailers. We've got to start looking somewhere, after all. Anybody asking for Madeira, have 'em say they'll make inquiries about ordering it, and ask for the customer's address. And let's get the Madeira into the press releases too, for nationwide coverage."

"Do you know how many places like that there *are* here?" Adler groaned. "O.K., O.K. And at the same time try to find out where he got that bottle, if it was at all recently."

49

"Yes. How much was gone out of it?"

"About two glassfuls," said Mendoza.

"Oh. And the press furor should make the job a little easier—a lot of the retailers will pick up the detail about the Madeira. If it *was* recently bought— Yes, and that's another thing, damn it. He may have got the girl to buy it for him."

"A little idea on that," said Mendoza. "Without wanting to interrupt, Mr. Waltham. Thorwald, under an alias, could have been a casual acquaintance of Valerie's. Overnight we've turned up the fact that Valerie knew a couple of people at least with little pedigrees—couple of girls charged with soliciting. She may have known other people in that category, who knows? If it was like that, maybe Thorwald just bought that Madeira as his contribution to a pleasant evening. If it was Thorwald with her on Friday evening, Mrs. Montague doesn't think he'd ever been there before. We don't know that it was, of course. And we don't know how long Thorwald's been here—"

"He's had seven months to get here from Berlin," agreed Waltham gloomily.

"Yes. Well, the fact that he left the bottle—or, of course, gave it to her elsewhere, because we don't know that he's ever been in her apartment—makes me think that he knows where he can buy a further supply."

Waltham thought that out. "All up in the air," he said. "There's another thing, damn it. We don't know how long that bottle's been sitting there. You see, we know quite a lot about Thorwald, from the caper six years back. One of his habits is trying to convert people to this Madeira. A lot of times we know about, he'd given one of his friends a bottle, urged them to try it. And it's not a wine everybody likes. Heavier and sweeter than port—like a liqueur, you know. While we were looking into him before, I ran across half a dozen people who had bottles of Madeira hanging around with a couple of glassfuls gone."

There was a gloomy silence. "Well, I guess that's it," said Waltham, getting up heavily. "We'll hope nationwide publicity will turn up something—because, though we'll take a damn good look around here, he might be anywhere, damn it."

"And," said Mendoza meditatively, "another interesting little thought occurs to me. Just an idea, maybe far-fetched. You said Thorwald isn't working for his former bosses any more. Just a stateless citizen. Well, wherever he is, or was, he couldn't live on air. People running from the Reds don't often manage to carry fortunes away with them. And I seem to recall that he had several engineering degrees which were, of course, canceled or destroyed or whatever happens to such things when a man's defrocked from the brotherhood. So he couldn't get work at his old regular job. We don't know what Valerie's latest racket was—could he have been in on it?"

"That's reaching," said Waltham. "I suppose it could be. But you said she's probably been on the bent for about three and a half years."

"Well"—Mendoza emptied the ash tray absently, brushed ash off the desk—"I've got another guess to make about Valerie. *Perdido por una, perdido por todo*—in for a penny, in for a pound. She'd been brought up to be honest—until she was nineteen, she associated with only nice upright people. When she succumbed to temptation and started shoplifting, her first venture off the rails, she was caught almost right away. Nobody turns into a suc-

51

cessful pro crook overnight. I think since she decided to live by her wits, she's drifted into several different capers, maybe steadily downhill. Maybe, teaming up with different people in that line she'd got to know. Maybe she did do a little hustling at some time or other—we'll ask her former landladies—she wasn't, by the autopsy, the nice innocent child she'd been."

"Well, that's up to you," said Waltham. "We'll get busy on our end of it."

"I trust any relevant leads to the murder will be passed on."

"Oh, sure, if we come across anything——" They left him en masse, leaving the office with extra chairs at odd angles, ashes on the floor, and reminiscent of a cheap cigar.

Mendoza reminded Sergeant Lake to remind Waltham that he'd like either the address book itself or a photostat of it back, and started for International Airport to see Paul Manton.

Miss Jane Freeman—forty-three, thin and ramrod-straight as a Grenadier Guard, with a no-nonsense face scrubbed with green soap twice a day and unenlivened by cosmetics—faced Alison frowning just a trifle.

"I'm afraid, Mrs. Mendoza, that psychological opinion does not bear that out, you know. You should simply leave them alone. Naturally, if they are given your whole attention every time they demand it, they will go from bad to worse. Babies are natural tyrants"—a wintry smile flickered across her pale lips briefly—"and one must be *firm* from the first."

"But I'd defy anybody to ignore them!" said Alison. "Do you mean you're simply going to let them yell?"

52

"Not at all, Mrs. Mendoza, not at all. One must always be thorough. Whenever a baby cries, one must check to see if there is valid reason. If he needs a diaper change, or has hurt himself in some way—you understand. But if he is simply anticipating his next feeding time, or asking for attention, no valid reason exists for spending time with him. The tendency must be checked at once, *or*," said Miss Freeman ominously, "one is asking for trouble later on. When the baby discovers that mere noise does not always get him the attention he wants, he soon stops. I'm sure you see what I mean."

Alison said reluctantly, "Well, yes, in a way. But—" That was all very well, she thought, for small children whom you could communicate with. Could discipline, try to reason with. But quite simply, what she felt was that babies who cried were unhappy, and needed comforting. You couldn't reason with a baby, say, look, you've got no reason to feel unhappy. Heavens, sometimes grown-up people couldn't explain why they felt unhappy. They just did. And she couldn't see why it was wrong to give a baby a little extra cuddling and loving.

"And another thing, Mrs. Mendoza—" Miss Freeman was definitely frowning now.

"Yes?" said Alison uneasily.

"I really am afraid we shall have to keep the nursery door shut at *all* times. Those cats keep coming in." If Miss Freeman had said *king cobras* she couldn't have sounded more portentous.

"Yes, Bast's taken a notion to sleep in one of the cribs, and— They're quite friendly cats, really, they're not doing any harm."

"*Harm!*" ejaculated Miss Freeman. "Why, not ten

minutes ago I turned my back for a moment and when I looked, that big black creature was actually licking the little girl's face!"

"That's El Señor," said Alison. "I know, he has a sort of compulsion about washing, he likes to—"

"Most insanitary!" said Miss Freeman severely. "One never knows what germs a pet animal is harboring."

"Well, that's nonsense," said Alison. "They don't. Actually, as Dr. Stocking says—our vet—cats and dogs catch more diseases from people than vice versa. They're perfectly clean cats—"

"I must disagree there, really. Personally I disapprove of keeping pets at all, any animal is bound to be insanitary. But I realize that some people will behave sentimentally. I'm afraid we must at least keep them out of the nursery," said Miss Freeman firmly.

At this point both twins began to yell. "They're hungry," said Alison, glancing at the clock. "I'll just—" She started for the kitchen.

"Now, now, Mrs. Mendoza!" said Miss Freeman archly. "What am I here for, after all? And it's half an hour before their regular time, there's no hurry. Leave it to me, I'll see to it."

"Well, I haven't been keeping to any regular schedule—" After all, thought Alison, even a baby knows when it's hungry!

"A regular routine is always best," said Miss Freeman. "Of course babies differ, some have slower digestions. We'll try a six-hour schedule at first, and see how it works out. Now don't you worry about a thing," and she bustled off kitchenwards.

Alison sighed. She wished she could have nursed them

longer; if she still were, she could simply walk into the nursery, whatever Miss Freeman said.

Well, after all she'd hired the woman; let her try her way and see how it worked out.

Bertha had been a silent witness to all this, vigorously polishing the big coffee table in the L of the sectional. "I don't figure," she said now, shaking her tight gray sausage-curls at Alison, "that it's just so natural for a born old maid to know what's best for children. Not that I ever had any myself, but I did bring up my niece Mabel. Just listen to them two yell! Hungry, all right. Well, personally speakin', Mis' Mendoza, the way I figure is, like the saying goes, catch more flies with honey than vinegar."

"How right you are," said Alison moodily.

"She was *what?*" said Paul Manton blankly. He stared at Mendoza incredulously.

Mendoza had located him without much trouble; InterState Airways occupied one of the smaller hangars scattered round the huge International Airport's perimeter. It wasn't a big outfit: ferried small cargo up and down the state. A busy general manager had pointed out Manton, working on a twin-engined plane at the far end of the hangar.

Manton was in his early thirties, tall and broad-shouldered, a good-looking young man in a rugged way; he had tawny blond hair, the same coloring as Valerie Ellis. He wore a once-white overall, oil-stained, and his big, well-shaped hands were dirty too.

"In some sort of crooked business," said Mendoza again. "No regular job. You didn't suspect that, Mr. Manton?"

"My God, no, of course not!" He had been, apparently,

genuinely astonished at the news of Valerie's murder. And, intriguingly, for just a flash Mendoza thought his eyes had held fear. News of her identification had been in last night's papers, but only a couple of paragraphs; he could have missed it. (After today it'd make headlines.) Now he was surprised all over again at this further news. His eyes narrowed a little on Mendoza. "For God's sake, are you sure? I mean—I thought—she told me she worked at some department store. Robinson's, I think it was. But, of course, I didn't know her very well. We'd had a few dates, but I wasn't the steady boy friend, like that. She went out with Cardenas more than with me."

"That's Ricardo Cardenas?"

"That's right. I met him at Val's, matter of fact. My God, are you sure about this? Ricardo'd have had seven fits if he'd known—Civil Service is kind of touchy about who employees associate with. What—what was she doing, anyway? She always seemed like an ordinary girl—" Unheeding of the dirt on his hand, he drove fingers through his crest of hair. "This really shakes me."

"Where'd you meet her, Mr. Manton, and when?" Mendoza dropped his cigarette and stepped on it carefully.

"It was about, oh, three-four months ago—another girl I know introduced us at a party. Maureen Moskovitch." He smiled briefly, showing very white teeth. "Sounds funny, but her maiden name was Kelly, she says. I don't know how she knew Val, or how long. But, my God— seemed an ordinary girl—"

"Her landlady tells us," said Mendoza, "that on several occasions two men came together to see her. By the descriptions, I'd make a guess that one was you and the other may have been—"

56

"Cardenas," said Manton. He blinked and disarranged his hair some more. "Sure. See, I—" He hesitated and looked a little embarrassed. "I guess this is going to sound kind of funny, Lieutenant. I mean, a guy like me—just a mechanic. But, see, I'm interested in folk music. I don't mean like hillbilly stuff, the American stuff, but—you know—the older foreign kind. The really old stuff. And Ricardo, he is too, he's got quite a collection of records—speaks six languages, bright guy—a lot more than I have. Well, I met him at a party Val had—"

"When?"

"Oh, call it a couple of months ago, bit more. And we got to talking, and found out we were both interested in this kind of thing, see? So one thing led to another, and about, oh, maybe three times we met there at Val's place and he brought along some of his records—he's got some really offbeat stuff—"

"And a phonograph?" There'd been no phonograph in the apartment.

"Sure, a portable. But—" Manton lit another cigarette nervously. "Look—"

"Why did you meet there? Why not your place or his?"

"Well—" said Manton. "Oh, hell, even if she is dead—even if she was a crook of some kind, like you say—— God, I can't take that one in yet!—hell of a thing to say, but there it was. Way I told you, I had a few dates with her but it wasn't anything serious, see? I was just somebody she knew. Like she knew Maureen and Bob and Linda Hausner—other people. But, first time I met Ricardo there, I could see—anybody could see—she'd really fallen for him. She was crazy about him, the big deal it was. And —well, it wasn't vice versa, see? He liked her O.K., but

57

she was just a girl *he* knew, if you get me. Well, that first time we met—Ricardo and I, I mean—and got to talking, Val—sort of dealt herself in. Claimed to be real interested too, wanted to hear his records, and so on. She wasn't really—she was just trying to impress Ricardo, get closer with him. See?"

Mendoza said he saw.

"Well, that was it. We met there a couple of times, but she was bored to death, you could see. He's got some great stuff," said Manton enthusiastically. "Really unusual— but I've got a couple of things he hadn't heard too. And lately we've been getting together at his place mostly, just the two of us." He dropped his cigarette, stepped on it, and said awkwardly, "Like I say, I guess it sounds funny, a guy like me interested in— But that was how it was."

"I see," said Mendoza. "Well, I understand a lot of people are interested in folk music."

"I guess so," agreed Manton.

"What does Mr. Cardenas do? You say he's in Civil Service?"

"Oh, he's a chief accountant in the Welfare office—pensions and so on."

"Mhmm. Would you mind telling me where you were on Sunday?"

"Last Sunday? That's when she—" Manton had an expressive face; it showed surprise, anger, nervousness in succession. "Hey," he said, "*I* didn't have any—what the hell, you think—Well, anyway, thank God, I've got an alibi." He laughed, suddenly relaxing. "I had Monday off, so I flew over to Vegas early on Sunday—came back Monday night."

"Yes? Where did you stay?"

"Oh, I didn't bother to check in anywhere—when I get in a hot game, what's a little sleep lost? Did myself some good, too."

"Mhmm. Names of anybody you played with? Friends?"

"Well, I guess not—I—you know how you pick up with people, casual— But, listen, I didn't have anything to do with—" He was uneasy again. "I didn't even know her very well! She was just—"

"A casual acquaintance, yes, I know," said Mendoza. "'That was quite a dangerous little spot you got yourself out of, a few days ago. That emergency landing. I read about it in the *Times*."

Suddenly a totally different man looked out of Paul Manton's steady blue eyes. A wholly adult, competent man, mature and sophisticated. A—what was the word? Something teasingly familiar about that expression . . . "Aren't you so right," he said. "I was saying to myself, Well, boy, here it is and don't you wish you'd said your prayers oftener, when I spotted that stretch of freeway. Damn tank springing a leak— It was God's grace there wasn't any traffic, that time of night. They do say, if you're born to be hanged you'll never be drowned."

"You do much private flying?"

"As much as I can." He gave Mendoza a rather shy smile; he was the awkward young mechanic again. "I just got in on the Korea thing—Air Force. So I got trained free, you might say. If I can ever get the capital together— which is about as likely as the Commies lifting the Iron Curtain—I'd like to start my own line, cargo hauling like this outfit I'm working for . . . Well, I'm sorry I can't tell you anything more about Val. The hell of a thing. Seemed like such an ordinary girl, you know—never

59

crossed my mind that she was anything else. And Ricardo will go straight up in the air. But then, neither of us really knew her very well."

Nobody, Mendoza reflected, starting back downtown, had known Valerie well. According to them. After the fact.

He saw the amber flick on on the signal ahead, jammed his foot down and made it across, illegally. And quite suddenly he knew what that expression had been on Manton's face. The look of the gambler saying, Let's take a long chance . . . It was—as Valerie's had been—a reckless face.

Yes?

But all that sounded straightforward. Very likely it was, but what proved it? In a way, his lack of corroboration over at Las Vegas was natural, if he was that kind of gambler.

Mrs. Farlow sounded genuine too (well, she very probably was), and the Dvorzhaks. But no proof.

There were, of course, Maureen Kelly Moskovitch and Gloria Litvak. . . .

Valerie Ellis—mixed up with the underground political thing, for God's sake? Thorwald . . . But the Feds said, Thorwald probably no longer involved with the Commies; on the run from them. Was this, could this be the complex spy story?

Just possibly? Thieves falling out. Thorwald, possibly, turning his coat again—and, having valuable information to pass on to, say, the C.I.A.? So the conspiracy here warned, and setting up a trap for him? Valerie one of the conspirators? And Thorwald getting wise, and—

Because, look at it from that angle—Valerie, spoiled, used to having money, and only nineteen—a lot of mixed-up kids that age got caught by the ideals of Communism. The impossible ideals. Communism, Socialism —two sides of the same coin. Sounding just fine, a wonderful idea—only the catch was, neither remotely workable until human nature got entirely changed around.

Could it be that—

No, he thought. Let the Feds work that angle all they pleased, it wasn't so. Thorwald be damned, this had been a private kill. A personal kill.

He got nuances from people—even from corpses. Valerie had been too much interested in Valerie to possess any ideals. What Valerie had been interested in was cold cash.

He left the Ferrari in the nearest public lot and walked half a block down to the Hall of Justice. After consulting the board in the lobby he rode the elevator up to the ninth floor and told the receptionist he'd like to see Mr. Cardenas.

"Oh, well, I don't know—" She cast him a doubtful look. "Mr. Cardenas in Accounting? Well, I'll see. Excuse me, what name did you—oh, yes." She went away, still looking doubtful. This was an old rabbit warren of an office, corridors leading in three directions from the main room. It seemed to be a busy office, people going and coming, clerks bustling by clutching armfuls of papers.

The receptionist came back and said Mr. Cardenas could see him now. Mendoza followed her down a dusty hall to a door with a frosted-glass panel that bore the simple legend, *Accounting*.

Inside, a large square room had been divided into a number of units by shoulder-high partitions. His guide led him to the one farthest on the left, opened the door set in the partition, and turned away with the air of washing her hands of him. Mendoza went in.

The cubicle was some ten feet square, and held a desk, two chairs and a couple of file cases. The man sitting at the desk looked up at him. "And what can I do for you, sir?" he asked in a pleasant baritone voice. "You're a *police* lieutenant? I haven't even had a traffic ticket that I can recall in— What's it all about?"

Five

Cardenas was obviously the boy friend described as "a little bit like you, sir." He was somewhat broader than Mendoza, and his face was rounder; he was in the process of losing his hair. Mendoza put him down as around forty.

He was pleasant and co-operative. As Manton had predicted, he was visibly shocked at the news that Valerie had been in some racket. "Good God, if the chief had found out!" he said. "What was it, anyway? I can't take it in—"

For the rest, he told exactly the same story that Manton had. Even down to confirming the fact—looking suitably embarrassed—that, yes, Valerie had, well, maybe been more interested in him than the other way round. "Not to sound conceited—and I don't deny that I was a little flattered." He laughed. "And also surprised! After all, I was a good deal older—" He'd known her only casually, and not long.

Naturally, naturally, thought Mendoza. And ask Mrs. Montague if she'd seen him, or Manton, calling there longer ago than a couple of months back—probably she couldn't be sure, she would just see their backs going in.

"Where did you meet her, Mr. Cardenas?"

"Through a mutual friend," said Cardenas easily. "A Mrs. Mandelbaum." He gave the address when asked, but looked rather shaken. "Lieutenant, I hope there won't be too much publicity over this—you know in my position, well, my chief— After all, I was a mere acquaintance, I hadn't anything to do with her death—"

"We have to check on everyone, you know," said Mendoza. When the Feds' press releases got out, there'd be publicity—like wildfire running loose there'd be publicity. "It doesn't necessarily mean we suspect you—or anyone else, Mr. Cardenas."

"Well, naturally not," said Cardenas a little stiffly. As if he found the mere suggestion that he could be suspected in bad taste.

"So I hope you won't take offense when I ask you where you were on Sunday from ten o'clock on."

"Where I— Well, I suppose you have to ask." Cardenas looked undecided whether to be angry or not. "Of course. And as far as that goes, I think you'll find it all—er—in order, Lieutenant. From ten, did you say? Yes, well, I was at home then, but I went out to eleven o'clock Mass at St. Mark's. I met a friend there, Dr. Gardner—he asked me to play golf with him that afternoon. Well, it was a nice day and I hadn't had a game in quite a while. We played a round and then had a drink at the clubhouse— that would be, let me see, about four o'clock . . . Yes, we'd gone straight from the church—that is, I stopped by to pick up my clubs, of course. And then we played another nine holes. He said his wife was away and he was going to have dinner at the clubhouse, asked me to join him.

64

Which I did, and later on we both played bridge with a couple of other fellows there, until nearly eleven. I got home about midnight." He gave the names readily. "So you see—" He tucked his round chin into his collar severely. "As if I could be remotely connected anyway—"

If it checked out, Cardenas was pretty definitely in the clear. Mendoza felt a little exasperated. No leads at all. "Thanks very much. As I said, we have to check."

"I just can't imagine who'd want to murder the girl. But of course, if she was involved with crooks of some kind—"

"Yes." Mendoza decided that Cardenas was a bore. The shirt well stuffed. And if that alibi checked, he was out of the picture. He thanked him politely and came away.

He drove up North Broadway to Federico's, and met Hackett and John Palliser just going in. They sat down together, and he brought them up to date on Valerie. "All up in the air, damn it. And what's worse, I'm beginning to have a hunch that it was a private kill in the sense that the motive hadn't any connection with whatever racket it was. So even when we do ferret that out— Well, how are you doing on Lover Boy?"

"We're waiting for Sacramento to send us another list," said Palliser resignedly. Palliser was the newest sergeant in Mendoza's office and a rather bright boy: promising. "I know it's the only way to get at it, but it takes time, and meanwhile all this mud thrown at us by the press—"

"I know. But it's an ill wind, et cetera. When this news breaks on Thorwald"—some of the afternoon papers already had it—"he and Valerie will probably occupy the headlines for a while and sidetrack the viewers-with-alarm . . . Small steak as usual, Adam, and coffee."

"Yes, sir." The tall waiter looked inquiringly at Hackett.

65

"Oh, hell," said Hackett unhappily. "I guess the same."

Palliser ordered and asked Hackett with respectful sympathy whether he'd lost any weight. "Three pounds," said Hackett gloomily. "The doctor says at least fifteen more."

Mendoza and Palliser looked at him with the conscious superiority of men not inclined to take on weight. Mendoza said, "You aren't firm enough with her, Art. After all, she did swear to obey you, didn't she? So she's a good cook —and she tells you you're a big man, you need a lot of food. She's heard what the doctor says and she's got a normal I.Q."

"It's not Angel, damn it, it's me. I mean it's not exactly Angel," said Hackett. "Sure, she gives me the high-protein diet, and I'm still trying to learn to drink coffee without sugar—but I can't expect her to go on a diet with me, can I? And, damn it, she's just like you two—eat anything and never gain a pound. Well, so she makes these things for herself, you know, like this special sour-cream dressing, and that wild-rice casserole with mushrooms and bacon, and last night"—a fond reminiscent gleam came into his eyes—"a really extra-special cheesecake—and, well, I get hungry, damn it. After all, I *am* six-three and a half, and only fifteen pounds—"

"No self-discipline," said Mendoza. "Deplorable. Keep the mind firmly fixed on your next physical."

"Thanks for the advice," said Hackett irritably. "The doctor's nuts. According to insurance statistics, I could go another five pounds and be inside the limit. He says they're way off base. But—"

"Never mind," said Mendoza soothingly. "Take your mind off food for a minute, and listen to me. I've had a small brainwave about Lover Boy." They both looked at him alertly. "That pock-marked complexion. All of the women said very definitely, pock-marked. Now, we hadn't thought too hard about it, except as another point of identification. But there's a couple of ways to acquire a pock-marked complexion. One, a bad case of adolescent acne sometimes leaves scars. But that's a little different than actual pockmarks, ¿no es verdad? And they were all quite definite—pockmarks. Well, smallpox is practically unheard-of in this country."

"So?" said Hackett.

"So," said Mendoza, "I suggest that you ask the Immigration people for a list of Negroes coming in from Mexico within the last—call it fifteen years. Calm down, it wouldn't be that long a list—ask them to do the screening. We know his approximate age."

"Well, it's an idea," agreed Palliser.

Mendoza had left instructions with Sergeant Lake that morning; when he came into the office after lunch, Maureen Kelly Moskovitch and her husband were waiting for him.

This kind, always a better chance of getting anything out of them if you brought them in to question. Their own familiar surroundings gave them a little confidence; but their past experience with cops and police stations turned them nervous in the proximity of either.

Overnight, as he'd told the Feds, routine had turned up Maureen—and Gloria—and a few interesting facts.

Maureen was twenty-eight, older than Valerie. She'd been picked up first as a juvenile, at seventeen, for soliciting. Ward of the court until she was of age. By that time

67

she was married to Mike Moskovitch, who had been clean of any record then. The year after that Moskovitch had been dropped on as the very successful daylight burglar who had for six months been taking nice parcels of loot from empty apartments. First offense, and he'd got a three-to-five; he'd served four and had been out for nearly four years. Rather certainly he was at some crook caper, holding no regular job, but they hadn't any evidence on him as of now.

Meanwhile, since about six years ago, Maureen had been picked up for soliciting three times, had served minimal sentences.

They were there waiting for him, brought in unwillingly, nervous and scared. And stubborn. He had them ushered into his office, asked Sergeant Lake to take notes. He started in on Maureen . . .

"All right, all right, so I got a little pedigree! That don't say—you're just nuts, trying to— Listen, Val was my *friend!* We were pals—I just cried buckets when I heard she was dead like that, didn't I, Mike? Honest, you got to believe me—" Maureen was little and dark, and if she'd left herself more or less as nature made her, would have been pretty. But she'd plucked out most of her eyebrows, and substituted outdated thin curves painted on, and exaggerated a small mouth with too dark a shade of lipstick; to a naturally buxom figure she'd added a much-padded bra. Her nails were long and mostly magenta, the polish chipped here and there; and her cherry-colored sweater was too tight. "Listen, we were pals from way back, Val and me! I didn't—"

"That's what I want to talk about," said Mendoza. "I'm not accusing you of anything, Mrs. Moskovitch. I just want all you know about her. Where'd you meet her, when, what was she doing then? Who did she know?"

"Oh," she said blankly. "You mean—you mean, like if I might know something that'd help you find out? But I don't! Gee, I'd tell you right off if I did, honest—Val was a good friend o' mine—" She looked at her husband. "You can say that, can't you, Mike? I never—"

He scowled at Mendoza, a big hefty young man, very dark, blue stubble of beard showing, dark eyes sullen under heavy brows. "We got nothing to hide," he said. "We're both clean, copper."

"You did know," asked Mendoza of private curiosity, "that your wife did a little time for prostitution while you were inside?"

"What the hell's it to you, bloodhound? So she did. I'm broad-minded, so what?"

"Nothing at all," said Mendoza equably. "So, let's hear what you know, Mrs. Moskovitch. When and where did you first meet Miss Ellis?"

She had calmed down a little. She said reluctantly, "'Bout three years back. She was living same place I did, on Masefield Avenue."

"What were you doing then?" And as she didn't reply, "You were earning a scratch living hustling, weren't you? I've seen the landlady at that place, she's damn easygoing. Weren't you?"

"You know all the answers," she said sullenly. "All right."

"How was Valerie Ellis living? She didn't have a regular job either. Was she in the same game? And you two got acquainted over—mhmm—mutual interests?"

69

"That's right," she said shortly. "Sure. She was kinda new at it, I give her some tips."

Mendoza looked at her, but he was seeing Valerie. Valerie, coming from the house in Bel-Air, a sorority up at Berkeley, to that. Within a year. Grant that she'd been spoiled, shocked to be left with nothing. Some fatal weakness of character there too, to slide so easily downhill. The go-getting Fred Ellis—yes, maybe she'd just naturally acquired the idea that money was all-important. Maybe some man getting hold of her, but— And the complacent honest Ellises, only relatives, believing whatever she said, because naturally Fred's girl couldn't do anything bad.

"Was she working alone?"

"I dunno what you mean."

"Let's not waste time, Maureen," he said, sharp and cold. "Was there somebody running her?"

"Not—then."

"All right. When and who?"

"I—she wasn't—she didn't take so good to it. It wasn't awful long she kept at it, see. I'm *trying* to tell you, give me a chance—"

Mike Moskovitch just sat and glowered.

"Who?" asked Mendoza patiently.

"Eddy Warren," said Maureen sulkily. "I didn't—don't know much about him. She sort of turned up with him about six months after I met her, an' after that she moved 'n' I didn't see so much of her."

"But you know what capers they were up to? The same thing, or something else? Did he run any other girls?"

"I dunno."

"Come on, come on—you knew, you kept up with her, she'd have said something. Out with it."

"I—guess it was mostly just the usual old game. You know. They'd hit—like conventions, and like that. Vegas, San Diego, all over."

"The tired old badger game? Shakedown. All right. Who's Eddy Warren, what do you know about him?"

"I don't know nothing about him. Honest I don't. He was just a guy. When I ran across Val again, she didn't say nothing about him, he wasn't around no more. Honest."

"What was she doing lately? Since dropping Eddy?"

"I don't know."

"You'll stay here until I get all the answers I want, you know," said Mendoza gently. "Don't make it so hard on yourself, Maureen. What was Valerie's latest racket?"

"I don't *know!*" she half screamed at him. "I'm not telling you no lies, copper— Jesus, I knew who took her off I'd tell you quick—she was a pal—but I just don't *know*. I saw she was really in the chips, clothes she had 'n' all—an' time goes on, even more—that color TV—I *asked* her—Jesus, wouldn't I ask her? But she'd just laugh an' say she was like a cat, always fell on her feet. I swear to God I don't know—it wasn't nothing like the other, I know that, but she wouldn't say!"

"Take it easy," said Moskovitch coldly. "He hasn't got a thing on you. He can't hold you, make you talk."

"Oh, don't be silly, Mike! I'd talk enough if I knew anything'd help 'em find whoever killed her! It don't seem it could be, somebody killing Val— But I just don't know, honest, Lieutenant. I asked her a lot of times, naturally. But she'd just pass it off."

"How?" he asked softly.

"Oh, any way. Like I remember once she said, Ask no questions, get told no lies. Kind of laughing. An' then,

71

'nother time, she said—she was serious about it then—she said, let me think back, she said, It's a swell caper, Maureen, a real offbeat one but it sure pays off. An' she said, But I can't talk about it. Be too dangerous. She said a funny thing—she said, about a old proverb—that three can keep a secret if two of them are dead—but she was sure about these other two. It was funny."

Mendoza regarded her in silence. He thought she was coming clean. One like this—no, Valerie wouldn't have confided in her. Maureen would have told the interesting news of Valerie's profitable caper to anybody she knew, if it occurred to her. And it probably would have . . . So, by inference, two other people in on it with Valerie? Whatever the hell it had been.

Looking at Maureen, where she sat huddled chewing her ragged lipstick off, he felt tired. Not for the first time he wondered why he stayed on this job, when he didn't have to. Sense of guilt, reneging on the oath once he had all that money? Not exactly . . . There was an inevitable gulf fixed between the police and the ordinary citizens. All those ordinary citizens clamoring for them to catch Lover Boy and stash him away behind bars . . . The police were the barrier, he thought, between the honest citizenry and the dirt. The incredible muck at the bottom of things. The average honest citizen saw the police in the person of the neat-uniformed traffic officer, white-gloved, his gun neatly sheathed at his hip. The average honest citizen hadn't any remote conception how very dirty the bottom of things was, that police had to probe, getting down in the muck themselves to do so.

They stood outside and complained and jeered. On the rare occasions when some cop got himself entangled in the muck, they rejoiced: knew it all along, corrupt cops. They wrote letters to the editor disapproving of the latest pay hike and telling about overbearing traffic cops.

They didn't know anything at all about the muck that policemen delved into, to keep the honest citizens safe and healthy and happy.

For some five seconds Mendoza succumbed to a prevalent disease among police officers and hated the honest citizenry with a beautiful savagery.

Remembering, say—the latest one—Patrolman Charles Haggerty, beaten and shot to death with his own gun by a gang of juveniles, while a crowd of adults looked on with never a move to help him.

Of course, that had been down on Skid Row.

He forced his mind back to Maureen. He asked, "You remember anything else she said?"

"No. She never told me nothing, for all I asked. Honest, I'd say if she had—I liked Val, she was a swell girl—we were *friends*—"

"All right," said Mendoza abruptly. "That's all. You can go." He didn't watch them out; he swiveled round in his chair and stared out over the panorama of the city, clear and crystal-sharp this February day, smogless. He could see the towers of the new California skyscraper, all of twenty-four stories, at the corner of Wilshire and Western. He could see, blue and sharp, the outlines of the Hollywood hills separating L.A. from the San Fernando Valley.

It was a prettier view than the Moskovitches.

He swiveled back. Sergeant Lake said, "Makes you wonder. But they come all sorts."

Mendoza felt better suddenly. Phlegmatic, comfortable

73

Sergeant Lake comforted him. There wasn't really much difference, he thought, between Sergeant Lake and any other youngish fellow in a white-collar job at six thousand a year, a fellow with a wife and three kids, buying a house on time, worrying about bills, about the kids' report cards. He said, "You're a philosopher, Jimmy. Set up a hunt for this Eddy Warren, will you? Ask Records. Ask Vice."

"Will do," said Sergeant Lake cheerfully. "Like you said, I had this Gloria Litvak fetched in too. She should be here by now, I'll go see. You want her right off?"

Mendoza made a grimace. "I suppose so . . . Why are we here, Jimmy? Deliberately playing in the mud? A lot of other ways to make a living."

Sergeant Lake, on his feet, regarded the question seriously, as he would any question. "Well, that's so, Lieutenant," he agreed. "And if you're not on inside detail, a lot of safer ways too. Like you know, I got shot up three times before I got out of uniform. But of course there's the pension and the hospital benefits. Hadn't been, I'd have had a time finding the cash to pay off the hospital when we had the third one. But, tell you the honest gospel truth, Lieutenant, what sort of tipped the scales for me was a second looie in the Air Force. When I joined up, I mean."

"Oh?"

Sergeant Lake rubbed his jaw, grinning. "He was after Caroline too," he said. "And don't we know, they always like a uniform."

Mendoza laughed "*¡De acuerdo!* You restore my faith in irrational human nature."

Sergeant Lake regarded him benignly and said, "Nor I don't see you've just all that right to look down your nose at Maureen Moskovitch. Seeing that before you got to be a respectable married man—"

"¡*Camarada, simpatía masculino!* I never stooped so low as the Maureens, I assure you!" said Mendoza, laughing. "O.K., go and see if Gloria's waiting." It was three o'clock; he swiveled around and looked out the window again, waiting. He wished he could go home to Alison and the twins and forget all this.

But, even as he thought that, he knew he never could; he wasn't built that way. Given the tangle, the mystery, he had to unravel it for his own satisfaction. Find all the answers, get it all tidily straightened out.

Six

Lake came back with Gloria Litvak, and Mendoza asked her to sit down. After a sullen moment she did. "I don't know anything about it," she said. "About Val's getting killed. I don't know who'd do a thing like that. I couldn't tell you anything."

"I haven't asked you anything yet," Mendoza pointed out. "I think you can answer the questions I'm going to ask. How long had you known Miss Ellis?"

"I don't see how that helps you on the murder." She was nervous. She fumbled in her bag, got out a cigarette. This one was younger, about Valerie's age. "I didn't have anything to do with that!"

"Nobody's said you did. When and how did you meet her?"

She started to protest again, shrugged, and said, "Cops. All right, I got to know Val about two and a half years ago, around there."

"How?"

She took her time over that one, probably doing some fast figuring as to whether the truth would be dangerous in some way; finally she said, "Oh, well, a guy I knew then introduced us."

"What's his name?"

"I lost touch with him since, I don't know—"

"What's his name?"

"Warren. Eddy Warren."

"Was he running you then?"

"I dunno what— No, for God's sake! I never let a man—" This one was platinum blond, buxom, not very pretty. All the usual accessories, from the dark-red nails to the cheap cologne.

"About that time, Eddy Warren and Val were working the shakedown racket. Were you in on that too?"

Her eyes moved; she had known about that, but she hadn't known that the police knew, by the way her mouth tightened. She'd only been picked up once, and got off with a fine; she wouldn't want to put herself in trouble by making any admissions. She said, "I don't know anything about that. I didn't know Eddy ever did anything wrong. Or Val either."

"Oh, come now," said Mendoza mildly. "Never had any little girlish chats about customers?"

"I'm clean!" she said hurriedly. "I been straight ever since that time your damn college-boy Vice cop tricked me! I never knew Val was—"

"But you'd kept up with her. You saw her fairly often. Don't tell me you just made light conversation about the latest fashions and the current best-sellers. Didn't you ever wonder how she was living, when she hadn't a regular job? Ask her about it? What'd she tell you? What was her racket?"

He didn't really think Gloria would know: another

77

one like Maureen, and Valerie wouldn't have confided. But he saw her eyes move again, before she dropped the lids, and one hand tightened its grasp on her shiny plastic bag. The other hand, holding her cigarette, trembled very slightly. She was scared to death, he saw. And she did know something.

Just scared of the cops? Or maybe, being involved in this just because she'd known Val, being looked at closer and dropped on again? No; she had been nervous, but not really frightened until he'd brought this up. She did know something about Val's racket.

Val and two others. Gloria one of them?

"I don't know what you mean," she was saying mechanically. "I thought she was straight."

"But you knew she hadn't always been. From the time you both knew Eddy Warren."

"No. No." She shook her head blindly. "I never knew that. I never knew her very well." A better education than Maureen; she spoke fairly well. But now her voice was shaking too. "I don't know anything about her getting killed."

"I'm not asking about that. When was the last time you saw her?"

She relaxed just a trifle; she wasn't afraid of that question. "It was a week ago last Tuesday. I just dropped by to ask her to a party. That Thursday it was, week ago today. I didn't stay long because somebody came—I mean, somebody was coming to see her." She'd nearly made a slip there, over something, and had scared herself again. Her eyes slid nervously away from his.

"Somebody came or somebody was coming. Which?"

She was flustered that he'd picked that up. "Somebody was coming, and she said it was private business so I left."

"I see. And you never asked yourself where her money came from, when she hadn't a regular job. Weren't curious enough to ask her about the private business."

"W-why should I? I mind my own business," she said breathlessly. "I thought she had a job at Robinson's, really I did, I thought she was straight. Just like m-me."

"Even when you found her home at—what time—in the afternoon? Well, of course she wouldn't tell you about the private business even if you'd asked. You're sure you never heard her drop any hints as to where the money came from?"

"Why sh-should I? No."

"Well, if you don't know, you don't," he said with a shrug. "At that, I don't suppose she'd talk about it." He let Gloria see that he'd accepted her denial, believed her all along the line. "And especially if you didn't know her very well, as you said. Pity you can't tell me any more, but thanks very much for coming in anyway." He stood up. She got to her feet in a hurry, anxious for release, open relief showing in her eyes. She'd put it across; he believed her, he didn't suspect anything.

"That's O.K.," she said almost happily, and turned to the door. He let her take a step, and then spoke quite casually.

"By the way, did she come to the party?"

"No, she had to be over at Vic's—" Gloria stopped dead still. In her sudden tremendous relief, her hurry to be gone, she'd forgotten to guard her tongue. She'd let out something else, and now she was terrified. Too terrified to open her mouth, try to cover up that slip, which was a pity—because if she did she'd probably tell several stupid lies and give him some lead.

She knew that what she'd just said was a slip; but it didn't mean one damned thing to Mendoza. *She had to be over at Vic's.* Vic who? No Vic had shown up in this case so far.

"Oh," he said, coming out from behind his desk and moving to face Gloria. "That's very interesting, Miss Litvak. So she had to be over at Vic's." He held her frightened eyes. "Vic who?"

Suddenly he thought she was going to faint. A greenish pallor spread over her complexion; she shut her eyes for a moment. He took her arm, but she shook him off. "I'm —all—right," she muttered. "Just kind of dizzy a minute, I got up too quick. Doctor says I need glasses."

"Vic who?"

"I don't know," she said. She was breathing rapidly, shallowly. "That's all Val said, just that she had to be at Vic's that night. I don't know any Vic. And, way I say, she was expecting somebody, so I just left then. And that's all I know."

She wasn't to be moved from that. He had to let her go. He went back to his desk and called Waltham. At least, on this one they were getting quite a lot of their work done for them. The Federal boys were taking a long close look at every individual mentioned in that book, and at their backgrounds and relatives too. Where only one name was mentioned, as was the case with those fourteen names embellished with dollar signs, they were taking a look at everybody in this territory who wore those names. It would take time and men, but they had the organization, and they were good. They would pass their information on, so there was no sense wasting his own men on that.

"I know it's early to ask," he said to Waltham, "but have you got around to Gloria Litvak yet?"

"Let's see," said Waltham. Mendoza heard papers rattle. "We're sending you a daily report, as we cover the list. Take a little time, of course. There's not much here yet. You know about her being picked up, naturally. She's twenty-four, never been married. Graduated from high school. Family looks respectable, nothing against any of 'em. Father's a bookkeeper at a manufacturing plant."

"Really? Well, the well-brought-up girls do go off the rails sometimes," said Mendoza, thinking of that case last year.

"So they do. Family consists of parents, one older and one younger brother, uncle—father's brother. Father emigrated from Poland when he was twenty. He's fifty-three now. Mother was born here, but is also Polish."

"You said not much? I'd call that plenty."

"Well, we're still looking at them for any political funny business. Father's a registered Democrat but that doesn't really say anything. Fellow who saw them says, by the way, that the family was terribly ashamed when he mentioned Gloria's little lapse. She doesn't live with them. Place where she does live, well, it's not very fancy, she could be still a subject for your Vice boys. That's about it, so far."

"Well, thanks very much. By the way, I saw Paul Manton and that Cardenas myself," and he told Waltham what they'd said. "You just might have a look to check on it. Just for fun. And I've got a new name for you. Eddy Warren." Sergeant Lake came in and laid a file card before him silently. Glancing at it, he told Waltham how Eddy Warren had turned up. "And I've just got his record. He's thirty-six—skip the description, rather ordinary type—two juvenile counts, dope, and three pickups as an adult. Procuring and resorting. He got a year on the second procuring charge. He's still on probation right now. I'll see his probation officer. Now I do wonder," he added suddenly.

"About what?"

"Those reefers. She might have been storing them for him. If her racket wasn't dope—which we don't know it wasn't, of course. How are you getting on with your end?"

Waltham sounded tired. "Not so hot. You sure run a lot of liquor stores out here. Of course it's a big town. We've been in touch with Interpol—nobody seems to have had a smell of Thorwald since he was seen in East Berlin last June. But he wouldn't have stayed there any longer than he had to, you know. It's not very likely he got into Britain, they keep a damn close check. Of course it's easier —an island. When I think of the thousands of miles of U.S. border right out in the howling wilderness— But my guess is that our Osgar got homesick, wasn't willing to settle for a quite anonymous life in Switzerland or somewhere. Also, there's another thing. We don't know whether they're still after him. Maybe he doesn't know. It could be they just got mad at him for some—er—indiscretion, and once he got away they just said good riddance and stopped chasing him. But maybe not, too. And he might feel a lot safer here at home, where if things got uncomfortably dangerous he could always run not walk to the nearest FBI office and ask asylum for a few Russian secrets."

"Yes, I see that. Well, I know a little more about Valerie now, and I doubt very much that she ever had a political idea in her head. Not a very nice girl, Valerie, but I really can't see her mixed up with a Communist front. Not the type to get idealistically converted—she wasn't given to ideals. And they've got their own experienced agents, why would they offer an outsider hard cash to do a job for them?"

"If," said Waltham, "she was already tied up to Thorwald some way and they saw they could get at him through her?"

"My God, the wild stories you cloak-and-dagger boys think up."

"You'd be surprised at some of the stuff we run into," said Waltham. "Straight out of the paperback spy stories. If she was Thorwald's mistress— Have you got anything on her on that angle?"

Mendoza told him what Maureen had said. "So she'd done a little hustling. Easiest way for a female to earn crooked money. But Maureen said," and he laughed, "she didn't take to it so good. I'll bet. Not just that she was essentially cold—most of that kind are—but she retained, maybe, a little fastidiousness from her expensive upbringing. She found it much more congenial, teaming up with Eddy, to play the old badger game. And it looks as if she graduated from that, and Eddy, to something a little bigger and more profitable. Anything went with Valerie, so long as it brought in the cold cash."

"But if Thorwald—"

"Wait a minute, I'm making a point. By what Maureen said, and by what I know of females, Valerie was essentially sexless. We know she was raking in a pretty good profit from somewhere, so she wouldn't have had to use her sex for money, against her inclinations. I don't think it's at all likely that she was shacking up with anybody."

"Well, by what you say that might be so," said Waltham. "Anything on Paul Manton yet?"

"No, sorry. We've only really been on it today."

"Yes. Well, I'll get onto Eddy Warren. Good luck." Mendoza put the phone down and got up. "I'll be down in Vice if anybody asks, Jimmy."

Vice was his old stamping-ground; he'd spent nearly eight years there; but it hadn't been in this clean, new, airy office because that had been before the big new head-quarters building went up. He drifted down to Lieutenant Percy Andrews' office and asked if he was in.

"Just as of now," said Andrews behind him. "Slumming, Luis?"

"Not exactly. One of your criminal types has showed up in a case of mine." He showed Andrews the file card on Eddy Warren. "Can you tell me anything about him?"

"Sit down. Eddy Warren—" Andrews searched his capacious memory and said, "a smalltimer. Sure, I remember a little. I picked him up that time he got put inside. Remember I was mad as hell because I had to go to court to give evidence on him on my day off . . . He's a little guy, very gentlemanly, and"—he grinned—"by what some of his ladies say, quite a boilermaker. Your type."

"A real Romeo," said Mendoza, translating the pro slang. "Know what he's up to now?"

Andrews shrugged. "He's on probation. Just makes it a little harder for them to carry on business as usual. You know the problem. There just aren't enough men to go round, to keep anything like a thorough check on where probationers live, whom they associate with, and so on. We go through the motions, you could put it. Get them in for the weekly chat, all nice and friendly. You're keeping straight, aren't you, Eddy? Oh, yes, sir, I sure am . . . We can ask his officer, but you won't get much."

"No. I know. The perennial-problem."

"But, listen, Luis. This Eddy Warren. Showing up in a homicide? Cross him off your list, boy. He's a rabbit when it comes to the rough stuff. Most pimps are, you know as well as me."

Mendoza grinned. "Well, I never associated so much with you low woman chasers, even when I was down here."

"So you didn't," returned Andrews amiably. "Being halfway a pro card sharp yourself, you got sent into the gambling-dens. You want me to tag along, see Warren with you?"

"Don't think it's necessary. I don't suppose he's involved in the murder, but he might possibly know a few additional facts about Valerie to hand me—if he'd kept up with her at all. Well, thanks very much . . ."

He sent Scarne out to pick up Eddy at his last recorded address. Forty minutes later Scarne called in to say that Eddy wasn't at home, or at a bowling-alley he was known to frequent, or at a bar ditto.

"Well, you wait at the home address, see if he shows by six. If not, I'll put one of the night-duty men on there," said Mendoza.

He spent a little while going over the current cases Sergeants Curraccio, Galeano, and Rolf were working. Nothing yet on that hit-and-run; damn. Probably nothing but an involuntary homicide on Galeano's case.

The new D.M.V. list from Sacramento, covering Orange,

Ventura, and San Bernardino counties, arrived by special delivery at five-thirty. Hackett, who had just come in, fell on it eagerly.

"He's just got to be somewhere here," he said. "He's just got to."

"Don't be too sure, Art," said Mendoza. "Seven crimes in ten weeks. He could be a truck driver who lives in San Francisco and hits L.A. once a week."

Hackett swore tiredly. "Don't discourage me. I know that, damn it. But, by God, if I have to go through a list of every light-blue pickup truck registered in all fifty-eight counties of California, I'll get him! I only hope he doesn't kill any more women before I do."

"*Es duro de pelar*," said Mendoza dryly. "He could also be a truck driver living in Tucson, Arizona, who crosses the border once a week or so with a cargo."

"*Entendámonos*," said Hackett dangerously, "when you say that, smile! Unless you're asking for an uppercut. Did you see what the *Citizen* said about us today?"

"Don't worry about the press boys. As from about seven hours ago, they're off on this new kick—Thorwald and Valerie. You'll get Lover Boy sooner or later. I wish I was as sure I'd get the X who took Valerie off."

"That's a tough one all right. No leads?"

"Except a hunch," said Mendoza. "And if I'm right, that turns it even tougher . . . a hunch that the motive hadn't one damned thing to do with whatever caper Valerie had been on lately. Damn it. Of course I've only seen a few of the people she knew. But—" He was silent, feeling his jaw. "Well, see what more the Feds turn up tomorrow." He got up and reached for his hat.

El Señor met him at the door, talking loudly. Mendoza caught him as he leaped for his shoulder, and finding the living room empty walked down the hall toward the new nursery, as yet undecorated.

"Alison?"

A tall scraggly gray-haired female bobbed up before him at the door of the room. "Mr. Mendoza? Mrs. Mendoza has gone out to the market, I expect she'll be back soon, sir."

"Oh." Mendoza wandered in. "The little monsters awake? Now, in broad daylight, you don't yell." He grinned down at Master John Luis, who returned the gaze dreamily. Master John, unlike his sister, had inherited his mother's hazel-green eyes, which looked oddly pale in his olive-skinned face. But his black hair grew into an uncanny duplication of his father's sharp widow's peak. "My own fault," said Mendoza severely, admiring him fondly, "such a combination." Master John had contorted his right leg into a comfortable position for sucking his big toe.

"Mr. Mendoza! You must *not*— The cats are *not* to be allowed in the nursery, and you must *not* touch the babies until you have washed—"

He swung around to face her. El Señor swore in his ear, in a bitter voice. "It's Lieutenant," he said. "And I am reasonably clean—is it Miss Freeman?"

"But one can*not* be too careful! I beg your pardon, but I cannot have these unsanitary creatures in the nursery. I must ask you—"

"The cats," said Mendoza, "are also reasonably clean. I don't—"

"Oh! *Another* of them! Get out, you nasty thing!" Miss Freeman clapped her hands at Bast, ambling up to welcome Mendoza. El Señor spat and leaped from Mendoza's shoulder, and Bast shied away down the hall. Master John began to cry.

Mendoza picked him up and patted him. "Miss Freeman, I'm afraid—"

"But you haven't *washed!*" she said distractedly. "I must ask you, Mr. Mendoza—after all, presumably I know my job—"

Belatedly, he got what Alison had been talking about. He said coldly, "Just whose children are these, Miss Freeman? And the cats have the run of the house. We all take baths at least once a day, I assure you." He heard Alison come in the kitchen door.

"Well, really, I didn't mean to imply—but after all, I am accustomed to having the routine I establish respected—"

Master John stopped crying and started to suck his thumb. Mendoza put him back in his crib. "Routine be damned," he said. "All you're hired for is to walk the floor with them in the middle of the night. I need my sleep." He went out to meet Alison.

"Luis?" She came down the hall.

"*Amada*—I've had the hell of a day, I need a little comforting—"

"*¡Querida, amada!*" She got her arms around him tight as he embraced her.

"*Cariña*—"

"Well, really!" said Miss Freeman pinkly, averting her eyes.

Seven

Mendoza was yawning again as he came into his office at a quarter of nine on Friday morning. He'd half waked when the twins went off on schedule, dimly, at two forty-five, but drifted back to sleep again. Miss Freeman might have some peculiar ideas but they could be ignored as long as she stayed up with the little monsters . . . He was awakened again half an hour later by Alison sitting up and lighting a cigarette.

" 'Smatter, they got you into the habit too?"

"I'm sorry, I didn't mean to wake you up," she said worriedly. "That woman and her valid reasons! I know she isn't with them at all, Luis—she's looked for her ridiculous valid reasons and not found any, and she's just letting them cry."

"At least she isn't asleep," said Mendoza. "Not with that next door." The yelling was blessedly dim, forty feet away behind two closed doors, and presently he drifted off again; but he suspected that Alison had stayed awake worrying . . .

89

He went into the office and found Sergeant Lake looking disgusted. "Women!" said Sergeant Lake.

"What now?"

"That Mrs. Montague. It does make you wonder. She just called up. She says she put it off because she was going on an all-day trip yesterday with her niece and nephew, up to Mount Wilson, and she didn't want us messing around making her miss it. I ask you! So just now she calls to tell us that somebody tried to get into Valerie's apartment again on Wednesday night."

"*¡Vaya por Dios!* Women, as you say. Details?"

"Some interesting ones," said Lake grimly. "She says about midnight Wednesday she was just going to bed when she heard the front door open. Being the kind she is, she listened at her door and heard somebody fumbling around at the door across the hall. So she looked out, and it's all just the way it was before on Sunday night. A man with a key to Valerie's door, just getting it open—and when he sees her there, he runs for it. Only this time he doesn't drop the key. And she says definitely it wasn't the same man. Smaller. Didn't get much of a look at him otherwise, the light's too dim, but that she'll swear to."

"Well, well. Somebody'd better chase up there sometime today, get a statement on that. I hope she enjoyed her trip to Mount Wilson."

"I almost asked her. And I don't suppose it's even any use to go and print that doorknob, in case he left any, because after he'd bolted, what did the silly old cow do but go across and shut the door!"

Mendoza shut his eyes resignedly in comment. "Can't be helped now—we'd better have a try all the same. Brief

Marx, will you?" He looked at his watch. "I trust somebody's sitting on Eddy Warren's doorstep?" Warren hadn't shown up at home last night at all: home being a cheap hotel room on Figueroa.

"Sure, Bert went out on it. The Feds are getting their full press coverage all right, aren't they?"

Mendoza agreed. Thorwald and Valerie were spread all over the front pages, since last night's editions. There were rehashes on the Thorwald case six years ago, a good many cuts. Not much detail on Valerie, but they'd gone to town with what they had. Even cuts of the James Ellises—*horrified relatives deny niece could have been involved in crime of any sort.* And they'd got onto Maureen and Gloria; there was a bad cut of the latter—*close friend of murdered girl, Miss Gloria Litvak, 1196-A Cherokee Drive.* And the news that both had been picked up for soliciting. The sly inference that maybe Valerie had been on the same lay. Big cuts of Thorwald, with HAVE YOU SEEN THIS MAN? in scare headlines below.

All that brought him, presently, James Ellis. A James Ellis looking sick and bewildered, and apologizing, "I know you're a busy man, Lieutenant, I don't want to waste your time. But what the papers are all saying—I've just got to ask you, have you found out for sure she—she was —like that? It doesn't seem possible—when she was brought up decent and honest—"

"Well, young people go off the rails rather easily sometimes," said Mendoza. "I know how you're feeling about it, Mr. Ellis. But by what we know of her, I think it's very possible that she'd have gone off the rails anyway, even without—"

"My wife's upset, no wonder. Keeps saying if we'd only

91

kept closer touch, tried to check on who she was running around with—"

"If it's any comfort to you, Mr. Ellis, I don't think you could have—changed her, just by that. You'd just have found out about her a little sooner. I don't know whether you agree with me, but I think we come equipped with our essential personalities. There was some flaw in her from the beginning . . ." Which wasn't very useful philosophy to Ellis right now, who might always feel partly responsible for Valerie's downfall. Not much to say to Ellis.

He got some interesting confirmation of his deductions about Valerie when Dwyer brought in Eddy Warren, who'd come wandering home about nine-thirty after a night out. Warren was a dapper little fellow not over five-four, good-looking, self-confident, and not at all worried.

"You've got nothing on me—Mr. Wayne knows that." His probation officer. "I'm being a good boy, I am."

"Staying out all night?" asked Mendoza.

Warren grinned. "Hell, Lieutenant, I'm not *that* good! I suppose you found out from somebody I used to know Valerie Ellis. Well, I don't know one blessed thing about how she came to get took off, but anything else you want to ask, go ahead." He lit a cigarette.

Since they'd never been dropped on for it at the time, he categorically denied the shakedown caper in collaboration with Valerie; she was "just a girl I knew, you know." Sure, he'd known she was a setup then; so what? After pressure he admitted that he'd scouted for her a little— just a while. He was quite frank on that. "Turnabout's fair play, gentlemen," he said cheerfully. "I like my clients to get value for their money."

"I had a hunch she was one like that," said Mendoza.

"Oh, yes, indeedy," said Warren thoughtfully. He looked at his cigarette. "I'll tell you no lie, gentlemen, that one was bad medicine. There was a streak in her kind of scared me, you want to know. A wild streak—real wild. Especially when she was lit up a little. I remember once she was telling me how a guy passed out on her, and she laughed and said all of a sudden she wondered how it'd feel to stick the bread knife into him. That kind of wild . . . And one day I said to myself, I said, Eddy, boy, you get shut of that female or she's gonna take you smack into bad trouble. She was Trouble in a big way." That came straight from the heart. He stabbed out his cigarette and cocked his head at Mendoza. "But you boys didn't know her. How come you decide right off it was murder? Sleeping-pills—it could've been suicide or accident and a boy friend or somebody got scared and dumped the body."

"Well," said Mendoza absently, "she got it all in one dose—bang. And there wasn't any codeine prescription in her apartment. And— Never mind. She wasn't a suicidal type?"

"Brother," said Warren in sole comment. "She was too interested in the long green . . . I hadn't seen her in a good long time, no."

"Is that so? Are you doing any business in reefers lately?"

"Who, me? On probation? Hell, are you kidding, Lieutenant?" His surprised dismay was exaggerated.

"Sure you hadn't kept in touch with Val? Maybe, since you're on probation, you were taking extra precautions— your own place apt to be searched at any time—and were maybe paying her a little rent to stash away your merchandize at her place?"

A muscle jerked in Warren's cheek. "You got one hell of an imagination, Lieutenant. That's crazy."

"Bert," said Mendoza, "let's just see what keys he has on him, shall we?"

Warren was on his feet like a cat, but he knew he hadn't a chance; sullenly he stood still while Dwyer went over him and produced a fat bunch of keys. Mendoza looked at them one by one. "This," he said, looking at the seventh one he came to, "looks very similar to me. Of course the Feds have got her key, but we can always take a little ride up to Mariposa Street and try it. Shall we?"

Warren sat down again. "All right," he said. "But about any reefers I don't know one blessed thing and you can't prove I ever did."

"You admit that this is a key to Valerie Ellis's apartment?" asked Mendoza formally.

"Yeah. Naturally I wasn't going to come out with this, gentlemen, especially as it hasn't anything to do with her getting killed. But as long as you've found out—" He shrugged and lit another cigarette. "It was like this, see. One of my lady friends has a jealous-type husband, and right now he's out of a job and sitting around their place all day. And my hotel mightn't be very fancy, but they stick to the ground rules, she can't come there. So I had this little arrangement with Val—oh, sure, I wasn't in close touch with her any more but I saw her around—you see what I mean, use her place. For a little extra change—it was anything to make a fast buck with that one." He faced them calmly.

He was an old hand. He knew they couldn't prove anything on him at all. They might be a hundred per cent sure that those reefers were his, that he'd paid Valerie to store

94

them for him while he was on probation; there was no proof. None of his prints in the apartment. They could get Mrs. Montague down, ask her if he was the Wednesday night intruder; she wouldn't be able to say.

"Yes, the first press stories about the identification of the body came out Wednesday night, didn't they?" said Mendoza. "That shook you, and you decided to take a chance that we hadn't looked at her apartment yet—try to rescue your stock in trade. But you didn't quite manage it, did you, Mr. Warren? You got scared off. Just like X on Sunday night. I don't know but what Mrs. Montague's been of some help to us, at that . . . And you underestimate us, we'd been over the apartment thoroughly by then."

"I don't know what you're talking about," said Warren indifferently. "I told you how it was."

"What's your lady friend's name?"

Warren grinned at him. "Why, hell, Lieutenant, I'm a gentleman, I am. You don't expect me to give her away, do you?"

Mendoza suppressed a grin. "O.K.," he said. "Out. Off the merry-go-round, Eddy. We could waste all day asking and answering, but I know when I'm beaten. I may be seeing you again."

"Any time at all, Lieutenant," said Warren, rising unhurriedly. He straightened his tie. "Nice to've met you."

Dwyer scowled after him. "What the hell do you do with the smart-aleck ones like that?"

But Mendoza leaned back in his chair and laughed. " 'I'm a gentleman, I am!' ¡Eso es hermoso sin pero!— beautiful. We'll never get him on those reefers, Bert. But at least we've deprived him of them. And damn it, I forgot to get that key—"

"I'll catch him," said Dwyer, and vanished, still looking angry.

A thinnish Manila envelope arrived by special messenger from the FBI. It contained the report on the Litvaks which Mendoza had already heard about, others on Robert and Linda Hausner, Cardenas, and a Marion Keller.

The Hausners were a young couple looking quite ordinary. Said they'd met Valerie by getting talking, casually, in the bar of The Black Cat about six months ago. Linda Hausner was German-born, had met her husband while he was doing his army service in Germany seven years ago. Both her parents were dead. They'd had no idea that Valerie was anything but respectable, but then they hadn't known her well (that phrase was beginning to ring in Mendoza's ears). Bob Hausner had a good job as an electrical engineer at a big manufacturing outfit in North Hollywood, made seven hundred a month. They sounded like honest citizens: buying a house, one kid four, another two, both boys; according to the neighbors no wild parties or fights. The Hausners said they'd been to a few parties at Valerie's place, that was all. Had met a couple of her friends casually, but not to *know* them.

They looked all right, but there was that little item: the wife was foreign-born.

Marion Keller was something else again. She dated from Valerie's Bel-Air days: a girl Valerie had gone to school with. Her father was a well-known TV director. Marion Keller, now happily married to a wealthy young businessman, said of course she'd always felt sorry for Val —they'd been friends for a long time, and she'd tried to keep in touch with her, to let her know "it hadn't made any difference." She said Val had changed; sometimes she'd be almost rude, say she didn't want any charity—"not that I ever offered her any, of course." And then again she'd be eager to have Marion come in and talk, reminiscing about old days. "To tell you the truth," Marion Keller had said, "we hadn't anything in common any more, it was more a guilt complex than anything else that made me keep in touch with her, especially since I've been married. But I did feel sorry for her, and I used to call her up—go to see her occasionally. Just for that reason."

Of course Marion had never suspected, et cetera.

Mendoza yawned and lit a cigarette.

Cardenas also looked like a very respectable civil servant. He was well thought of by his superiors, got on well with his juniors, was "very conscientious." He certainly was interested in folk music; his apartment living-room bore ample evidence in the form of an expensive stereo outfit and some hundreds of L.P. records. He lived with his sister Maria, also unmarried, also employed in Civil Service, as an accountant.

He had been employed by the Welfare Department for seventeen years. He had been married; his wife had died in childbirth, with the baby. He lived within his means, attended church regularly, was not known to run around with women or overdrink. He had no close relatives except the sister. He was a native Californian.

It was all very depressingly respectable. So unproductive of any suggestive lead. Mendoza yawned again.

They had not found a single Vardas in the county. They had found over a hundred Glessners, sixty-four Imarosas, over two hundred Monteux', and a dismaying number of

Hoesses, while the figure on the Wilanowskis—Mendoza could imagine Waltham clutching his brow and groaning. Like the L.A.P.D., they had only so many men . . . If Hackett had not stripped the office bare on his hunt for Lover Boy, Mendoza would have offered to take over part of that list. On the other hand, he knew the Feds: they never felt a job was well done unless they'd done it themselves. He sympathized; he felt the same way himself.

He was curious as to what they'd turn up on Paul Manton.

But so far, absolutely nothing to suggest a lead to X. Absolutely nothing to point to what Valerie's latest racket had been.

She had to be over at Vic's. He shook his head. It might have some significance, but not for him. He made a note to pass it on to Waltham.

Another messenger dropped by with his requested photostat of Valerie's address book, and he studied it earnestly all over again.

Glessner—meet Rikki's 5 p.m., get $5000.

Five thousand dollars. Split three ways? A nice little take, but nothing spectacular. What did that say?

He thought, say those fourteen mentioned names were marks they had taken. (They?) Glessner was the first. All right. Was five thousand the average take? That made it—he scribbled figures—seventy thousand, a very nice piece of change indeed, even split three ways. It was all supposition, however, because that was the only time a figure was mentioned. And, by the comment in the address book, maybe "s.o.b." meant Wilanowski hadn't paid up.

Another thing the book said to him now was, it hadn't been used as an address book. It had been in use as a

98

daily diary, where she'd jotted down reminders to herself. There wasn't a date noted throughout. How long had it been in use? Anybody's guess—three months, six months, a year.

Possibly, other little address books might have got filled up with her scrawls, and been tossed away? No reason to keep them; she'd leaf through for any phone numbers she'd want, recopy them in the new book.

So, in those other books (maybe other books), how many other little jottings embellished with dollar signs? He sighed. Just no clue at all as to the racket, how often they'd taken a mark, or how, or for what.

Could he pinpoint anything at all definite about Valerie's murder yet? Not much. She hadn't thought she was in any danger, could you say that? Dr. Bainbridge said she'd got the whole massive dose of codeine at once, he was pretty sure, and probably in a drink of some kind. There was alcohol in her stomach: not much. Call it about as much as in a Martini. And not much else: she hadn't had a solid meal in about twenty hours. That was odd, or was it? Not necessarily: a good many young women conscious of their figures didn't eat much breakfast or lunch. She'd died probably before dinnertime on Sunday. Bainbridge had put the outside limit at midnight to be on the safe side.

Why the hell had she been left where she was? And how?

He thought he'd go and look at that Garey Street school.

It was a quarter of twelve. He wondered how Alison was getting on with Miss Freeman. Damned fool of a woman, calling the cats insanitary. Oh, well, so long as she was the one to get up and walk the floor with the twins—

He took up his hat and went out. "Jimmy, I'm going down to—"

The outside phone rang and Lake picked it up. "Headquarters, Homicide," he said mechanically. And then, "I beg your pardon, I don't—" A variety of expressions chased over his face; he said sharply, "Who is this speaking, please?" and began to scribble on his memo pad.

Even Mendoza beside him heard the violent click as the other phone was banged down.

"I will be damned," said Lake blankly. "Probably just a nut, but—"

"What'd she say? I could hear it was a woman's voice."

"Yes. Must have been a nut of some kind. First off she said, 'You tell whoever's investigating the Valerie Ellis murder, it wasn't nothing to do with this Thorwald, see?' That's when I interrupted her. She said, kind of sharp, 'You just listen! I would so tell them! I know why she was killed, she was killed because they murdered that woman six years ago—' And then you heard the phone banged down. Just a crank, you always get them calling in, but it's—"

"*¡Parece mentira!*" said Mendoza. "That's a funny one, all right. 'Because they murdered that woman six years ago.' They."

"You think it means anything?"

"*¿Quién sabe? ¡Sabe Dios!* It's just damned funny . . . It's so damned funny, Jimmy, that I'm going to ask you to go and collect the files for me on every first- and second-degree homicide of a female that's still pending, for—what

100

year'd that be?—1958. A nice afternoon's occupation for you."

"Thanks very much," said Sergeant Lake gloomily. "I remember one offhand, Lieutenant. That Overton woman was murdered in 1958—January. We never could pin it to the husband. He married his secretary afterward."

"Maybe a starting-point. Go and look out the files, just for fun," said Mendoza; and, thinking hard, went out to take a look along Garey Street.

At five-twenty that afternoon, just as Hackett plodded wearily into the office after yet another abortive day's routine checking on light-blue pickup trucks, a new homicide was reported. The call came from the Wilcox Street precinct; the sergeant there said, "After a first look, we figured for pretty sure it's one of your colored boy friend's jobs. Looks like the same set-up. So we thought we'd pass it on—with sympathy and all that. How near are you getting? Oh, well, bound to get him sooner or later, routine'll turn him up . . . Yeah . . . Mrs. Gertrude Dasher, 1114 Sierra Bonita in Hollywood. Friend of hers was invited to dinner, knew she'd be there, so when she couldn't raise her she made a fuss and called us. No, not raped, but killed the same way, and stuff missing—so the friend says . . . You're welcome to it."

Hackett put the phone down and passed a hand across his eyes; broke the news to Palliser.

"I've got all these damn reports to make up," he said. "Will you go out on it, John? Start to get the details anyway. God, who is there to take with you? All the damn paper work—"

"All right, don't worry, I'll get on it," said Palliser. "I

think Higgins is on night tour now." Sergeant Hackett had been putting in long hours on this one, he thought: so had they all; they were all feeling the needling from the press, and were savagely anxious to catch up to their boy. "You take a break," he said, "have a good dinner, relax. I'm on it."

"I wish to God I could go home," said Hackett heavily. Palliser, on the way out, heard him on the phone, saying, "I know, Angel, but—for the love of God don't tell me what you're having for dinner, darling, I'll break the oath and come home anyway—"

Hackett's wife was one of those inspired cooks. Palliser grinned to himself sympathetically.

He didn't mind the overtime; he kind of had his teeth in this thing now. And he hadn't had a date with Roberta tonight; she was involved with beginning-of-term exams for her fourth-grade pupils.

Eight

"I knew there was something wrong, I just felt it in my bones!" exclaimed Mrs. Powell dramatically.

Since Mrs. Dasher had expected her to dinner at five-thirty and would normally have been there to let her in, Palliser reflected that common sense rather than second sight might have led her to suspect something wrong. But he'd met a lot of Mrs. Powells, and he just made a polite murmur. Higgins was poking around the room. They had just come for the body, and the Hollywood boys had left with it, wishing them luck.

"I just don't know why you can't catch this awful fiend! A nigger, too," said Mrs. Powell, as if that logically made it easier.

"Well, we're working on it," said Palliser. The Hollywood boys said that it certainly looked like Lover Boy again. Same setup; back door lock broken in by force, the woman attacked when she saw him, and afterwards the house ransacked. The only discrepancy, of course, was the house itself. This Hollywood street was in a middle-class but not wealthy part of town; the houses were modest, most of them neatly maintained, but not affluent by any means.

Mrs. Dasher's house was an old bastard-Spanish stucco painted cream, with a red tile roof. Two bedrooms, very modest furniture.

He'd taken a look at the back door; the screen door had a piece cut out with a sharp knife, so the hook could be lifted, and the old-fashioned four-ward lock on the wooden door had been forced with crude violence. Across the driveway, there was a thick, tall privet hedge a good ten feet high, which successfully hid any view of Mrs. Dasher's back door from that other house so close there; Palliser couldn't see its windows, only the upper third of it. It had a nearly flat pseudo-shingle roof. He glanced down the drive. It was a longish drive; these were old-fashioned deep lots and Mrs. Dasher's house was built farther back from the street than either of her neighbors'. If anyone had been passing on the sidewalk, or casually watching from across the street, about all he'd have seen would have been a man fumbling at the door, maybe over a stiff lock. The screen-slashing wouldn't have taken five seconds.

"Well," said Palliser to himself now. And to Mrs. Powell, "Now let's go over this again. We want to be as exact as we can. I realize you can't be sure of every single item." That was a lie; he'd take a bet that she could rattle off an inventory of the place. She and Gertrude Dasher had been close friends for over twenty years, and Mrs. Dasher had lived here for almost that long—since before she'd been left a widow. ("And good riddance," Mrs. Powell had said with a sniff. "He Drank.") Mrs. Dasher had obviously not been the kind who redecorated every few years, or spent much on the house at any time. The

104

furniture was well cared for but old—just old, not antique. The rugs were worn. The refrigerator and stove were clean, but far from new. The clothes in the closet of the front bedroom—or rather scattered on the floor and about the room, now—were the typical clothes of an elderly woman with enough money but not a surplus.

"Better write it down so you won't forget it!" snapped Mrs. Powell. "Policemen! This fiend in human form running around killing helpless women, and you just dawdle around asking silly questions!"

"We're working on it," said Palliser patiently. "Now, you said there was an antique silver tea service—"

"On the sideboard in the dining room, where it always stayed. It belonged to Gertrude's grandmother. Real English silver, teapot and sugar 'n' creamer. And a set of a dozen German silver teaspoons, in the top right-hand drawer of the buffet. Don't you be silly, young man, since we were both left widows I knew this house almost like my own, and I've been through it—with those other policemen practically ready to put handcuffs on me, saying don't touch anything! Impudence. I know what's missing. Her fur coat—a beaver coat it was, three-quarter, and only ten years old, perfectly good, she paid three hundred for it on sale. And her jewelry. She didn't have an awful lot but what she had was good. Her grandmother's cameo brooch and a set of garnets—sunburst pin and a ring and a pair of drop earrings and a pendant—and her mother's engagement ring, and one of those old-fashioned wide hoop bracelets, real gold, and her own engagement ring, and an onyx ring with a diamond set in it, and an amethyst ring that was her twenty-first birthday present because it's her birthstone. *All* gone!" said Mrs. Powell. "*And* her wrist watch!"

"Yes," said Palliser. He thought about the loot Lover Boy had got away with in other instances. A new mink coat, a diamond necklace valued at ten thousand dollars; at another place, miscellaneous jewelry to the value of fifteen thousand: expensive clothes, a diamond wrist watch, another mink coat. Small doubt rose in his mind; he looked around Gertrude Dasher's living-room. *Sunburst pin and a ring and*— He remembered his mother turning over his grandmother's jewelry after the funeral, and talking about garnets. ("Never worth much, they're inexpensive stones, but I always liked them all the same.")

He also thought about his and Hackett's joint deduction about Lover Boy. Obviously, he was a wild one, maybe a little or a lot unhinged; leave that to the head-doctors. But Hackett thought the burglaries were just afterthoughts—just wild snatching at whatever he easily found lying around, and not anything systematic. Because at that place he'd got away with the diamond necklace, there'd been a good deal more valuable jewelry untouched; and at another place, one of those in Beverly Hills, he'd taken a fourteen-carat cigarette case from one bedroom— the owner was positive as to where it had been—and left it in another room where he ransacked a jewel case, taking a lot of costume jewelry as well as real stuff. Just grabbing wildly, said Hackett, and maybe—if he was unhinged— not even attempting to profit by it.

My God, *had* they worked this one. They'd even drawn up solemn maps, with little dotted lines drawn between the addresses of jobs he'd pulled. West Hollywood, Beverly Hills. Palliser thought about that now. Like any cop, he knew the city; and visualizing the map, he saw that the distance between here and West Hollywood was about the same as between West Hollywood and Beverly Hills, only in the opposite direction. There was nothing impossible about all this: if Lover Boy was as unhinged as Hackett thought, he might just have happened to be driving his light-blue pickup truck down Sierra Bonita when the urge hit him, and he— Yes, thought Palliser, there was that. Those places in West Hollywood and Beverly Hills, wealthy homes: larger lots, and any curious neighbors farther away. Here, where houses were set close—Lover Boy retained some natural caution, maybe?—he'd chosen a house very well protected by that tall hedge, by being set back farther from the street. Was that logical?

"Well, thank you very much," he said to Mrs. Powell; and had a little time getting rid of her. The boys from Prints arrived, and he left them to it while he questioned the neighbors.

The people next door, where there was no hedge between, gave him a little surprise but not much help. The householder was one of the sheriff's boys, Deputy Harry Lee. He offered Palliser sympathy—"This is the tough kind, don't we know!"—and nothing else. He hadn't come home until after Mrs. Dasher had been found. Mrs. Lee had been out to market. Home alone had been Davy Lee, out of school with a cold. And Davy Lee, aged eleven, said importantly, "I saw the man who must've been the one. I did too, Dad, I'm *not* making it up! Honest, mister, I did!"

"You saw him come down the drive? Saw his car?"

"Naw, he went to the front door. He came walkin' up the street and he went up and rung the front doorbell."

"That was the salesman, honey," said pretty Mrs. Lee. "The one the Flesches told about." The Flesches lived on the other side of Mrs. Dasher.

"It wasn't either! I saw him 'n' I saw the salesman, didn't I? I answered the door when the salesman rang an' said you wasn't—weren't home an' he gave me the catalogue to give you."

"That was the same man, Dave, because it was about the same time the Flesches said he came." Lee nodded and winked at Palliser, and shrugged.

"It was *not*! I saw him! He wasn't as old as the one rang Mrs. Dasher's bell first—it was afterward the salesman came! Honest, I—"

Lee took Palliser's arm and led him out to the entrance hall. "Don't get confused by all that," he said. "I'm afraid the boy's at that stage—not only wanting in on the act, to look important, but we've caught him out in a couple of—call it exaggerations—lately." He grinned. "You know. They all go through it."

"Sure," said Palliser. He didn't know much about kids; without much doubt Lee knew more about his son than Palliser did.

The people beyond the hedge couldn't tell him anything helpful either. They were people in their sixties, Flesch retired, and they'd been having lunch in the kitchen between about twelve and twelve-thirty, not in sight of Mrs. Dasher's house. The Fuller Brush man had come by, they said, at about noon, maybe a few minutes before.

The surgeon said she had died between eleven and one. Technically of strangulation, though she'd been beaten too—head banged in (probably against furniture, the floor) and so on.

The Fuller Brush man—they left brochures, didn't they? No brochure in Mrs. Dasher's house. So—had she been dead when the man rang the bell? And her killer holding his breath, until the salesman went away?

Palliser sat down on Mrs. Dasher's tapestry-upholstered couch and stared earnestly at the picture on the opposite wall. It was a brightly colored print of a young woman in a long red dress, playing a piano, and it was in an ornate gilded frame.

"Dreaming of the girl friend?" asked Higgins.

"Well—" said Palliser. Actually he was thinking about Mendoza. Mendoza and his reputation. They joked about it: Luis and his crystal ball. And the hunches didn't always work out, of course. But sometimes—surprisingly often— they did.

He thought about Mendoza saying, "Routine—sure, we have to go by routine. Facts. But don't ever ignore your feelings, John. This I say to you personally. There are a lot of good cops on this force—any force—I wouldn't say it to. Good men, but not men who have enough empathy to get the nuances, if you know what I mean. You have. So any time you have a feeling about something, follow it up. It might mean something."

Palliser was naturally a rather diffident man; he didn't lack self-confidence or strength of character, but he'd risen rather rapidly from uniform, to be the associate of men like Art Hackett who'd had a lot more experience. When he offered some idea of his own, it was usually hesitantly.

But in the last six months or so he'd found Hackett and Mendoza to be easy, reasonable fellows to deal with. He thought he'd bare his feelings to Hackett on this one, see what Hackett thought.

109

There wasn't much of Garey Street, Mendoza had found. Two blocks of it along here, between Third and First, and it picked up again a couple of blocks on, to run for another three blocks between Turner and Commercial. It was a rather dreary little street, interspersing old houses with small businesses. The parochial school was an old one, shabby and showing its age: not as large a playground as a public school would have.

Why the hell had X gone to some trouble to leave the body in such a funny spot? Or, come to think, had he gone to much trouble? Maybe somebody who'd once worked as a janitor or night watchman here, still had a key to the gate? Farfetched, but—

Nowhere to park along here, not only because it was a narrow street and parking was allowed on only one side, but because at the moment half this block was filled with workmen and large yellow-painted machines doing something about either the water or the gas mains. They had a deep trench dug along the curb opposite the school fence, lengths of pipe stood about waiting—by their diameter, it was the water, not the gas—mounds of earth made the street a one-way maze for a car. He negotiated it carefully, turned the corner onto Third Street and found that solidly lined with parked cars. Well, a little exercise wouldn't hurt him; a lieutenant's job was too sedentary. He went on up to Santa Fe, and nearly down to the corner of Second Street he found a slot. He maneuvered the Ferrari in, fished for small change, discovered he had no pennies or nickels, swore mildly, and—a solecism big-city dwellers are learning to commit without shame—accosted the first passer-by for change for a quarter. He put a nickel in the parking-meter; nothing happened; he shook it severely, and a little reluctantly the red *Violation* sign disappeared and the needle slid over to *60 min.* On second thought he locked the Ferrari, and started back down Santa Fe.

Ten minutes later he was staring through the schoolyard fence at the place where Valerie Ellis's body had been found last Monday morning.

This was the side of the school, which faced on Third Street. The body had been close inside the fence, behind a small bleachers erected for the baseball diamond there. He had seen the photographs: body awkwardly sprawled out. As if dropped, say, from the top of the fence? He had asked Dr. Bainbridge, who had shrugged. "What with the post-mortem cyanosis, you know, difficult to say. A dead body would fall like an unconscious person, of course— limp—unless rigor had set in—and probably wouldn't sustain the injuries a conscious person would from any considerable fall. There weren't any bones broken, anyway."

The fence—now he looked at it—wouldn't be as high as most public-schoolyard fences. Call it fifteen feet. It was a very solid chain-link fence, probably newer than the school buildings, supported by very solid steel posts at intervals.

Mendoza sighed to himself. Generally speaking, anybody with a corpse on his hands to get rid of got rid of it in the handiest dark place. Which there were plenty of in any big city . . . Had he brought along his own ladder?

He turned around and looked thoughtfully at the men and machines working in the street. He strolled down to where the trench was; sure enough, a ladder propped in the hole. A deep hole. So, a long ladder.

Most of the men were working stripped to the waist: even in February, in California, the sun was hot. They

111

were deeply tanned; there were several Negroes among them. Lover Boy flitted across his mind and he sighed again. He waited until a man came nearer the curb, and called, "Excuse me, who's the foreman on this job?"

Everybody in hearing stared at him. The man approaching looked him up and down and said, "I am, and what's it to you, bud?" He was a big hefty fellow about forty, burned almost as brown as the grinning milk-chocolate Negro peering at them out of the hole. The foreman stared at Mendoza's exquisitely cut Italian silk suit with contempt.

Mendoza produced identification. "You remember that body found inside the school fence on Monday?"

"Well, I didn't put it there, anyway. Sure, some excitement, cops all around. What about it? . . . Sure we were working here then. Ever since last week, why?"

"You see, it's a peculiar place to dump a body. Not so easy a place to get a body into. And I was just wondering—what do you do with all this at night?" He gestured at the machines. "Take them all back to your—er—headquarters, or park them here?"

"You think the company's crazy, mister, waste time trundling these things back to the garage every night? They come on a job, they stay until the job's finished. Left parked up against the curb, sure."

"Yes." Irrelevantly Mendoza thought that the machines looked like Martian monsters. There was one that had a great iron claw with sharp teeth, at the end of a cranelike jointed arm: the thing had a sinister expression, he thought. "That ladder down the hole—is it left there overnight?"

The foreman laughed. "Mister, you think *we're* crazy?

112

Anything you leave out loose, neighborhood like this, you don't expect to find it there next morning! All that sort of thing gets locked into one o' the trucks." There were a couple of ordinary trucks there too, with closed bodies, probably for transporting and storing the smaller tools.

"Well, I'd just like to be sure," said Mendoza. "Who's the one responsible for seeing to that? Was the ladder definitely locked in a truck over last weekend?"

"Oh, hell," said the foreman. "Sure it was! You cops! Hey, Tony?"

"What's up?"

"Come here a minute." A lithe young Negro climbed out of the hole, his bare chest glistening with sweat, and came over. "Look, when we quit work Saturday noon, you pulled up that ladder and put her in No. 2 truck, didn't you?"

"That I did," said Tony. "Why? We always do."

"Like I said. This cop here asking. On account of that body they found in the schoolyard, see? You're sure you locked up the ladder?"

"Sure," said Tony absently. "You a cop, sir? Looking into that, like? I don't want to butt in, Mr. Davies, but you reckon maybe the cop oughta hear what Barney says? I mean, nobody ever asked us anything, but if he's right it might have something to do—"

"Oh, for God's sakes," said the foreman disgustedly. "Barney had his mind on a Saturday night spree and that blonde of his—he don't know what he's talking about! How *could* his rig get moved around? It's—"

"Well, but he's pretty sure, Mr. Davies—we never thought as how it might have something to do with that body, but you know, it could be—"

113

Mendoza said, "I think I'd like very much to hear what Barney says. Please, Mr. Davies."

"For God's *sakes!*" said the foreman. "Wasting time! *Barney! Come here!* Taking men off the job! Listen, mister, all the time we hear nothing but complaints—the damn public—city men take forever on a job, leaning on their shovels—good union wages an' they work about half the time, loaf the rest. Let me tell *you*, mister, we get damn sick 'n' tired of hearing complaints. We work, God knows. Job like this got to be done, we *do* it. You think we *like* tying up traffic, just to make things hard for people? We earn our money, mister, and we earn it honest! I tell you—" It was automatic complaint, uncalled for.

Maybe every trade, thought Mendoza, has its grievances against the rest of humanity.

"I'm not doubting you," he said. Barney was the operator of the sinister-looking machine with the single claw. He left the claw suspended in mid-air, clambered down from the cab, and joined them.

"What's up?"

"All right, all right," said Davies angrily. "So tell your fairy story about last Monday morning to the cop. About the rig."

"You a cop? What about? . . . That body! Jesus, I never thought of that body! But now I *do* think, I bet you —I just bet you that was *it!*" Barney, squat and broad, didn't look as if he thought much about anything. Now he was suddenly excited. "I just bet you! So O.K., I'm imagining things—my God, *I* know how I left the rig, don't I? She isn't exactly the easiest rig made to maneuver, and ain't we got strict orders, don't block traffic no more'n we can help? Well? Listen," he said to Mendoza fiercely,

114

"*I* know how I left her on Saturday noon, I can show you! Right bang up against that right-hand curb I left her"—he pointed—"about the legal distance from the fire hydrant. I checked, on accounta the hydrant. Wouldn't I check? I ask you! And you can say I'm as crazy as the boss here thinks, it makes no never mind, on Mond'y morning that rig was a good ten feet, maybe fifteen, further back from that hydrant 'n I'd left her! I got *eyes*, ain't I? I got—"

"Now that's very interesting indeed," said Mendoza. The foreman made a disgusted sound in his throat. "Tell me—those things aren't so easy to operate, you say—the ordinary citizen couldn't climb right into one and start it up?"

"Jesus, no. You got to know where everything is—all the levers and so on. *You* believe me, mister? I'd swear it on a stack o' Bibles—rest of 'em say I'm just imagining, because how the hell *could* she've been moved? I mean, the ignition was locked, naturally."

"There's an ignition, like that on a car? Yes." And almost any man with a very little know-how, even if he hadn't started out a pro career by borrowing cars, might know how to start a locked ignition—those two little wires— "And once the engine's on," he said, "the power's available to work that claw thing? I don't know your technical terms—"

"That's right, sure, only like I say you'd hafta know which levers—there's one to bend her down, and open her, and close her, and raise her up—"

Eso si está bueno, thought Mendoza irritably. What a setup! It got more and more complicated—and no leads at all! *Was* Barney right? It seemed too big a coincidence if he wasn't. Had that Martian monster been the convenient means of hoisting the body over the fence? Grant that X knew how to operate it, of course, a very easy means. That great claw was a good eight to ten feet long. Open it at ground level: lift the body in: close it, and swing the crane over the fence—within easy reach of the twenty-foot-long arm: open it, and there you were.

But who that they knew of in this case (so far) might possess that knowledge?

A man who didn't know how to work the machine, but had sufficient mechanical ability to figure it out by trial and error? Why go to the trouble?

And—he looked across the street—a good many of the old houses used as business offices: a chiropractor, a dentist, an herb-doctor—maybe nobody there at night—but down the block a few houses still used as residences. Wouldn't the protracted noise of this heavy engine, the creak and groan of that crane, have aroused some curiosity, say, at nine o'clock on Sunday night?

And how had X known this convenient means was waiting here for him? That was easy enough: if he had by chance passed this way recently—

And—hell and damnation—if this astonishing and curious thing was true, there'd be absolutely no traces left inside that monstrous claw, to prove it—after five days of use in between.

And—once again—why the hell had X gone to the bother?

Nine

Mendoza went home, after a brief return to the office, in an exasperated frame of mind. Lover Boy pulling another one, God, that one they had to catch up with—and this very funny new development on Valerie . . . He garaged the Ferrari, kissed Alison at the back door.

"Well, happier with the sanitary Miss Freeman, *amada?*"

"No," said Alison. "She's gone."

"Gone? *¿Como dice—qué se yo?*"

"What else could I do?" she demanded. "That woman! Her and her established routines! I didn't like her, but I *had* hired her, I was willing to try her out a few days, but then she kicked Bast, and I—"

" *Porvida!* She's not hurt? *Mi cariña—*" He let Alison go and went to pick up Bast, who was limping pathetically across the kitchen telling him all about it at the top of her voice. "*¡Mi gatita cara! ¡Queridita!* That scraggly old bitch—"

Bast, always pleased for a chance to be the center of attention, uttered a satisfied *Nyeouh* and lay back in his arms with closed eyes. "No, she's not hurt," said Alison, "she's just being a hypochondriac because she's feeling sorry for herself. The limp's all put on. I had her over to Dr. Stocking, she's perfectly all right. But—"

"*Nyah!*" said Bast indignantly.

"She was just innocently walking into the room—that woman had been acting worse all the time, Luis, the most impossible ideas—I think she's got a neurosis about hygiene—and then she tripped over El Señor and he spat at her— Well, it may strike you funny now, but at the time—! I know some people just don't like cats, but after all— All of a sudden she started saying 'you nasty creature' and so on, and I turned round just in time to see her kick Bast—a good hard kick too. Naturally I blew up—"

"*¡Probrecita!* I should think so indeed!" He fondled Bast. "These neurotic females. You're sure—?"

"I said I took her to the hospital to be sure. She's just feeling sorry for herself, and I can't say I blame her," said Alison, still angry. "Ask me, all that woman's funny ideas, she'd have ended up giving the twins a trauma or something. But they can't all be like that, surely there must be at least one kind motherly nursemaid available, among seven million people! I thought I'd try another agency tomorrow."

"By all means. But meanwhile, we're stuck with them tonight," said Mendoza. "I suppose they're asleep now. Of course. *Naturalmente.*"

"Yes, well, I thought," said Alison, "that just for tonight—I'm sure to find somebody else tomorrow, you know—I could sleep in there next to them. To be handy when they start. And then—"

"*¡Valgáme Dios—es el colmo!* What's all this? I forbid it, *absolutamente!* I've put up with these twin monsters so far, but enough is enough! When it comes to you moving out on me—"

"Don't be silly, *querido*, if you weren't so self-conscious about it you'd be acting as sentimental and boastful as any other parent. And it's only for one night—I'm bound to find somebody else—and besides, it's ridiculous to move the nursery furniture back just for one—"

"*Nyaouh*," said Bast plaintively, aware that attention had shifted from her.

"*Gata hermosa*," said Mendoza absently, patting her. "I will not allow it. We can, God knows, hear them plain enough anywhere in the house. As a lawful obedient wife, your first duty is to your husband—"

"If you remember," said Alison, "it was a civil ceremony at the Hall of Justice and I never said one word about obeying you."

"*Impudente*. I still say—"

"Of course," she added, "I shouldn't expect a man of your advanced years to change your habits, and you never have taken kindly to sleeping alone—I gather, though I've only known you, what, four years—"

"*¡Qué pronto pasa el tiempo*—how fast time goes!" said Mendoza. "You will stay where you belong, no argument. Now go and see to dinner."

"I'm going, I'm going. Autocrat," said Alison. He opened the cupboard over the sink, poured himself a small drink; and El Señor materialized from nowhere, demanding his share. "There you are, setting bad examples—he's turning into a drunkard."

"Nonsense," said Mendoza, pouring El Señor an ounce

119

of rye in a saucer. "He needs it after putting up with that woman for twenty-four hours." El Señor, licking his chops, uttered a sound of distinct agreement and leaped down to find Sheba or Nefertiti to cuff, that being how alcohol affected him . . .

Alison stayed where she belonged, in the king-size bed in the master bedroom. But inevitably she got out of it, with a sleepy muttered "damn" at 2:45 A.M.

Fumbling into her slippers and robe, she said crossly, "I'm *coming!*" And added to Mendoza, "You go back to sleep, I'll see to them."

He pulled the blanket over his head and tried to go back to sleep. It was, of course, useless. He sat up and smoked a cigarette, ruminating sleepily about Valerie—this curious new twist, that machine—and Lover Boy—and what Valerie's profitable racket might have been—

Until his conscience got to bothering him. After all, he was fifty per cent responsible for the existence of that pair of little monsters down the hall.

He got up resignedly, put on his robe and slippers, and went to join Alison and the twins.

Somewhere there must be a nice motherly experienced nursemaid—like all those nannies in the British novels—for present hire?

"Tomorrow—" he said to Alison. He joggled Miss Teresa determinedly.

"Tomorrow," said Alison somnolently, patting Master John.

He sat at his desk next morning and studied all those files Lake had turned up for him—homicides from six years back, of females: cases still labeled *Pending.* Was this woolgathering? That phone call: "Because they murdered that woman six years ago—" . . . They.

There weren't too many of them. This was a crack force, but also, the average homicide didn't present much of a mystery in the crime-fiction sense. When X wasn't pretty obvious on the known facts—and he usually was—the mystery arose because of his anonymity: the casual mugger, the casual rapist, the lunatic. In most of these cases, that was the reason the case was still pending: there just hadn't been enough evidence at the scene or elsewhere to point to anybody.

The Overton woman, first of all. Rose Overton. Husband Gerald vice-president of a small company that manufactured cardboard boxes of all kinds. Reasonably affluent: Mrs. Overton had a little jewelry, her own car, spent her time playing bridge, shopping, entertaining. She was forty-three, he was a year older. No children. They'd been married for nineteen years. Nobody had ever suspected any trouble between them: no public arguments. They had seemed, to everyone who knew them, to be an ordinary couple. And then, one cold January evening, while Mr. Overton was detained in his office, dictating to his secretary Miss Norma Walsh, somebody had forced the back door of the Overton home in Bel-Air and bashed Mrs. Overton's head in with a blunt instrument. It had looked at first glance like a burglary—burglar seen by Mrs. Overton, he hit her to shut her up. But several little things said no. A burglar would know someone was home from the lights; it happened between eight and nine, and that was the wrong time for a burglar to pick. And the burglar hadn't acted like a burglar, dumping whole drawers on the floor to get at the contents in a hurry, tearing clothes off hangers at random. He'd left a few drawers open, that was all, and he had missed an expensive set of golf clubs and other valuables—all belonging to Overton.

Overton, of course, was openly shocked and grieved. He'd been in his office from seven to nine-thirty, and the secretary backed him up. It was a big office-building with a night watchman, who'd seen them both come in at seven, and said Overton didn't leave until they both left at nine-thirty. But he couldn't watch all the exits at once, and there was a fire escape.

Mrs. Overton had been a devout Catholic. Overton wasn't. And a discreet eight months after the murder, Overton had married Miss Walsh.

So, you could spot him as X—there just wasn't any evidence at all. Weapon never found. If Overton had wanted a divorce, wanted to be rid of his wife, nobody had ever heard either of them say so; there was no evidence of any discord between them.

Mendoza thought about the Overton case again now for two reasons. They had lived in Bel-Air—where Valerie had lived at the time. L.A. Headquarters had come into it by being asked by the Beverly Hills boys to check the downtown alibi. And the anonymous woman on the phone had said "they" killed the woman. And if Overton had killed his wife, the secretary must have been an accomplice.

On the other hand, it could have been a "they" who was responsible for Marion Carlson. Attacked and raped and strangled in an alley off Venice Boulevard, not a very good section of town, as she walked toward home after leaving the bus. Absolutely no clue left on the scene: a very anonymous kill.

There were two others like that, only the women hadn't

122

been raped. Agnes Fletcher, aged fifty-one; Ellen Draper, aged thirty. Far apart: Fletcher in Boyle Heights, Draper in Palms. It had looked like a mugger in both cases, maybe hopped-up on dope and hitting a little too hard, just to get the handbag.

Then, Ruth Ganner. High-school kid living in Hollywood. The Hollywood boys had asked for help on it. Nobody had got anywhere. The Ganner girl hadn't been a very nice girl. Had played around with several boys she knew at school, and got herself in trouble. And that was about all they knew for certain. One dark night somebody had stabbed her several times with a very sharp knife and left her body rather casually on the front lawn of the Ganner house. It might have been one of the boys she'd played with, or it might, of course, have been a couple of them. A "They."

But what possible connection with Valerie, then attending a different high school? Of course, kids got around these days . . .

And that left Dorothy Clark. Who had been divorced from her husband George and was living with a boy friend, Brian Lavalliere. None of them very savory characters. Dorothy had a little pedigree for shoplifting and habitual drunkenness; George had been inside twice for robbery; Lavalliere, despite his aristocratic name, was a pro burglar. Dorothy and Lavalliere had been living in a ramshackle rooming-house a couple of blocks off Skid Row. Other tenants said Clark had come around a couple of times, threatening both of them; and said also that Lavalliere and Dorothy had had a few fights. So, when somebody ambushed and stabbed Dorothy from the mouth of an alley a few doors from the house, as she came home late one night—late, and a little drunk—it might have been

123

either man, or it might have been a mugger. A good many types in that section of town carried knives; a certain proportion of them wouldn't think twice about using a knife on the chance that there was five or ten bucks in the handbag. Nobody knew exactly how much she'd been carrying. Insufficient evidence to show who was guilty.

Mendoza really couldn't see those three having any connection with Valerie Ellis. He couldn't see any of these cases having any connection with Valerie Ellis. Except, just remotely possible, the Overton case. The Overtons living in Bel-Air . . .

Six years ago Valerie Ellis had been seventeen, a high-school student: her parents still alive, she'd been the spoiled darling, with everything she wanted.

The anonymous woman on the telephone hadn't got around to saying what the connection had been between Valerie and the murdered woman, but the implication was that she had known something damaging about the "they" who had allegedly done the murder. Maybe had tried blackmail? Well, the blackmail bit would ring true enough: Valerie had liked money however it came. But how had a still-innocent high-school kid stumbled across a criminal secret? And why had she kept silent about it then?

It didn't make sense. Probably the phone call hadn't one damned thing to do with it: just a crank, a nut. Nothing in this whole peculiar business made sense. The place the body was left. That really wild one, the Martian machine used (maybe) to get the body over the fence . . . He made a note to have somebody ask around there, whether anyone had heard it on Sunday night. The mysteriousness of Valerie's latest racket . . .

She had to be over at Vic's. Vic. No Vic visible.

That Gloria female knew something. Bring her in as a material witness, try to scare her into coming out with it? No, thought Mendoza. There was an old saying, catch more flies with honey— Go to see her, try to coax it out of her.

He put out his cigarette and got up, deciding to do just that. And just as abruptly decided first to go and see this Marion Keller, who'd been Valerie's best friend in high school. In high school, six years ago . . .

But he hadn't got to the door before it opened and Hackett and Palliser came in. "Sit down, Luis," said Hackett. "John's got something to tell you. We need your expert opinion."

"Later on," said Mendoza. "Right now I—"

"Now," said Hackett. "You're the expert on hunches. John has a beautiful hunch to lay before you. Look at it and tell us if there's anything in it, *por favor.*"

Mendoza sat down again resignedly.

"It's just an idea," said Palliser. His long dark face, normally grave, lit up when he smiled, and made him look younger; he smiled apologetically now. "Nothing really to say one way or the other."

"In fact, a hunch," said Mendoza. "About what?"

"That Mrs. Dasher. Sure, it looks like the boy we're chasing—same M.O. House broken into, woman assaulted—he's not particular, he's already assaulted one older than Gertrude Dasher—she was sixty-six—and a few things stolen. He didn't actually rape Mrs. Dasher, but then he didn't rape two others. Only they fought and got away, or he would have. All right. But I've got a hunch it

125

wasn't him. That somebody set it up to look like that. For one thing, the other seven women all lived in West Hollywood or Beverly Hills—wealthier sections of town. Mrs. Dasher was off his beat, so to speak. And I know we all think the burglaries are a kind of afterthought, he just snatches up what he finds on a hurried search. Well, here he took everything of any remote value Mrs. Dasher had— and it didn't amount to very much. Apparently he took a good long look through the house. But after all, a dozen German silver teaspoons, and a handful of old jewelry that never had been worth much—" Palliser gestured. "And then there's the kid. There's this hedge hiding the Dasher house from the next house—those people can't see her front walk or porch. All they do say is that at about twelve o'clock a Fuller Brush man came by. But in the house on the other side, there was a bright kid home alone. And he says he saw two men go up and ring Mrs. Dasher's doorbell, one after the other. Says the first man was older than the Fuller Brush man, who came afterward. His parents—father's one of the sheriff's boys, by the way, nice fellow—think he's imagining it, just to sound important. Say he's given to telling stories. Well, I don't know. For one thing, I should think that Lee, being a conscientious fellow, would have impressed on the boy some—you know —understanding of the job. And wouldn't a kid that age, a boy, be pretty proud of a father who's on the sheriff's squad, and not want to let him down? You can see it's all odds and ends—"

"Yes," said Mendoza, "but they might add up. I see what you mean. Very strong hunch, John?"

"Well, I guess I'd say so. When I get to thinking it over."

"And I don't know but what I go along," said Hackett

126

soberly. "I had a little thought of my own about it." He lit a new cigarette. "We haven't given the press all the details, just some. As per usual. And what the Dasher setup looks like—if it wasn't our boy—is that whoever did it and arranged things to look like one of Lover Boy's jobs, knew what's been in the papers but not a couple of other things we know."

"Details, please?"

"Well, it's been in the papers that he robbed the houses after assaulting the women, but not that he's just snatched up a few things at random, on the run, so to speak. And here, as John says, whoever it was ransacked the house for anything of remote value. Then, it's been in the papers that he's broken in by forcing locks, but not that we're pretty sure he uses a pro burglar's jemmy. And Mrs. Dasher's back door—I've just been taking a look at it—wasn't forced that way. We don't think. Somebody just poked something like a pair of scissors, or a strong knife, in and worried around until the lock broke. Crude violence, you could say. And it *is* a break in the pattern, an entirely different part of town."

"So it is," said Mendoza. "And if you're right, something else on our plates. Another mysterious murder. Of course there's an obvious explanation."

"Yes, I saw that," said Hackett, "but it's no help looking for him."

"What?" asked Palliser blankly.

Mendoza leaned back and shut his eyes. "*Esto es otro cantar*," he said. "You get a series of crimes like this—as you'll discover with more experience—and sometimes you get some nut or hophead imitating the original X. You'll remember the Black Dahlia, for instance—" He shuddered. "In a town this size, anything can happen. And on this series, what a nice cover-up for serious burglary. What a nice excuse for some borderline lunatic to let out the repressed violence."

"Oh," said Palliser. "I get you. That could be, I suppose. Well, I just thought—"

"An excellent thing for a smart detective to do," said Mendoza a little sleepily. "And a little maxim it's a good idea to remember is, No stone unturned. Always go on the assumption that the worst is so—from our viewpoint— and look at every possibility. ¿Como no? In this case, the worst that could be so from our viewpoint is that this was a private kill, somebody who had some personal motive for killing Mrs. Dasher. That'd be a tough one to unravel, probably. She doesn't sound a likely victim for that kind of murder. But you've got to consider the possibility. Look into her background—look at her friends. If nothing suggestive shows up—well, it could be an imitator, or of course it could still be Lover Boy on an off day."

"Yes, I see that," said Palliser. "My God, on top of everything else—" He sounded dispirited, with reason. "What did she do, by the way? Still working?"

"I heard a little bit from that Mrs. Powell— I'll want to see her again. She was retired—Dasher, I mean. She'd been a practical nurse. The last few years she'd worked, she'd taken mostly baby cases."

"Really," said Mendoza. He hoped to God Alison was finding that nice motherly nurse. Or was it a dying breed?

"She got a legacy from one of her former patients and retired. She already owned the house. I'll look into it deeper now. As you say, just in case." Palliser got up, looking tired.

"How are you coming along with your little puzzle?" asked Hackett.

"I'm not," said Mendoza exasperatedly. "Some of the damnedest things showing up—I might even lay a couple of problems before you and ask your opinion. Say Federico's, twelve-thirty? I'll tell you all about it."

"*Déjème tomarle el pulso*," said Hackett in mock astonishment, "let me feel your pulse! The great Mendoza, asking advice?"

"Or maybe," said Mendoza, "it's these damned infants. I'm not operating on all cylinders. Maybe the answer's staring me in the face, only I just don't see it. All right, let's all get busy—see you at lunch."

He looked up the number and called Mrs. Keller. Yes, Mrs. Keller was at home and would be happy to tell Lieutenant Mendoza whatever she could about Valerie. Not that she thought she'd be much help, but— Yes, she'd be expecting him then, in half an hour.

"Another batch of stuff from the Feds," said Sergeant Lake.

"Leave it on my desk—I'll see it later."

129

Ten

"Looking back, I can see now she was always sort of wild," said Marion Keller thoughtfully. "Well, kids haven't much judgment of people, and then too it's only natural—you make friends among the—the available people. Proximity. The Ellises just lived one house down from us, and Val and I being the same age, we naturally teamed up. And maybe too because we were just opposite in some ways." She smiled at Mendoza a little shyly.

Marion Keller was an ordinarily nice-looking young woman, very smartly dressed; her house, on Maybrook Drive in Bel-Air, was a big one, beautifully decorated by someone of individual taste. Marion? She was dark, with a warmly tanned complexion and steady blue eyes; a good deal more mature for her age than Valerie would have been. She had rather large, capable-looking hands. She looked healthy, happy, and good-tempered; and she had the natural poise, the self-confidence, of someone who has always had plenty of money.

She said, "All this awful row in the papers. On account of the Thorwald man, of course. But awful all the same—

do you know they even came here? Hal was furious. I'm awfully sorry for that poor ultra-respectable aunt and uncle of hers . . . I never did suspect about her, really, you know. Of course I didn't see her very often. But all the same, I don't think it was the—the usual sort of—"

"No, she wouldn't have been walking the streets, she'd have had a man out picking up clients for her." Maybe Eddy Warren, for a little while; another, or others, afterward. But he didn't think Valerie had lived on that trade very long; she'd found an easier, more congenial racket in the shakedown. And after that, what? "Mrs. Keller," he said, "I'd like you to cast your mind back six years, to 1958. What was Valerie like then? Do you remember anything special, or unusual, happening that year, to her or about her?"

She looked at him in surprise. "Well, we were both just kids then, in high school. I can't remember anything—I don't know what you mean."

"Well, what was she like then?"

Marion clasped her long fingers together, staring at them, and then abruptly sat up and lit a cigarette. "Yes, looking back, I can see there was always a reckless streak in her," she said abstractedly. "At the time, I suppose, it seemed to me like—oh, vivacity, a sort of crazy zest for life I didn't have. I've always been cautious, for one thing, but Val would take any dare. I remember she jumped into the Allens' swimming-pool one night with all her clothes on, just because one of the boys dared her. Like that. And she loved to drive fast. I was always nervous, driving with her."

"Wild," said Mendoza, "meaning also the forbidden drinks and maybe dope?"

"Oh, *no*," said Marion quickly. And then, "I don't

think so. Oh, I'm sure not—I'd have known, we were together so much. The Ellises—well, looking back at them, he was one of those hearty men, you know the kind I mean, and Mrs. Ellis was, oh, pretty, and just ordinary. They weren't especially strict with Val, I don't think, but I do know that—like my own parents, well, like most parents—she wasn't allowed to drink or smoke. A lot of the older boys—college boys—we knew did smoke, and we'd take a cigarette sometimes, but not regularly. Then." She regarded the tip of her cigarette a little ruefully. "There wasn't anything like dope, Lieutenant. As teen-agers go nowadays, I think we were fairly moral ones."

"Steady boy friend?"

"No, she never went steady with anyone . . . Well, popular? She wasn't the most popular girl in school, I wouldn't say, but she had dates—with a lot of different boys . . . In some ways she was older than her age, and in others younger. And that's hindsight too," said Marion. "One thing I've just realized, thinking about her—since. She wanted to be grown-up, to do all the grown-up things —very much. She was so anxious to—to get there, if you see what I mean. She argued and complained about her parents being old fogies, even when they weren't terribly strict, because they wouldn't let her do some things, tried to keep some authority over her. Well, maybe that's standard practice for seventeen-year-olds. But she was—intense about it. There was that Pitman woman—looking back," said Marion thoughtfully, "I expect the Ellises were quite right."

"Who was that?"

"Oh, now I can see it was just silly, and very likely they *were* right. At the time, of course, I was all on Val's side."

132

She smiled faintly. "You know how girls that age get crushes on glamorous older women? Well, the Pitmans lived next door to the Ellises until they were divorced, and Val had quite a crush on Nan Pitman. To tell you the truth, I don't remember her too well—tall and blond—anyway, she got the custody of the child and moved away. Maybe the divorce was a particularly nasty one and the Ellises knew it, or maybe they just didn't like her, or approve of Val liking her, anyway they told her she mustn't go to see the woman any more. Val used to go there quite a lot. She got in a temper over that all right, said she was old enough to pick her own friends and so on."

"I see. Tempest in a teacup."

"Sort of. Though I guess maybe the Ellises were right, she wasn't exactly a desirable companion, so to speak. Because some time after that—it was after Val had sort of forgotten her, got over it—it was an awful thing, she got drunk one night and accidentally set the place afire and she and the child were both burned to death. I remember Val being dramatic about it, even though she'd got over the crush . . . No, I don't think she was ever very serious about any of the boys she went with. I—as a matter of fact, I don't think she was—capable of any very deep emotion. She just liked a good time—excitement. All I can say is, when that FBI man told me, I was shocked, but I wasn't surprised. That she'd gone down that far."

"Yes. Six years ago— Do you know the name of Overton?"

"No," said Marion. "No, I don't."

"You don't remember any even slightly unusual incident, connected with Valerie, that happened about then?" He tried to jog her memory. "You'd both have been in—

what, the second year of high school. Having dates—doing homework—all the teen-age things . . ." Marion went on shaking her head, looking politely puzzled. "I don't suppose you were in the habit of reading the papers much? Following the latest sensational murder?"

"No, I'm afraid not." She looked more puzzled. "Valerie never read much of anything, it was one of the ways we were opposite. She couldn't understand what anyone got out of it."

"Not a very good student, then?"

"Oh, fair. She wasn't much interested in any of her classes, but she was a good parrot, if you know what I mean. She was only going to college because it was expected of her. She was more interested in—" She hesitated, and finished, "Just living."

"Yes," said Mendoza. He felt frustrated. Every faintly suggestive little lead led him to a blank wall. He got up. "Well, thanks very much anyway, Mrs. Keller."

She ushered him politely to the door. "You can understand why she—went the way she did, when you knew her. Having everything, and then suddenly nothing. Somebody more stable would have—accepted it. But possessions—having things—meant a lot to Valerie. And I suppose, once she had got into a—a crowd of people like that, real criminals that is, well, violence—"

Mendoza didn't tell her that the incidence of homicide among small time pros was practically nil. He thanked her again and left.

That Gloria girl knew something. See her next. She had an apartment on Cherokee Drive in Hollywood. He drove up there, but got no answer to his knock. Out. Feeling more frustrated, he went back to his office to look over the latest FBI report.

He wondered how Alison was doing on her hunt for a nursemaid.

Alison was feeling frustrated too. It appeared that nursemaids were as obsolete as scullery maids. These days, there were women prepared to take care of babies but only during the day. The times when servants lived in had passed. No matter how much money you had, evidently, you were expected to look after your own offspring between midnight and dawn; all very democratic, of course, but all the same—

Bertha, now, would have been just fine; Alison wouldn't in the least mind washing the dishes and doing the dusting and so on, Bertha's normal duties, if stout, kind, competent Bertha would walk the floor with the twins at night. But unfortunately Bertha wasn't available, being tied to her own home by what she called her Germing Shepherd, the ubiquitous Fritz.

"Of course, you could hire a practical nurse," said the employment-agency clerk.

"I don't care what she calls herself," said Alison. "That's fine, if you—"

"But there's hardly ever one free," said the clerk. "A constant demand, you know, and not all of them will take baby cases. I can put your name down." She sounded doubtful.

Alison very nearly lost the temper that accompanies red hair. Instead she thanked the clerk and walked out. After all, she thought, this was a roundabout way to go at it. There were such things as classified ads. No harm in *looking*.

She walked up to the corner and bought a *Times*, to save driving all the way home for the morning paper. She walked down to the public lot where she'd left the Facel-Vega, got in and began to look at the classified ads.

And there, under *Child Care*, she found what sounded like the very ideal nursemaid she was looking for. *Widow, no ties, will care for baby or children, any hrs. your home, exp.* And a phone number. Fired with eager hope, Alison jotted down the number, folded the paper tidily, and walked up to the corner drugstore to call the woman . . .

Now she was sizing her up in person, and feeling thankfully that she looked just the thing—just the kind of nursemaid she'd hoped to find. Mrs. Thelma Cole was English. Not quite Cockney, but a humble accent. She was small and thin, but jolly for all of that. About fifty: very neat and clean and respectable-looking. Salt-and-pepper hair in a tidy bun, old-fashioned rimless spectacles. Her modest apartment was tidy and clean too.

"Oh, yes, mum, they can be trying at that stage, I know," she was saying sympathetically. "Do seem to be a thing you got to teach 'em, like, sleeping at night . . . Yes, mum, I've had a deal of experience with babies. I can give you good references, mum. Not so recent, but you see, 'tisn't since I lost me husband I had to go to work again. I'm sure I'd be real pleased to come to you, they do sound like lovely babies, mum . . . Well, living in like, I thought maybe—a hundred dollars a month, p'raps?"

Quite too good to be true, thought Alison, happily writing a check. Luis would be so pleased . . .

Mendoza read the FBI reports before going out to lunch. If there was anything suggestive in them, he didn't spot it. This was slow work, looking out backgrounds, and this they had so far was just surface—what the subjects themselves said, what neighbors and friends said—lawyers and doctors; in some cases relatives.

The Dvorzhaks looked like just what they said they were. Genuine Hungarian refugees. Jan Dvorzhak had been a professor of languages: they were superior, educated people. Had come here two years ago under the quota, after escaping into Austria. Dvorzhak had known other professional men here through correspondence, and had been accepted as a teacher in a private language school. He earned a fair living at that, but had besides an enviable capital investment in securities. He said quite frankly that for years, anticipating the chance to escape the Communist regime, he had been secretly acquiring unset stones, which he had managed to bring away with him. The transactions had been looked into and were all above-board; he had paid duty on the jewels, and eventually sold them for a tidy sum. He was one of the lucky refugees. His daughter Anya was attending college with the intention of becoming a teacher.

The Moskovitches—other end of the scale—an unsavory family. Mike's record—Maureen's record—Mendoza skimmed through that: nothing.

The Farlows. Even though the connection was so nebulous, the Feds were looking at everybody. Mrs. Farlow had been a Grace Eininger. Her older brother, Thomas Eininger, had been a money-maker: whatever he touched turned prosperous. Oil stock, real-estate investments, mining—he'd amassed quite a fortune while he was still a young man, having started with nothing. He hadn't married until he was forty, and then he had married a wife twenty years younger than himself. There had been a baby—a boy; and Thomas Eininger had made a will. Among many other provisions, it provided that in case of his death and that of his wife, his sister be appointed legal guardian of the boy, and co-trustee with his lawyer of his entire estate, held in trust for the boy, John. The unexpected had come to pass; Eininger was an ardent amateur yachtsman, and he and his wife had drowned together in a sailing accident when the boy was two years old.

Meanwhile, Grace Eininger had married Jack Farlow. He might be an amiable weakling; he seemed to be well liked. He'd held a good many different jobs before he and Grace fell into this soft place. Nothing said he was anything but a good-looking lazy charmer; and she seemed to be a perfectly ordinary straightforward woman, maybe the stronger character of the two. The co-trustee, a busy Los Angeles attorney, said he was quite happy about the home the Farlows made for the boy, and what the hell business was it of the FBI anyway? The neighbors said they were nice quiet neighbors, and good to the boy. Parties sometimes, but nothing wild. They also said that Farlow seemed "good" with the boy: the boy seemed quite happy, looking on them as parents.

Nothing, nothing . . . But Mendoza sat up a little over the report on Paul Manton.

Manton's employers said frankly they were thinking seriously of firing him. Again. He was, said his immediate boss with equal frankness, one hell of a good mechanic, but he wouldn't stand routine. Work a couple of weeks honest and regular as you please, and then all of a sudden he wouldn't show; and when he eventually came back on the job, he'd just say, Oh, he'd taken a notion to drop over to Vegas a couple of days, or, Well, he met up with this blonde. Erratic, in other words . . . Like, his boss went on to say, just this last week, he takes off a couple of days without a word, and just when they were particularly swamped, too.

His Air Force record was excellent; he'd won a couple of medals. He'd only been twenty, twenty-one then. Yes, thought Mendoza, remembering that good-looking, strong, reckless face, he'd be that type. Maybe he should have stayed in the service. But again, in peacetime, not the kind who could live with any discipline.

He didn't seem to have any close friends or a regular girl. "Oh, Paul, hell, he plays the field," his boss had said cynically. Which figured. A man with a face like that, thought Mendoza, wouldn't be an ascetic. He drank very little. People who ought to know said he was a very good pilot.

He lived in a middle-aged Hollywood apartment, nothing fancy, and the manageress said he wasn't there much. Just to sleep, and not always that. He very seldom got any letters. He'd lived there for three years and had always paid the rent regularly. Always been a quiet tenant. Apparently he was interested in folk music: a phonograph and quite a few L.P. records around. He didn't seem to live extravagantly; as a top mechanic, of course, he made good wages.

His previous record was predictable; he'd been fired from several good jobs for taking a few days off whenever he felt like it. But he was good enough so that employers had hired him back several times too, and he always managed to get another job if they didn't.

He hadn't seemed nervous in any way at being questioned; said he realized they had to take a look at everybody, and though he hadn't known her well—

It was interesting, but not altogether surprising. And as for linking Manton any closer to Valerie, useless.

That girl Gloria—

Mendoza swore, and took himself out to lunch. At Federico's he met Hackett gloomily contemplating the Dieters' Special Steak, sat down opposite and presented his problem to him.

"Just a great big blank. Nobody admits to knowing where she was going on Sunday, or to seeing her at all. She didn't come home again after Mrs. Montague saw her leave at ten o'clock. And that damned machine— And what the hell was her racket? None of the usual things is indicated."

"No," agreed Hackett. "Offbeat one all right. Funny way to take her off, too—in a way. Unusual. No inspiration hits me offhand, I'm afraid. And as for your anonymous phone call—these six-year-old murders—"

"Well, of course that's a wild one," agreed Mendoza. "Six years ago Valerie was a giggling seventeen-year-old, never opening a newspaper to hear about the latest murder. Though there's always the radio."

"On the other hand—" Hackett picked up his fork. "We like to think we're pretty good," he said inconsequentially, "and mostly when we get a new homicide, whatever variety, eventually we collect evidence on who's responsible. But once in a while—there was that Burnham—something turns up to make us blush a little."

"Burnham," nodded Mendoza. Another offbeat one. One out of the books. A suspicious neighbor coming to the police, and the body found buried in the back yard; and Burnham calmly confessing that he'd murdered eight wives in the last fifteen years—and the bodies showing up where he said they were. "Burnham?"

"It just occurs to me," said Hackett, "and it's not very likely, but it could be—granting that your anonymous caller wasn't just a crank of some sort—that the murder she mentioned never got into the papers. Never got into our files. Got itself written off as accident, suicide, natural death, or never got noticed at all. In a big city, frightening to think how somebody can drop out of sight and never be missed."

Mendoza stared at him. "That's so," he said slowly. "As you say, not very likely, but— And at this late date, how hopeless to make any check! Where to look? Your bright ideas just confuse the issue some more, damn it."

"Just occurred to me," said Hackett.

When he got back to the office, he called Gloria Litvak's apartment. She answered; when he announced himself, told her to stay in and expect him, he thought at first she'd fainted. "Miss Litvak?"

"A-all right," she said tremulously. "I don't know anything more to tell you—honest, I—"

"I'll see you in half an hour," said Mendoza. "Just routine, Miss Litvak."

As he came out of his office, Sergeant Lake stopped him. "I think you'd like to hear what this young fellow has to say, sir," he said formally. A tall gangling young man, looking nervous, was standing beside his desk. "He's got something to tell us about Miss Ellis."

141

"Oh, yes?"

What young Mr. Jorgensen had to say wasn't very important. He was a clerk at a Thrifty drugstore on Hollywood Boulevard, and he was pretty sure it had been Valerie Ellis who had come into the store last Sunday and he'd waited on her. About eleven o'clock in the morning. He couldn't remember exactly what she'd bought, but something small, inexpensive—maybe a package of aspirin, something like that. "I guess I shoulda come in before, but I wasn't just so sure it was her, I had to study on it, make up my mind—"

"All right, you take a statement, Jimmy." Mendoza cut him short; it wasn't important, but of course you never knew what might turn out to be important, so you took statements. He went on out, and drove up to Hollywood to see Gloria. Try to coax what she knew out of her.

Both he and the Feds thought that Gloria was probably earning a living as a call girl. No proof; they hadn't the manpower to tail all these people. If only some lead would show up to point to somebody definite, use the tails, but so far—Gloria was calling herself a model these days. He'd passed her name on to Perce Andrews; maybe he was taking a look at her . . .

Mendoza put out all his persuasive charm, which was considerable. But, looking as terrified as the proverbial bird hypnotized by a snake, Gloria remained stubborn.

"I've told you all I know—honest I have—it was all just like I told you and I don't know anything more about it."

"I think you do, Miss Litvak. I wish you'd think twice and tell me what it is." He smiled at her. "Did you know what her latest racket was? I think so. Unless you were involved in it, you know, we couldn't do anything to you for—" She went on shaking her head stubbornly. She was green with fright. "Look, Miss Litvak. Just because you've had one brush with the police, you needn't be afraid we'll automatically suspect you, or do any railroading. We've looked up your family, and know that they're all quite respectable people, that you don't belong to—" He stopped. She had fainted now, slumping awkwardly from chair to floor. "Damnation!" said Mendoza, annoyed.

He picked her up and laid her on the couch, propping her feet up. He brought her a glass of water when she came to, asked if she wanted a doctor.

"I'm—all—right," she said weakly, turning her face away into the back of the couch. "If you'll just—stop bothering me, and go away. I *told* you all I know."

He couldn't go on pressing her, by the humane rules.

He walked down the stairs, thinking about Gloria, who knew something. Gloria, possibly in on the racket? Not a very brainy accomplice.

She had to be over at Vic's. The phrase haunted him.

He wondered if he'd turn up anything setting a tail on Gloria.

He came out of the apartment-house door, fishing absently for his car keys; a woman brushed past him, up the steps to the front door. He turned right, up toward where he'd left the Ferrari half a block up the street; and then a belated vague memory touched him, and he turned and looked back.

The woman had stopped, with one hand holding the door open, and he thought she had been looking after him. He had no more than started to turn his head—he saw

143

out of the corner of his eye—when she shoved the door wider and ducked in and was gone.

An impression of youth, smartness, lithe energy.

And he thought that had been Anya Dvorzhak. He wasn't sure. He wasn't sure at all, but— A dark, pretty girl like Anya, anyway. Had it been?

Mendoza went back, rapidly. Nobody in the lobby or on the stairs. When he got to Gloria's apartment, she faced him woodenly, her face tear-stained, and said No, there wasn't anybody there. Why should there be?

And maybe there wasn't, then. Maybe it hadn't been Anya Dvorzhak at all. If it had been, maybe Anya knew somebody else who lived here. Coincidence, but they did happen. And Anya just didn't like cops, didn't care to be recognized and questioned. Anybody who had grown up under a Communist regime might very understandably dislike official police.

And also, reflected Mendoza, anybody like that—who had managed to escape—was probably quite experienced at dodging and evading and telling the plausible lies and covering up in general.

What the hell was all this about? Could the Feds be right after all—did the Communists come into this? But the Dvorzhaks would have been thoroughly screened before they were let in—

Maybe, for God's sake, he was getting old. Losing his touch. Floundering around like a new ranker, with no more idea of what had gone on here, what the case was all about—!

Eleven

He went back to his office and called Waltham. Unavoidably, he'd noticed the headlines the last two days; he wasn't surprised that Waltham sounded harassed.

"Surprising how many doubles Thorwald has, isn't it?" he asked.

Waltham didn't laugh. "If that's suposed to be funny—" Thorwald had been seen by excited honest citizens in fifty different places between Honolulu and New York, in the last forty-eight hours. As any one of them might really be Thorwald, all the tips had to be followed up.

"Well, we've had a little of that ourselves," said Mendoza. They had. Half a dozen people had called in to say they'd seen Valerie Ellis at such and such a place on Sunday. They had all been checked out, because any of them might be so; but they'd all been proved duds (by men taking valuable time to check) except one report that she'd been seen at one o'clock buying a ticket to the Hawaii Theater. And he thought they'd find that one had been mistaken identity too. He thought Valerie had had something more profitable to do with her time that afternoon than attend a movie . . . Very probably, of all those reports, young Mr. Jorgensen was the only one they could believe; he'd been so diffident about coming in. And what did that say, that she'd dropped into a drugstore?

"What I called about is something a little funny," he said, and told Waltham about the Martian machine. Waltham grunted. "Say anything to you?"

"Yes, damn it," said Waltham, "or it might. Thorwald is an engineer. I wouldn't doubt he could figure out with no trouble at all how to operate a thing like that. He was right at the top of the class, after all."

"¡Por Dios!" said Mendoza softly. "That I never thought of. What a tangle . . . Are you getting anywhere?"

"Odds and ends. This stage, largely eliminating—you know how it goes. We've got leads on about a dozen people who've bought Madeira wine fairly recently, or habitually buy it. We've got all the liquor retailers briefed to watch for that. Oh"—Mendoza heard papers rattle—"that Mrs. Mandelbaum. Report just came in."

"What Mrs.—oh, yes." Cardenas had said a Mrs. Mandelbaum had introduced him to Valerie. "Yes?"

"Well, it doesn't take us very far." Waltham sighed. "Need a month of Sundays to really check all these people, damn it. She looks perfectly level. Widow, living alone at a nice apartment in Santa Monica. German accent you could cut with a knife. Says she met Valerie at a fashion show at The May Company, they just got to talking. She was such a nice bright girl, says Mrs. Mandelbaum; she likes cheerful young things around, she used to invite her to parties and so on. Very shocked—as isn't everybody!— to hear that Valerie was a bad girl. Fellow who looked at her says she's a nice fat old lady, kind of simple. She's lived there about five years, neighbors say the same thing."

"I can't remember another case I ever worked," said Mendoza, "when *some* lead didn't show up within this length of time. Even when we couldn't get evidence for the D.A. Damn it, what was the girl up to? Of course, come to think, it could have been more than one caper. Here a little, there a little. Yes." He told Waltham about his doubtful identification of Anya Dvorzhak at the apartment where Gloria Litvak lived. "No, I'm not a hundred per cent sure, but—"

"Well, I'm bound to say," said Waltham, "just because they are who they are, I think we can mark the Dvorzhaks off—if it is anything political. People coming in like that are very thoroughly screened, after all."

Mendoza said irritably, "I thought you boys were supposed to be hot shots. As a confirmed capitalist, I get worried sometimes. For God's sake, how long are we going to go on being blind? So it takes two to start a fight, it also takes two or more—of honest intent—to create an atmosphere of brotherly love. Can you tell me that, with all our noble democratic sympathy for the poor downtrodden refugees, one or two or more couldn't slip in who are fakes? Provided with the convincing proofs by the Kremlin?"

"Well, no. Of course we've picked up a few like that," said Waltham mildly. "But I assure you, they are looked at. Just for that reason. And this Professor Dvorzhak seems to be a well-known man. I've seen them myself, and checked. Are you coming round to the idea that the murder was political?"

"I am not. I think it was a very private kill. I can't figure the political tie-up." Mendoza was silent and then asked, "You said you knew a good deal about Thorwald. When he landed back in this country, what do you think he'd do? Where would he go? Just as an intelligent guess? Any old friends he could trust?"

"Not old professional friends, no. I'd say nobody he knew, before, except— It depends on whether his friends from Moscow were chasing him. There was an old girl friend—he was quite the ladies' man, in a discreet way— who stayed by him. In fact, if you recall, she got a year's term for sheltering him. Would have been more, but we couldn't prove she knew he was guilty of treason at the time. Lisa Thorne. She was executive secretary to a big firm of attorneys in town—"

"By town meaning Washington?"

"Sure. They didn't take her back when she got out— she's dropped out of sight. If he could have got a message to her before or after he got here—providing he knew where to reach her—it's in the cards she'd have been ready to team up with him again. But no leads on it . . . What would he do? I'd say, if he knew they weren't chasing him, he'd go to ground—with or without the girl friend—in some big city, take an inconspicuous job, look as inconspicuous as possible. Very probably that's what he'd do if they were after him, too."

"Yes," said Mendoza. "I think so too. Well—wish each other luck." He hung up, swiveled around, and looked at the panorama of the city spread before him.

He thought, Paul Manton. A hell of a good mechanic. Very likely he could have taken a long look at the Martian machine's dashboard or whatever it was called, and seen how to operate it. But why? No close tie-up with Valerie

148

that showed . . . And that was another thing. Introduced to Valerie by Maureen Moskovitch. Could a sophisticated man like Manton not have known what Maureen was? So, would he have been so very surprised to hear that a friend of Maureen's was on the bent? It was a little thing, of course.

He swiveled back and looked at the pile of reports on his desk. Odds and ends were coming in. He had Dwyer, Scarne, Piggott, Glasser on it, asking the questions, poking around. And there were the reports from Prints.

No identifiable prints on the doorknob of Valerie's apartment. But they knew who the intruder on Wednesday night had been—Eddy Warren. After, pretty certainly, his reefers stored with Valerie.

A lot of prints in her white Dodge, inside and outside. Tiresome work eliminating the unimportant ones, the garage-hands and so on. And collecting prints to compare, from her circle of acquaintances, the gas station where she had the tank filled, et cetera. Most of those people raised a fuss, expectably, at being treated like criminals. But two rather interesting little facts had just shown up from that. First, as they'd known since first looking at the car, the steering wheel was virginally clean of any prints at all, even smudged ones, as were the push buttons for the automatic transmission, the light switch, and the directional signal switch. And second, there were a couple of Paul Manton's prints on the dashboard and outside of the car.

That rather canceled itself out, thought Mendoza. That said that Paul Manton wasn't X, who'd so carefully removed his prints—after driving the Dodge.

Yes. Build it up. She had been unsuspectingly fed the

doped drink, elsewhere. Most probably in a private residence. And had died there. Dr. Bainbridge had said she'd pass out in about half an hour, and probably be dead within four hours. X had planned, had hoped, to get her back into her own apartment, set up an obvious suicide or accident. The safest way, if he could manage it. It wouldn't matter that she hadn't a prescription for those sleeping-tablets; there were ways things like that could be acquired under the counter. So he had, after dark, got her into her own car, probably rolled in a blanket, and driven to her apartment house.

He could find out which garage was hers, if he didn't already know, by trying the padlocks: which one she had the key to. And then he'd gone to get the apartment door open. Mendoza didn't think X had planned to carry her in openly through the front door. Entirely too dangerous. It was a ground-floor apartment, on the driveway side of the building; the best way to get her in would be to open a window, unhook the screen and prop it open, carry her up the dark driveway and hoist her through the window . . . A little job, carrying a body around like that. X a pretty hefty fellow?

Only Mrs. Montague had startled him as he opened the door . . . Yes, *how* he must have cursed himself for dropping those keys—those invaluable keys!

So then he couldn't stage the fake suicide. And for some reason he had decided to leave her—

Despacio, aguarda un momento—wait a minute here. He'd brought her back home in her own car, and the car had stayed in her garage. Well, he could have driven her down to Garey Street and brought the Dodge back again afterward. But also, he might already have got the car all polished up, removing his prints thoroughly, and not wanted to do the job over again. He might have called an accomplice to bring up another car. "They" again . . .

She had to be over at Vic's. Damn it, it seemed almost to mean something, but he couldn't catch the significance.

Rikki's bar, mentioned in the notebook. Ordinary place out on Vernon Avenue in Huntington Park. Yes, she'd been in; the barman, a waiter, somewhat vaguely recognized her picture. She'd been there at least once with another woman, and they thought several times with men. No remotely useful description of the men, of course. But then, most bars were kept so dark. Influence of Prohibition still holding, thought Mendoza irritably.

The patient Dwyer had rung doorbells all along that block of Garey Street. Had anybody heard one of those big construction machines running on Sunday evening?

He had found people who had been watching TV and really couldn't say. He had found people who had been listening to the radio and couldn't say. He had found people who had been away from home until late and couldn't say. The chiropractor lived in a couple of rooms behind his office; he was an amateur photographer and had been in his makeshift darkroom most of Sunday evening, developing a negative and making some prints—he didn't recall. The herb-doctor, a polite young Chinese, was a devout Methodist and had been at some church affair. The dentist had been at the movies with his wife. And then, down at the corner of Second Street, Dwyer had found ancient Mrs. Modjeska. Mrs. Modjeska, eighty-seven and retaining all her faculties if she had lost most of her teeth, said that indeed there had been one of those machines running that night. Only for a very short time, but it amounted to the same thing— Heathens, she said, shaking a finger under Dwyer's nose, breaking the Sabbath. As if it wasn't bad enough to come tearing up the street, making all this dust and commotion—half-naked men out there in broad daylight—they must come back on the Sabbath! It was an outrage.

Dwyer tried to pin her down to a time, but the best he could get out of her was between nine and ten.

So, the Martian machine had been used to get the body over the fence.

That scrawl in Valerie's address book which might have been either Frank or Fred had turned out, by the phone number, to be one Fran Schwartz. The report said tersely, *Another model, question mark*. Address on Bronson in Hollywood. He had phoned a query down to Vice; maybe they knew something about her.

By what Gloria, and Valerie's Aunt Mabel, said, a week ago Tuesday afternoon Valerie had been expecting a caller. Gloria may have seen the caller, wasn't admitting it. A new mark? Something to do with the racket? Then, on Wednesday, she went off in her car, and didn't come home until Friday evening.

In her car . . . The Dodge convertible was four years and four months old; it had been given to her by her father three months before his fatal accident. And it had nearly forty thousand miles on it. That was a little unusual right there, because a girl like Valerie, using a car for the casual little errands around town, calls on friends, wouldn't as a rule average over a couple of hundred miles a month. Of course in this metropolis even the casual little errands could pile up mileage, but even so—

And the funny thing about it was, it wasn't a struck average. They'd found the garage where she always took the Dodge for servicing. The garage kept a record, of course, of oil changes and so on. What the mileage had been when. And up to about twenty months ago, Valerie hadn't driven the Dodge two hundred miles a month. Twenty months ago or thereabouts, the Dodge had had upwards of eight thousand miles on it, an average figure for its age. She'd piled up all the rest of the mileage since. How and why? Connected with the racket?

Odds and ends, odds and ends. Nothing pointing anywhere . . . He wondered how Hackett and Palliser were doing. No sign of either of them in the office this morning . . .

"Too good to be true," said Alison contentedly. "Tell me how clever I am, darling."

"I knew there must be one somewhere," agreed Mendoza. "She seems eminently satisfactory, but of course it's early to be sure." He leaned back, stroking Bast on his lap. The steak had been done just as he liked it, there had been wild rice and mushrooms to accompany it, Alison's copper head gleamed above a favorite topaz-colored gown, the twins were asleep, Bast purred under his hand, and altogether if he'd had any glimmering of an idea about this damned case he'd feel wholly at peace. As it was—

El Señor was washing Sheba, holding her down with one paw. Nefertiti lay purring on Alison's lap. "They've been neglected lately, poor things, what with the twins . . . She likes cats, Luis. She made friends with El Señor right away, and you know he's usually standoffish. And the babies took to her too, I could tell—she's very good with them." Alison heaved a peaceful sigh. "I really think our worries are over."

"For the moment," said Mendoza lazily. "I ran into Saul Goldberg this afternoon, as I was leaving—he said something that struck me. I was complaining, you know, and he came out with this—old Hebrew proverb—'*Small children disturb your sleep, big children your life.*' A sobering thought, and probably true."

"Nonsense," said Alison robustly. She threaded a needle, tongue protruding delicately, and bent over the small blue sweater. He waited for the inevitable explosion. "Oh, damn! Of *all* the—"

"You do amuse me," he said. "You know you can't sew. It arouses all your most unladylike instincts when you try. Another thing like the nursemaid business—going all conventional just because you have produced a couple of very ordinary infants."

"You be quiet," said Alison crossly. "You'd think anybody could sew a simple appliqué to a sweater. All I'm trying to *do*. It doesn't help for you to sit there and heckle me— *Oh!*"

"Nothing to do with me. I'm not heckling. I'm just saying you amuse me, *querida* . . . Put that down for a minute and pay attention. Imagine that you are a young woman very greedy for money, who has in fact engaged in prostitution for same, and is now involved in a very lucrative racket of some kind. You are essentially a rather sexless young woman, not much interested in that sort of thing—"

"Well, I'm trying," said Alison obediently. "Yes?"

"Would you be, could you be, very romantically interested in a balding civil servant who probably doesn't

154

make over ten thousand a year? Even if he looked a little like me?"

"This is Valerie? I certainly shouldn't think so," said Alison. "Was she?"

"I don't think so either. But when you come to that kind of thing, it's a No Man's Land. Who can say what A sees in B? She could have been, damn it. The two people who say so look very much on the level . . . And those other girls, who probably would know, are being so damn cagey —afraid of being involved—keeping back even innocent information—" He got up, Bast cradled in his arms, and began to pace restlessly, up and down Alison's handsome big living room. "And then there's another thing—"

Distantly, one of the twins began to cry, and stopped almost immediately. "A jewel," said Alison. "Now I know what the phrase means. A perfect jewel. Such a nice little woman."

"Is Mrs. Mandelbaum what she seems to be? Did Gloria see whoever came to see Valerie a week ago Tuesday? Who the hell is Vic?"

Alison took up her needle again. "You sound exactly like the announcer for a soap opera . . . What fascinates *me*, if there's anything in it at all, is who the woman was who was murdered six years ago."

"That's a wild card, for God's sake."

"I don't think so . . . Oh, Lord, what have I—oh, I see, it has to go under, not over . . . Suppose—you said they're much the same coloring—this Paul Manton is really Valerie's mother's illegitimate son, and the woman who was killed was a friend of hers who knew all about it, and was going to tell her husband, and—"

"¡Zape—*vaya historia!* Now who sounds like a soap
155

opera?" Mendoza laughed. "I'll tell you one thing just occurs to me—damn it, this lack of sleep *is* affecting my mind! That phone call. If it wasn't a crank, if it was the genuine article, it tells us that X is probably being blackmailed. That somebody has guessed he is X, and why."

"Oh. Why?"

Bast leaped lightly down to tumble her big blond son away from Sheba and take over the wash job. El Señor withdrew coldly to sit on the credenza and polish his blond paws and face. "What she said on the phone," said Mendoza. "We should have picked that one up right away. She said at one point, 'I would so tell them!' Meaning us. That call was made as a last dead-serious threat to X that if he didn't pay up she'd pass on what she knew. Without any doubt, X was standing right beside her when she made that call. He'd been dickering with her—or refusing to come across—so she showed him she meant business."

"That's—yes, I see what you mean."

Mendoza wandered out to the kitchen to pour himself a scant jigger of rye. El Señor hurried after hopefully and received his ounce in a saucer. Green eyes shut tight, he lapped happily. "*Señor Atroz*," said Mendoza. "Talk about bad examples." He wandered back to the living room, glass in hand. "And where the hell does Thorwald come in?" he asked.

"She was his mistress," said Alison. "Or, all right, you say she wasn't interested in being anybody's. Then she'd found out about him—who he was. He was paying her to keep quiet about it. That was her racket."

"But there's an implication there were a couple of other people in it."

"Only by what Maureen said," Alison pointed out.

"That Valerie had quoted that proverb about three keeping a secret if two of them were dead, and adding that she was sure of these two. Well, I ask you, *amado*, who could she have been surer of than Thorwald and his old girl friend, who had probably joined him? . . . Oh, damn! This abominable thread—"

Mendoza stopped in his tracks and stared at her. "Now that's an angle I never— That could be so. That could be so indeed. Only if it is so, where did Thorwald get the money? By all appearances, a very substantial sum of money."

"Well," said Alison, her red head bent over the sweater, "I wouldn't know if any of the cloak-and-dagger stories are plausible. But we all know that some fantastic things have happened in the last twenty years—things that sound like Ian Fleming at his wildest. Haven't there? Caches of prewar gold—stolen hoards tucked away— It could be something like that. And as to how Valerie might have spotted him—you say she wasn't the political animal, as the saying goes—I wouldn't guess, but you've just heard that this old flame of Thorwald's dropped out of sight after she got out of jail. She didn't get her old job back— she'd have no references. Probably she wouldn't stay in Washington. How would a woman like that earn a living? You said yourself, the easiest way— And it could have been here."

Mendoza finished the rye. "You're building a story," he said softly. "So?"

Alison cocked her head at him. "L.A.'s getting to be like that place in Egypt—sooner or later everybody gets here. Isn't it? You know Thorwald was here, wherever he is now. Quite possibly his former girl friend was here, to

157

meet him—or he came here because she was here already. Maybe Valerie knew her, and—they'd be very cautious, wouldn't they?—acted as a messenger, a go-between, some way. And found out about Thorwald—maybe because the girl friend trusted her too far—"

"*Un momento*," said Mendoza. "Grant that Thorwald came back with a fortune in hand. From somewhere. I don't see him paying out hush-money at that rate over a period of eighteen or twenty months—he can't have been here that long anyway—before finally deciding to get rid of her."

"So the Thorwald business was—extracurricular," said Alison. "Maybe quite recent, only a couple of weeks or a month ago."

"Another thing. That bottle of Madeira in Valerie's kitchen cupboard. So she was putting the bite on him— or them—to keep quiet. It hangs together after a fashion. And that was apart from the regular racket she was working. This I like, because I've had a hunch all along that the motive hadn't a thing to do with her racket. All right. Would Thorwald make her a present of that bottle? 'Do try some of this excellent wine just to please me, my dear.' "

"And I've had a thought about that too," said Alison. She stuck her needle in the sweater and looked at him. "That could have been before she began the blackmail. When she was still being friendly to them. And also— Have you had the Madeira analyzed? To see if there's any codeine in it? Because, say Thorwald had spiked it before he gave it to her—or afterward, when she tried blackmail. Maybe he'd given her a bottle of it before and knew she liked it, would drink it of her own volition, maybe a glass before going to bed. She could have drunk a fatal

158

dose—how melodramatic that sounds—and then gone out somewhere, on Sunday. The doctor says she mightn't feel it for a half-hour or so. She could have gone out somewhere, and collapsed and died in, say, the Moskovitches' apartment or somewhere, so whoever it was was scared of being involved and simply carted the body off, not to be associated—"

Mendoza stared at her. He said absently, "I must be losing my touch, all right. *Porvida*, I never thought of that. An entirely new angle—" He wheeled and made for the telephone, to contact Waltham.

Talk about soap opera. But it was *possible*, damn it. It wouldn't do any harm, to have that bottle of Madeira analyzed . . .

Twelve

Palliser came into the office after six on Saturday night, feeling low. With reason. He'd taken the rest of the day, after they'd talked to Mendoza about it, looking into this Dasher thing. In one way he hadn't got much, and in another way he'd got too much.

There was this and that in Mrs. Dasher's background that looked odd. It could still be that her killer was an utter stranger, imitating Lover Boy; but at least one thing he'd come across might point to—what was Mendoza's phrase?—a private kill.

He found Hackett drinking black coffee out of a cardboard mug and staring glassy-eyed at a pile of reports. "Anything show up?"

"Not yet. And the hell of a list still to get through. What've you got?" asked Hackett dully.

Palliser sat down and started to tell him what he'd got.

He'd been handicapped by the fact that it was Saturday. Not infrequently, police officers resent the five-day week; it not only delays investigations, but the fact that they often work a couple of weeks or more straight without a day off, all to protect the honest citizenry, makes the idea of the honest citizenry lazing around at home a bitter one.

After talking to Mrs. Powell again, and a few friends and neighbors of Mrs. Dasher's, Palliser had found he wanted urgently to see Mrs. Dasher's bank record . . . She had, everyone who knew her agreed, been one to keep her affairs to herself. She hadn't had any really close friends aside from Mrs. Powell. Oh, several women she knew from church, and other nurses she'd known—Mrs. Dasher had had an address book too, but not very full.

"She never gossiped about her cases," said pleasant-faced Myra Thompson. "That I will say. It was a living to her, was all—she wasn't really interested in people, I don't think . . . Why? I mean, I thought it was this awful colored man who—"

"Well, we like to be thorough, Mrs. Thompson," said Palliser vaguely. "You'd known her long?"

She nodded, eying him curiously: a woman in her fifties, stout and amiable. "We took the practical-nursing course together, that's how we met. That's twenty years ago. I'd just lost my first husband and she'd just lost hers, and we'd both thought that was a sensible sort of job to learn. She was ten years older than me, of course . . . Well, we didn't see each other too often, especially since I remarried. Even if she was retired, she wasn't one for gadding around much, you see. Wish somebody'd leave *me* a legacy! Not that I grudged her the luck—she was a hard worker—but I was a little surprised at that. Because, well, she couldn't help it, poor thing, but she wasn't really very sympathetic —just do the work she was supposed to, but no little

161

personal fussing, know what I mean . . . Oh, I don't know any of the details about that, she was pretty close-mouthed."

Gradually a picture built up in Palliser's mind . . . "Well, when I say I knew her, I'm bound to say it was kind of casual. We've both lived on the same block a good many years, and she was friendly enough, but kept herself to herself like they say." And a church friend: "Oh, it was just her way, to be secretive. I guess people who live alone get that way. Nobody expected any different, knowing her." And: "I don't say she was mean about money, but she was careful. She'd had to be, I guess, and got in the habit." A picture of a rather house-proud old woman, conventional and solitary, with no close emotional ties and perhaps not wanting any. Closemouthed, close with money.

Mrs. Powell told him a good deal; she had known more about Gertrude Dasher than anyone else; but she couldn't tell him a few essentials.

"Closemouthed, so she was, and hadn't she learned to be! That husband of hers, tell him anything, he'd go letting out real personal things at the nearest bar! And expecting her to manage on practically nothing. What? Well, he was a plasterer, but they wasn't making the wages they do now, twenty years back, you know . . . Well, Gertrude tried hard enough, the good Lord knows, to stop his drinking. Lifelong member of the W.C.T.U., *as* I am myself . . . Drunk? That's not the point, young man —he didn't exactly get *drunk*, but it's the principle—"

Palliser suppressed a twinge of sympathy for the late Harry Dasher, plasterer, who had liked a couple of beers with the boys after work.

"No, she never had any children, she was alone in the

162

world, poor woman. And had the arthritis coming on bad, the last few years, so it was a mercy she could afford to retire."

He asked about that: the fortunate legacy. "Well, she never said the name, I don't know who it was. Some old patient. Nor I don't know how much. Gertrude liked to keep her affairs private, and I respected that, I do myself. I just know it was enough so she could live pretty well, better than before. She wasn't extravagant, I don't mean that, but I noticed she'd buy things she couldn't afford before. Like frozen vegetables instead of canned, and round steak instead of stewing beef, and she sent her coat to be cleaned instead of doing it herself—'"

Palliser's picture grew clearer. A little more than close, Gertrude Dasher. He often did the shopping for his mother on his days off, and he had some idea of prices. Not all that much difference these days between round steak and stewing-beef; call it twenty cents a pound. And one old lady, a pound lasting maybe three days. Fifty cents to have the coat cleaned . . .

"Was she working on a case when she heard about the legacy?"

"I couldn't say," said Mrs. Powell. "She never said much about the people she worked for, but I do know she'd been mostly taking baby cases, about then. Taking care of babies for people could afford to pay a nursemaid. So I don't expect it'd be one of them—"

"But she must have told you something about it," said Palliser. She had been Mrs. Dasher's one relatively close friend; they had, she said, usually had dinner together at least once a week.

"Well, she didn't," snapped Mrs. Powell. "For one thing,
163

I wasn't here when it happened. I was on a visit to my married daughter back in Pennsylvania, from February to April that year, and it was when I got back Gertrude told me about her legacy. She wasn't much of a letter writer and neither am I."

Palliser tapped his ballpoint pen reflectively on his front teeth. Grant that Gertrude Dasher had been a secretive, solitary old woman: surely that was a little unnatural? She'd had to work hard all her life; she'd learned to be very close with money (though maybe that had come natural to her). When out of the blue she got a sufficiently substantial legacy that she could stop working, live a little better than she had before, surely she'd have made a few comments on it to a close friend? That nice old Mr. Smith, fancy him remembering me, or, that lovely old Mrs. Jones, I never thought she'd be so kind . . .

And aside from what Mrs. Thompson said about her lack of sympathy, he definitely got that impression himself at second hand: a rather sour, embittered old woman, not likely to have impressed a patient as so kind a nurse that a legacy was in order.

So he wanted to see what her bank record looked like. Find out where the money had come from, in what form. And it was Saturday, damn it. He asked Mrs. Powell if she knew where Mrs. Dasher banked. The Security-First National, the one nearest on Hollywood Boulevard.

To hell with Saturday. Bankers could be forced to do a little work on Saturday without bringing the world to an end. Palliser used the telephone, got names and phone numbers. Made more calls, patient and polite. After a good deal of delay and argument, bank officialdom finally produced for him an annoyed junior vice-president by the unlikely name of Rumpeldorf, who met him outside the doors of the branch in question.

"I suppose you know what a nuisance you're being—" Mr. Rumpeldorf paused inquiringly.

"Sergeant Palliser. I'm very sorry, but we need the information urgently." Mr. Rumpeldorf was trying keys and swearing.

"At whatever inconvenience. Damn the door. I suppose you realize this meant my running around collecting different keys from several people? And that I shall have to disconnect the alarm while we're inside, and I know very little about it? Damn Scobey—they should have sent Nichols down with me—" He got the door open at last.

It was Palliser who disconnected the alarm system; with Mr. Rumpeldorf dithering around at it, he had visions of bringing the nearest squad car down on them. But when it came to looking up files, Mr. Rumpeldorf seemed to know what he was doing, and produced Gertrude Dasher's records at once. The current file showed all of last year's statements.

"We are in the process of microfilming records for 1963 now," said the junior vice-president stiffly.

"Yes." Early in every month, never later than the fifth, Mrs. Dasher had deposited five hundred dollars cash in a checking account. She didn't write many checks. Some time each month, around the middle, she'd usually written a check for fifty or sixty dollars. Household expenses? The account at present contained seven thousand, three hundred and twenty-one dollars and ninety-four cents.

Mr. Rumpeldorf stood sighing and jangling his keys irritably. "I'd like to see back further than this," said Palliser.

165

"Oh, my God!" wailed Mr. Rumpeldorf. "The *microfilms*? Listen, damn it, we're giving a party tonight—my wife—"

It was very petty and small of him, Palliser acknowledged, but he couldn't help feeling a little pleased at the thought of somebody besides a police officer maybe having an evening spoiled because duty called. The times he'd had to break a date with Roberta—

"And," he said to Hackett, "all those years, five hundred in cash paid in regular as clockwork every month. Nothing to show how she got it. Never any incoming checks. And she lived on less than half that, letting it mount up. Well, it looks funny. I mean, a legacy might come all in one piece or in the form of a trust or an annuity, but I never heard of a trust or annuity that paid in nice crisp green cash."

Hackett rubbed his sandy unshaven jaw and said neither had he. "So she stashed the legacy away in cash in a safety-deposit box? Or, no, of course not, when she kept a checking account."

"She didn't have a box. Not there anyway. Probably not anywhere else, though we'll have to look."

"And you couldn't get into the Hall of Justice to look up the possible record of the legacy."

"No, not until Monday. But if there was a legacy the record's bound to be there. She'd never been out of the state, hardly out of the county."

Hackett looked even more tired. "Well, you may as well go on doing the looking. It's possible, if she was as secretive as you say, that she kept it in some form at another bank—queer old ladies do that kind of thing. But it's also possible

166

that she got that nice bundle of cash through the mail every month. In which case it looks like—"

"Blackmail money. I know."

"A very nice motive for murder," said Hackett. He looked at the reports. "On top of everything else."

Mendoza went to the office on Sunday morning, but he wondered why. Just to await the latest FBI report? There wasn't much more they could do on this, on Sunday. Waste of time seeing these people over again, hearing the same stories.

He wandered around rereading reports, thinking in circles. Not one smell of a lead—

One thing they'd been using men on was the banks, because that was a little mystery on top of the big mystery: what had Valerie done with the money? If he read those notations right, somebody or a group of somebodies had taken around seventy thousand bucks over an unspecified length of time. Say it had been split three ways, as hinted by Maureen's information. She'd spent a lot, Valerie had, but she couldn't—or could she?—have got through twenty-three thousand in—well, how long a time? Eleven dollars and some odd cents in cash in the apartment. They'd talked to sales clerks at that Little Shoppe in Robinson's, at other places she'd shopped; the clerks said she had always paid in cash—where they remembered. No charge accounts. No bank in town had a checking account, a savings account, for her. Or a safety-deposit box. Surely she'd have had some of it left?

Maybe an account under a false name. A certain basic cold shrewdness in Valerie. So, take her picture around, ask.

167

See if anybody remembered. And it might be a bank any-where in the county, and the number of them—

And it might look unimportant to find out what she'd done with the money; on a thing like this, you looked everywhere, because you never knew where a lead might show.

Hackett and Palliser came in and gave him the news about Mrs. Dasher. Mendoza all but snarled. What looked like another mysterious murder, and maybe a tough one to untangle. With this other thing still up in the air— "It could be hush-money all right. What was the Dasher woman doing at the time it started coming?"

"Nobody knows," said Palliser. "Or claims they don't. And none of her friends are all that prosperous, I think they're on the level. She was secretive. Didn't write let-ters. If she ever got any, she didn't keep them. Hadn't any relatives. Never talked about her cases—nobody even re-members her mentioning a name, saying she was taking care of a Mrs. Jones or a Mr. Johnson. And, damn it, we can say, maybe hush-money—we see so much dirt, do we suspect it when it isn't there? For all we know, she had an illegitimate daughter who married a millionaire and was taking care of mama. But—"

Mendoza looked at them. At big broad sandy Hackett, eyes red-rimmed from weeks of poring over reports and lists, and at grave dark Palliser looking tired and doleful. He laughed and said, "*Ora esta, ora est otro*—we've just struck a bad patch. It's a long lane, et cetera. Tell you what, boys—it's only just eleven, but I'll take you out and buy us all a drink. I think we need it."

Alison patted Miss Teresa's small rump under the blanket and glanced at her watch; it was twelve forty-five. "Well, that's fine then," she said. "I won't be back until around five-thirty or six, but you needn't do a thing but look after the babies, Mrs. Cole—we're going out for dinner."

"Yes, mum. Sleeping lovely, aren't they?" Little Mrs. Cole beamed at the twins. "You don't need to worry, mum."

Alison smiled at her. A perfect jewel. She said good-by and went out to the garage. She was on her way to see Angel Hackett, just for a casual chat—what with the twins, somehow, she hadn't had a nice long gossip with Angel in ages—and Roberta Silverman had asked her to drop in for coffee and a chat later on. She had an idea that Roberta, whom she liked very much, wanted to ask her this and that about how it was, married to a police officer. She wondered if Roberta and John Palliser were engaged yet. A nice young man, Palliser, thought Alison, backing out the Facel-Vega.

She found Angel home—as predictable, in the midst of stirring up a brand-new recipe. Alison sat down at the kitchen table and told her all about that perfect jewel, Mrs. Cole. Angel congratulated her warmly, breaking off to dive on sixteen-month-old Mark as he started to clamber up on a chair.

"He always falls off—too much ambition," said Angel. "After all, he's only started to walk. Because he's so big, the doctor says. I expect it's only natural, Art being so out-size, but it's embarrassing—he looks a good three years old, and people expect— Do the twins like her?"

"She's marvelous with them—you've no idea what a

wonderful feeling it is, just walk out and know they're being looked after so well."

Angel was going out to a wedding shower for an old school friend, and Alison left when the baby-sitter came. She'd just turned onto York Boulevard, on her way to South Pasadena and Roberta's apartment, when she remembered that recipe. One of Angel's, a rather exotic one, something special to do with lamb. She'd promised to bring it, when Roberta called, and had forgotten. Damn.

Undecided, she pulled over to the curb. She could go back and ask Angel, but she'd be in the middle of dressing for the wedding shower, and besides it was early. Roberta had said, about four, and it was only five to three now. Better not bother Angel. Better go back home and get it. What a bore. She'd put it out, ready, right there on the dressing-table, and then just walked off and left it.

Oh, well.

She turned off at the next side street, Avenue 63, and drove around the block to start back on York in the opposite direction. Got onto Eagle Rock Boulevard, and then the Golden State Freeway, and off that onto Los Feliz. Followed Los Feliz on up into Hollywood, down to Franklin, and turned up through the winding little streets north to Rayo Grande Avenue . . . Luis and his absurd fancy to live on a street called Great Thunderbolt. But it had turned out a nice house, after they'd had the lots leveled. Say it though she shouldn't, most of the design being her idea, a very handsome house . . . Twenty past three. Just nice time, to get the recipe and be at Roberta's by four.

As she turned onto Rayo Grande, a taxi passed her, turning fast down Sunset Plaza. She glanced after it because it was going too fast, and her one glimpse of the single passenger—of course that was absurd, just someone who looked a little like neat Mrs. Cole—

She pulled into the drive, duly careful for cats: went in by the kitchen door. Both the twins were yelling their heads off. Alison went down the hall. "Mrs. Cole, it's just me—"

Nobody with the twins. "Mrs. Cole?" She looked into the next bedroom, went down the hall toward the living-room. And stopped dead as she glanced casually into the master bedroom, passing.

Drawers of the dressing-table dumped in the middle of the floor—closet doors open—*her jewel case*—

Hardly hearing the twins, she rushed into the room. Jewel case open, face-down on the bed—*all the emeralds!* —thank God most of the diamonds at the bank, she didn't often—but— She stared in dismay at the havoc in the closet. She hadn't a fur coat, an affectation in this climate, but her newest evening-dress gone, the imported suit, the—

She whirled to the bureau. Drawers dumped on the floor. All Luis' extra links, that fourteen-carat cigarette case he never carried—

"A jewel!" said Alison semi-hysterically to herself. "Just a jewel!" She ran for the phone down the hall . . . . . . And after a calm voice had assured her there'd be an officer there directly, she dialed again . . . "Is the lieutenant there? This is . . . *Luis*, the most *awful* thing—"

"Well, well," said Sergeant Albers of the Wilcox Street precinct, "baby-sitting Betty again. Where'd you say the

171

ad was? The *Times*. Get 'em to cancel it, Ed, huh? Oh, sure, we know that one."

"I can describe her exactly—Luis, you can too— Of *all* the— She seemed so nice! Really, Luis—"

"I'm sorry, *amada*—just the last straw—" Mendoza lay back on the couch and laughed. "Your perfect jewel of a nursemaid!"

"All the emeralds!" wailed Alison. And one of Sergeant Albers' minions stepped on El Señor's tail; El Señor wailed too, and spat loudly. Mendoza doubled up in another paroxysm. The twins yelled down the hall.

"Well, she won't be looking much like when you saw her by now," said Albers. "She could've been a star actress in the movies, you know. Quick-change artist, and she can put on any of half a dozen accents and make you believe it. Of course, we're on her a lot sooner than she'd expect. Good chance we'll catch her before she gets rid of the loot, or has a chance to put on the blond wig or whatever. Damn lucky you came home early, and spotted that taxi." He eyed Mendoza a little worriedly. "Excuse me, but—"

Mendoza pulled himself together and sat up. "Don't mind me. Don't fuss, *querida*, they'll get your emeralds back. I was just visualizing tomorrow's little human-interest story, VETERAN OFFICER ROBBED. They will call me a veteran. So you know her? A long-time pro?"

"Sure," said Albers. "Quite a nice little racket. Baby-sitting Betty. Betty Bellew. She's only got dropped on once. I mean arrested, sir. She—"

"You needn't translate," said Mendoza, mopping his eyes. "I graduated from the academy while you were studying algebra, boy. Headquarters, Homicide. As you say, a

172

nice little racket. Get into the house by being hired as the eminently suitable servant—"

"She mostly hires out as a baby nurse. Sometimes as a maid. Sure," said Albers, and added, "sir. Excuse me, I didn't know—er—"

"Lieutenant. Don't fuss, Alison. They'll rescue the emeralds, you getting home early and finding out. It's just"—he started to laugh again—"such a jewel!"

"Excuse me," said Albers, looking a little puzzled and interested, looking around the obviously expensive living-room, "you said—some emeralds? I see you're wearing an emerald ring, Mrs. Mendoza. She'd have gone by that sort of thing, you know. How you were dressed, and the address, and all. Made it look as if it'd be worth her while, get into the house. Oh, yes, she's an old hand, is Betty. Slippery as all hell—she'll be intending to go to ground now, while she gets rid of the loot."

"But how can you be sure you'll—"

"The cab company," said Albers. "We got on it so soon, probably before the cab took her wherever she was going. They'll know where she went—there they are now," and he dived for the phone.

Alison said bitterly, "It isn't as funny as *that!*"

Mendoza straightened and put his handkerchief away. "It was just—on top of everything else—! My darling, I hesitate to mention it, but our offspring are raising the roof. Shouldn't you go and see if there's a valid reason?"

Alison uttered a very rude word in Spanish dialect and marched out.

Thirteen

They had Betty spotted in a hotel on Fourth Street half an hour after she'd checked in. She'd made no stops on the way, and had four suitcases with her—two of them Alison's. Being a prudent man, Sergeant Albers waited until she came out, had her tailed, and picked up not only Betty but a mild-looking little fellow who kept a dingy jewelry shop on Main Street and had never been suspected as a fence.

Both Mendoza and Alison went down to Wilcox Street to make a formal identification: redundant, since they had her prints and all the loot intact. All the same, Alison said, she might have been doubtful. Gone was the respectable Mrs. Cole with her neat bun and rimless glasses. Betty Bellew was a much made-up Hollywood blonde; she'd even taken the time to paint her nails.

She was reasonably philosophic, if understandably annoyed. "All in the game, you can't win all the time," she said in a flat middle-western accent evidently native to her. "Best haul I'd made in months, too." And then she looked curiously at Alison and said, "Like to ask you just one thing, dearie—if you don't mind—how come, every-

174

thing else in your place so new and nice, how come you only got those two old beat-up suitcases?"

Well, maybe it was as funny as Luis thought . . . and thank God they'd got everything back; though all that mess to straighten up at home—

"If I know Bertha," said Mendoza as they walked back to the car, "she's busy straightening it up now." They'd had to call her to come and stay with the twins. "I'll take you out to dinner."

"Luis, we can't! Just wish all that on her—" In the end, to prove it to her, he let her phone home.

"Perfeckly all right, Mis' Mendoza," said Bertha. "Lands' sakes, after an upset like that you need to relax some . . . Not touch anything? Why, Mis' Mendoza, you don't rightly think I could sit 'n' look at such a mess 'n' not do nothing about it? Everything's all straight as pie now, and no harm done, barring one o' your best lace brassieres as that El Saynyor got hold of before I did, I'm that sorry. Just you go on to dinner 'n' don't fuss about me. I'd already fed Fritz, like I say."

Mendoza's forebodings came true; and it wasn't a two-paragraph story on the third page, but a second head on the first, because, of course, he was the officer on the Ellis-Thorwald case.

VETERAN OFFICER INVESTIGATING ELLIS MURDER ROBBED, said the head in the *Times*; they'd even dug out pictures. The most prominent was the candid shot of Alison and him an enterprising press photographer had snapped as they'd emerged from the Hall of Justice the morning they were married. It was one of those chance shots that turn out astonishingly sharp: Mendoza was looking toward the camera in obvious irritation, Alison was looking impossibly demure, and there on the steps behind them loomed Hackett with his Angel, and the Lockharts. VETERAN OFFICER LT. MENDOZA AS HE WEDS RESCUED VICTIM OF RAPIST. Mendoza frowned over that persistent *veteran*. All right, damn it, so he had twenty-one years' service, he wasn't senile yet . . .

Naturally he got needled from the time he stepped in the front door of the headquarters building. "Having servant problems, I see, Lieutenant," said the uniformed sergeant at the main Information desk. Lieutenant Goldberg of Burglary joined him at the elevators and repeated this original sally.

"Very funny," said Mendoza. "How could Alison know? A thing that might happen to anybody."

"One problem we don't have to cope with," said Goldberg, blowing his nose. "Who can afford it?" The elevator came and they got in. Mendoza pressed the button for Goldberg's floor, but the elevator stopped at the second floor and Captain Duvalle of Vice got in.

"Well, Luis, I see you're having a servant problem," he said, eyes twinkling. "You millionaires."

"Just one of those things," said Mendoza. "At least we got it all back. Look, Jack, you've got a couple of grandchildren, haven't you—where do you find a good nursemaid, for God's sake?"

"Ask my daughter," said Duvalle. "She's found a couple of dandy ones—free, too. Elvira and me." He got off, still shaking with laughter.

Mendoza walked down the corridor to his office. Sergeant Lake looked up and said, "Morning. See you had a little excitement yesterday. That's quite a racket that female has, isn't it? What won't they think up next?"

"Isn't it? The Hollywood boys were touchingly grate-

176

ful to Alison for coming home early, so they could get on it so soon and pick her up again." He went on into his office; Hackett was standing beside the desk looking through some papers.

"I see by the papers you're having servant problems," he said, grinning.

"It wasn't funny the first time," said Mendoza. "Anything new in?"

"Not on Lover Boy. John's down at the Hall of Justice looking to see if Mrs. Dasher really got a legacy. Somehow I don't think she did. They just sent up a report on your bottle of Madeira, from the lab. Here it is. What was that idea?"

Mendoza told him, scanning the report. Negative. Simply an innocent bottle of Madeira wine. Well, it had been a wild idea; and come to think, he should have known it was, because there was the drug clerk saying she'd been walking around normally at about eleven o'clock on Sunday morning, and they knew she'd left the house at ten. If she'd had the dose before she left, she'd have passed out long before eleven.

Hackett went out to get on with processing his lists, and Mendoza started to look over the latest FBI report. Sergeant Lake put his head in the door and said, "That Fed's on the wire, Lieutenant." Mendoza picked up the outside phone and said hello to Waltham.

"And if you mention my servant problem I'll hang up on you."

Waltham laughed. "You made the press boys happy, anyway—they haven't had much new on this for a couple of days . . . Something interesting just showed I thought you'd like to hear. Arrived at by some very smart detective work, all on his own, by one of our local boys, Adler."

"Yes?"

"It was Adler who went to see this Paul Manton, among other people. And he didn't like his smell. Adler's a bright boy, he gets the feelings from people. You know? He said to me, Manton's a wild one—of any of the people Valerie knew, he thinks, the one most likely to be mixed up in something wrong. Well, God knows none of us have had time to spare, but Adler's been sniffing around Manton at odd moments when he could, and he's found out a few things. You went to see Manton last Thursday, and one of the things Adler's found out is that as soon as you left, Manton lost no time getting to a telephone box."

"You don't tell me."

"And then he just walked off the job and drove away from the airport in his car. In a hurry."

"I take it there's no finding out where?"

"Well, Adler thinks he knows one place he went. It's a damn funny thing," said Waltham, "how coincidence does play a part in detective work sometimes. You know we talked to Manton in his apartment. Adler and another local, I should say. And as it happens Adler goes in for stereo and knows something about it. He said Manton was nice and easy, very co-operative, looked very level, but he still didn't like him. And he took a good long look around the room, for anything suggestive. Two things he noticed, and that's what started him looking other places. A good boy, Adler."

"Has this story got a point?"

"I'm getting there. What he noticed was that the phonograph in Manton's apartment is brand-new, and that the L.P. albums visible also looked new. And the top ones in the two racks of 'em both had a label saying they'd come from Delancey's—big music store downtown."

"I know it."

"So he went and asked. Unfortunately he didn't have a photograph—we'll get one now, to clinch this for sure—but Manton's a fairly distinctive guy, not a type. He didn't get anything Saturday, but there was a clerk not on that day, so he went back to ask her this morning. And she says that Manton—or somebody an awful lot like him—came in at about three o'clock Thursday and bought a phonograph and about a hundred bucks' worth of records. All folk-music records. He didn't take much time making up his mind, she said, didn't listen to any of the records—maybe what made her remember him. Just asked to be directed to the folk-music section, and picked out records almost at random. And he didn't bother to try out the phonograph before he bought it, either—test its tone or whatever. Just said, I'll take that one. And paid cash, and took everything away with him. To the tune of two hundred and forty-nine bucks and fifty cents, plus tax."

"*¿Para qué es esto?*" said Mendoza. "What the hell?" And then he said, "Now don't tell me. I see. I see. How nice. Is this starting to come unraveled at last? I wonder—"

"I'm not just sure what it says, but it looked to me as if it had more to do with your end than ours."

"Hasn't it indeed! Thanks very much. I'll let you know what comes of it, if anything. Tell Adler when he has any spare time I'll be happy to buy him a drink." Mendoza put the phone down and went out fast to the sergeants' room to see who was in.

"Morning," said Dwyer. "I see you're having servant problems, Lieutenant."

"The low humor around here— Chase out to International Airport, Bert. Locate Paul Manton and bring him

179

in for questioning. You needn't be too polite if he objects."

"Right," and Dwyer went out.

Indeed, how nice, thought Mendoza. Things starting to break at last?

There had been discrepancies between what Mrs. Montague said and what Manton said, but Mrs. Montague had been fairly vague and Mendoza hadn't thought much of it. She had said "a lot of times" Manton and Cardenas came to Valerie's apartment. Manton had said maybe three times. And what a nice artistic little tale he'd produced, almost on the spur of the moment (if he had missed that Wednesday night story on the identification of Valerie) to account for it! The mutual interest in folk music. And the minute Mendoza left him, he'd contacted Cardenas and passed on the story to him, and then—anticipating a visit from the police, if not the FBI—dashed out to buy the phonograph and records to back up the story.

Cardenas the one genuinely interested in folk music, with the long-time collection, which Manton had known.

Paul Manton was a very astute young man, in some ways.

But, Cardenas?

Manton and Cardenas in the racket with Valerie? How and why? Neither of them was even on the borderline of pro crime. And what caper would those two fit into, anyway?

In a way, he could see it. Cardenas, in Civil Service—notoriously the sort of job that was underpaid, supposedly making up for it in security of tenure. He thought his guess at ten thousand a year might be an overestimate;

more likely six to seven. Cardenas might not be averse to making a little side money, if it looked safe. Very safe. Because he'd be a very cautious man about his own safety.

Manton—it wouldn't have to look like a safe gamble to him. He'd said he'd like to start his own airline; maybe that was so. He was a gambler, he'd take long chances not just for the stakes but for the hell of it.

Did this say definitely that Manton and Cardenas had been in some racket with Valerie? Damn it, thought Mendoza, as Alison had pointed out, he didn't *know* that anybody else had been in on it: that was just implication, from what Valerie had said to Maureen, and Maureen not being the brainiest female alive she might not have heard right, or repeated it right.

What this did say was that Manton and Cardenas were in some caper together. Those two . . . There was an old Spanish proverb, appropriate: *Everyone is as God made him and very often worse.* And money sure as hell talked.

And Eddy Warren. Don't forget Eddy Warren, he thought. Without much doubt, paying Valerie a little fee to store his reefers for him safe. (*De paso,* better pass that on to Pat Callaghan up in Narcotics, because it could be that Eddy had some H. stored away with some other obliging pal.) Could it be that Manton and Cardenas had just used Valerie's apartment as a convenient, semi-secret meeting place? Used Valerie as a convenient excuse for foregathering?

It was a thought, anyway.

And—yes, that was a thought too, by God—maybe Valerie hadn't originally known one damn thing about whatever it was they were up to; maybe they'd underesti-

181

mated her intelligence—and greed; and, finding out, she'd wanted to cut herself in, so they— Not *they*; Cardenas wouldn't have the guts. If so, that had been Manton. Yes.

(That phone call: "Because they murdered that woman six years ago." All right: a lunatic. Even if it wasn't, he didn't know what Manton and Cardenas had been doing six years ago. Conceivably their caper had been running that long; conceivably they had done a murder in the course of it, and Valerie had found out about it—or the woman on the phone thought she had. All right. Ten to one the phone call hadn't a thing to do with it.)

One thing, Paul Manton could very probably have operated that machine.

Only, why? Why, for God's sake?

He looked at his watch. Quite a drive out to International, through traffic. He hoped Manton would be there, and not off playing hooky somewhere again. It would be another hour at least before Bert got back with him, if he was there . . . Mendoza picked up the FBI report and began to study it, but his mind kept straying back to Manton . . . and Cardenas, of all people . . .

At about the same moment, Mr. William Gunn was reaching the deliberate conclusion that something would have to be done about Number Six. Later on people were to say that Mr. Gunn should have realized there was something wrong and investigated Number Six long before; but as the late Mrs. Gunn could have testified, William Gunn was not a precipitate man. He thought things over thoroughly before reaching any decision.

He had been thinking, off and on, about Number Six ever since last Tuesday, but a little harder since last Thursday.

182

Mr. Gunn owned and managed a small motel on San Fernando Road in Glendale. He did a fair-to-middling business; if it wasn't one of the classy places with a pool, well, he charged fair rates and everything was kept clean and nice. And no funny business. Mr. Gunn had a very sharp eye for funny business, the nervous teen-age couple, the brash salesman with a chippy he claimed was his wife.

Otherwise, well, you got all sorts, running a motel; one thing he'd learned was, you sure couldn't judge people by their looks. People who looked decent and clean as you please, they'd leave the place in a shambles. There'd been that couple from Oregon: woman looked a nice respectable woman, and the husband an ordinary white-collar type. Leaving all those empty whiskey bottles when they left, and a lamp smashed, and all that stuff scrawled on the bathroom wall with lipstick. The hell of a job it had been, cleaning it off. People . . .

Then—Mr. Gunn always smiled faintly when he remembered that—there'd been those hillbillies. He'd been of two minds whether to admit he had a vacancy. Oklahoma plates on the old Model-A Ford, stuff tied on top, three kids in patched-up clothes—but the woman had had nice eyes and was sort of shy. Migratory workers, some kind, with a bit more than usual saved up. Woman about ready to have another baby, and the man had been nice and kind with her, sort of anxious. And in the end Mr. Gunn had rented them Number Eight, hoping they wouldn't leave it in too much of a mess . . . When they'd pulled out next morning, the woman had thanked him and said what a nice place he had, it was the first time they'd ever stayed at a motel and they'd sure liked it. And they hadn't left the place in a mess at all; they'd made up the

183

beds nice and smooth all ready for the next guest, and hung up the towels neatly, and left the tiny used bars of soap handy— Mr. Gunn remembered how he'd laughed, but not really laughing *at* them, as the maid stripped off the used sheets.

So, after twelve years of running a motel, he wasn't really surprised at anything. His present Number Six had showed up, alone and without a car, at about nine o'clock a week ago last Friday evening. A man around forty-five to fifty, ordinary-looking fellow except that he had a little short beard. Couple of suitcases with him. Said he was just moving out to California from Iowa, and he'd left the car with his wife back home, he wanted a place to stay a couple of weeks, maybe longer, until he found a house to rent.

Well, Mr. Gunn sometimes had semi-permanent people like that, and the fellow looked respectable and paid him for a week in advance right off, forty-nine bucks, so he led him down to Number Six and showed him about the lights and so on. Four of the units had kitchenettes, and Number Six was one of them.

He hadn't seen much of Mr. Robertson—that was how he registered, James Robertson, of 112 Elm Street, Cedar Rapids, Iowa—since. Naturally, his own apartment and office being right up front, all the guests passed his place going and coming; he wasn't nosy enough to watch for them, but he could hardly help noticing.

Mr. Robertson had gone out, walking, the next morning; of course they were right in the middle of town, stores all around, and Mr. Robertson had evidently visited the market a couple of blocks away—he came back with two big bags of groceries. And stayed in.

Well, Mr. Gunn thought, he *could* have missed seeing him go out and come back—there were times he was out himself, or in one of the other units, or just not noticing —but he didn't think Mr. Robertson had set foot outside Number Six from that Saturday morning until last Tuesday. Then he'd gone out again, and again come back with a big bag of groceries.

And that bag at least had apparently contained something alcoholic. Because at about half-past eleven that night the people in Number Five, who'd driven all the way from Santa Rosa that day (they'd only checked in an hour before), phoned the office to complain about the singing next door. "I'm as patriotic a man as the next," the man had said dryly, "but when it comes to 'The Star-Spangled Banner' at nearly midnight—and not just once, but over and over—and he can't carry a tune." So Mr. Gunn had pulled on his pants over his pajamas and gone down to Number Six and found Mr. Robertson riding very high indeed.

Mr. Robertson had leaned on the doorpost and apologized with the earnest solemnity of the drunk. "Ver' sorry cause any dis—disturbance," he'd said. "Shelebratin', 's all. You know how 'tis. You p-pull off shomethin'—been plannin'— C'me on in, have a drink with me, friend—my friend!"

"No, thank you, sir," Gunn had said. "Now don't you think, sir—"

"Pasht time for thinkin'. Shelebrate," said Mr. Robertson rather wildly. "Great shelebrashun. I made it. I got home." He reached out and clutched Mr. Gunn's pajama top. "Tell you a shecret," he said. "Ivory tower, they shaid —grow up, get wise. I thought I wash sho smart. Idealsh. C'me on in, have a drink. I did it. I made it."

"Now, Mr. Robertson, if you'll just quiet down, please—"

"Tell you—tell you—shecret," said Mr. Robertson. He swayed toward Mr. Gunn, but caught himself. And for one brief moment he seemed completely sober; he said in a perfectly normal, articulate voice, "Dear God, I could have kissed the ground. Corny. Laugh at it. You don't know until you've been there."

"Mr. Robertson—"

The other man blinked and swayed again, and the moment was past. "Wash gonna tell you a shecret. My friend. You promise me—remember it. Wanta tell—lotsh 'n' lotsh o' people. Gotta tell. Shee? They're a bunch of bashtards! Thatsh the shecret—bunch o' bashtards. You remember it, shee?"

"Sure, I'll remember it," said Gunn patiently. He had been just faintly surprised, because Mr. Robertson had looked so respectable, so conventional; but of course you never knew. He had finally persuaded him back into Number Six, and to quiet down. Presumably he'd passed out; there were no more complaints.

And the next morning, looking about as you'd expect, he had come to the office and apologized very nicely. "I've been kind of worried," he said, "having to switch jobs at my age—I don't drink much as a rule. I hope I didn't say anything—er—?"

Mr. Gunn, reassuring him, had figured to keep an eye on him: if he pulled that again, toss him out.

But since then, Number Six had been very quiet. Too quiet, since last Thursday night.

On Thursday morning Robertson had gone out shopping again. It was about then that Mr. Gunn began seri-

186

ously wondering about him. Changing jobs; waiting for his wife; looking for a house. Oh, yes? He didn't seem to be doing any house hunting.

He had come back with a bag of groceries, at about eleven, and stayed in.

About eight o'clock on Thursday evening, Mr. Gunn and his old friend Mr. Peters had been playing backgammon over a companionable glass of beer when Mr. Peters glanced up and said, "What was that? Customers? Somebody outside—"

Mr. Gunn had opened the door and looked out. Two men were walking down the open court, backs to him—vague in the half shadow, but he saw them. He called, "Can I help you?" but they just kept on going. He hadn't thought much about it. Guests coming back from a little walk, or friends calling on somebody, car left in the street.

A few minutes later, it seemed that among Mr. Robertson's purchases had been a radio of some kind; the people in both Number Five and Number Seven called to complain. And no wonder; he could hear it from up in front, it was so loud. He'd gone down and knocked on the door of Number Six, hard, and the radio had been turned down right away.

And since then, he hadn't seen Mr. Robertson at all. Coming or going. He'd expected him to drop in at the office on Friday, to pay another week's rent. When Robertson hadn't showed up by Saturday night, Mr. Gunn had gone down and knocked on the door, but got no answer. He'd tried again on Sunday morning, with the same result.

And now, on Monday morning, he had reached the decision that he must do something about Number Six. He didn't know quite what he felt was wrong, or might be, but he thought it was all a bit funny. And Robertson owed him for three nights.

Mr. Gunn knocked out his pipe, rummaged for his extra keys, and plodded deliberately down the court to Number Six. He knocked and called, "Mr. Robertson?" No answer. No stir from inside. He fitted the key into the lock and opened the door . . .

At first, of course, Mr. Gunn got the Glendale police: a couple of big fellows in tan uniform. He got more and more police. From the minute, about half an hour after he'd first called them, when a wide-shouldered tough in plain-clothes said suddenly, "Hey, take away that beard— and look at his ears— Jesus H. Christ, I'd take my oath that's—" and plunged for the phone.

Mr. Gunn, eventually, got the FBI crowding into Number Six. It was a while before he made out who Mr. Robertson had been. Mr. Robertson, lying wide-eyed with a bullet in his brain, five days dead.

When he understood, Mr. Gunn went back to his own place, shaken, and gave himself a drink. He thought about what that man had said, drunk, last Tuesday night. And he said aloud, soberly, to his jigger of bourbon, "Well, at least he died at home. They couldn't take that away from him."

Fourteen

Odds and ends, odds and ends . . . Jack Farlow was a member of something called Americans All. So what? Sounded like one of those ultra-conservative groups. Linda Hausner corresponded with several old friends in Germany. This Fran Schwartz—so Vice said—had the expectable record; you could piece it together, and it was possible that Eddy Warren was the link. Gloria, Fran, Maureen and Valerie, working as call girls and at one time Eddy scouting for them. But Valerie breaking away . . . Another small thing, thought Mendoza; the Hausners honest citizens, so, wouldn't they have spotted something a little funny about a couple of Valerie's friends, if not Valerie herself? Maureen at least looked like what she was, if Gloria didn't, quite. Well, maybe they'd never met Maureen . . .

"Scarne's back with Cardenas," said Sergeant Lake.

"O.K.," said Mendoza. "Keep him on ice. I want Manton first."

He got him fifteen minutes later. He had Manton wait

in the outer office, opposite Cardenas under Sergeant Lake's eye, while he talked to Bert and Scarne.

"Never batted an eyelid," said Dwyer. "Said, sure, anything he could do, though he hadn't known much about her. He's a very cool customer."

"Not like the other one," said Scarne. "He raised a little fuss. All pompous and blustering. He'd told you all he knew, et cetera. At that, he sounded natural. I mean, a guy in his job—he'd be nervous, just to be associated. Wouldn't he?"

Which was, of course, true. "Manton first," said Mendoza. He was lighting a cigarette when Manton came in; he took time to get it burning nicely, and smiled at Manton slowly, not asking him to sit down. "You're an impulsive young man, aren't you, Mr. Manton?"

"Am I?" said Manton. "In what way d'you mean?" He was in matching tan shirt and slacks today, cleaner and neater. A ruggedly good-looking man, blue eyes pale in his tanned face, and that reckless tilt to his heavy brows.

"You acquire hobbies so suddenly," said Mendoza. "Such as folk music. After I'd talked to you last Thursday, dashing out to acquire the—mmh—appurtenances of the hobby you'd claimed. The phonograph and all the folk-music records. Down at Delancey's."

"Sorry, don't see what you're driving at," said Manton. "Mind if I sit down?" He dropped into the chair beside the desk, pulled out cigarettes and lit one. His strong mechanic's hands were perfectly steady. "Sure, I bought a new phonograph and a few records lately. What's that got to do with Val getting murdered?"

"You never had a phonograph or any records up to last

Thursday, did you? Only you'd told me that pretty little story about you and Cardenas having the mutual interest, and you knew we might be checking—us or the Feds—so you provided the local color."

"I don't get you," said Manton. "I'd been planning on getting a new phonograph for some while, my old one was shot. No good even as a trade-in. What the hell is it to you? I told you all I knew about Val. So I knew her—it was the casual thing, I didn't know she was mixed up with crooks of some sort, and Ricardo sure as hell didn't, or he'd— Look, what do you want with him, anyway? We told you how it was, and you know how the Civil Service is, one little hint of any—"

"It's a nice act, Manton, but I'm not buying it. You and Cardenas are in some caper together. You and Cardenas and Valerie were in it. You—"

Manton said angrily, "I don't have to take this, damn it! I don't know what you think you've found out, but that's just crazy! Ricardo—that stuffed shirt? Risking his job? We've told you all we know about Val—damn all—and I'm wishing to God now I'd never met the female! So I've incriminated myself by buying a new phonograph —maybe they've changed the laws since I went to school?" Impatiently he stabbed out the cigarette.

Mendoza stared at him. No, this one wouldn't scare easy. "Maureen Moskovitch introduced you to Valerie," he said abruptly. "So you said. Not being a schoolboy any more, Manton, you read Maureen?"

Manton smiled at him amusedly. "Hell, how d'you think I met Maureen? Sure. But I figured it was a part-time thing with her—that Val didn't know about it. She seemed ordinary, way I said, nice enough girl. Why the

191

hell you're making a deal of this— I hadn't known her long, or very well, it was all just the way I told you." But that wasn't too emphatic; he didn't overplay it. He was a little angry, a little surprised, a little indignant.

A very tough boy indeed, Paul Manton.

"Not just a few records," said Mendoza, "added to a collection already existing. All the records you've got, Manton. Bought last Thursday. As a cover. To back up that story you'd told me."

"I'd really like to see you prove that," said Manton. And Mendoza read his mind; he knew they couldn't hold him or Cardenas, and as soon as they got away, he'd figure on somehow transferring some of Cardenas' older records to his apartment, pending another police look. Verisimilitude. "This is all damn silly," he said. "Why the hell aren't you looking in the likely directions? What possible reason would I have to—a girl I hardly knew? And Ricardo, that's just damn nonsense!" He laughed contemptuously. "He hasn't got the guts to swat a fly!"

And all right, say that Manton and Cardenas had been in the caper with her—which he wasn't at all sure of— that was perfectly true, on what showed: they'd have had no reason to want her dead. By the evidence of the notebook, the racket had been yielding handsome profits, and depending on what it was, maybe Valerie had been a vital ingredient. "I thought you and Cardenas were pals," he said.

Manton's little cold smile didn't waver. "For God's sake," he said wearily. "We both happen to be interested in folk music, but that's about all we've got in common. I don't stop seeing people as they are because we share an interest."

Mendoza sat back in his chair. No longer the awkward, ambitious young mechanic: Manton was acting his age, letting a little education show. Otherwise, a tough: a very hard one to crack. Mendoza had seen more details of his record by now. He'd been in Communist hands, in Korea, for several months without breaking. He wasn't at all likely to be faced down by a mere L.A.P.D. officer.

Mendoza buzzed Sergeant Lake and asked for Cardenas. The weaker member of the team.

Cardenas came in blustering. But it was natural-sounding bluster. "Really, I cannot understand—a man in my position—you must realize that my superiors— The publicity so far has been outrageous, but to—"

"Mr. Cardenas." Manton had made no attempt to speak to Cardenas, signal him; he sat smoking, looking angrily bored. "Mr. Cardenas—to your knowledge, has Mr. Manton been intending to buy a new phonograph lately?"

Cardenas stopped short and looked bewildered. "A new— Why, yes, he did mention it. But why on earth are you—" He looked at Manton. "Have you got it yet? Which did you get, the R.C.A. or the Silvertone?"

"The Silvertone," said Manton. "I liked the tone better."

Very nicely fielded, thought Mendoza sardonically. Cardenas was smarter than he looked.

"But you didn't listen to the tone," he said gently. "You just said, I'll take that one, and paid for it. Rather a hasty choice, Manton, wasn't it?"

Manton knocked ash off his new cigarette. "Oh, for God's sake," he said. "Talk about a tempest in a teacup. I'd tried out several models at different times, a few days before, at a couple of other places. Been mulling it over in

193

my mind. I decided that was the one I liked, why bother to test it out again? Very nice tone indeed," he added to Cardenas, "you'll have to come over and hear it."

"I only said I thought the changing mechanism on the R.C.A. is more efficient, I— But why the *police* should be interested—! And really, Lieutenant, I don't think you realize how unfortunate it is for a man in my position, even to seem involved in such a— I scarcely knew the girl, after all! Really—"

Cardenas a good deal smarter than he looked. And maybe more guts than Manton had expected. He was sweating, but he sounded natural, the touchy civil servant — And the whole thing was still sufficiently up in the air that— A lot more evidence needed.

Mendoza stared at them another long moment. Manton returned the stare with almost open impudence. A single drop of sweat rolled down Cardenas' round olive-skinned cheek; but his faintly indignant, pompous expression held stiff.

"All right," said Mendoza tautly. "That's all—out. I'll be seeing both of you."

They went, unhurriedly. He followed them as far as the door to the sergeants' office. Dwyer and Scarne were there, talking idly. Mendoza jerked a thumb. "After them. Call in when you can and we'll set up reliefs."

He went back to his desk feeling savage. Take it easy, he told himself, maybe a tail would turn up something usable. Maybe—

"Waltham on the phone, Lieutenant."

"O.K. . . . Yes?"

"They got him," said Waltham sadly. "Thorwald. We just got a positive ident. The Green Tree Motel, San

Fernando Road, Glendale. Dead about four-five days. Shot. A very professional taking-off. You like to come and poke around for anything on your end?"

"You don't say," said Mendoza. "How come he wasn't found sooner?"

Waltham sounded sadder. "Motel owner's not a fellow to rush into things. He had a couple of interesting things to tell us. Not that it's of much importance now, I guess, but by what Mr. Gunn says, it seems that our Osgar had repented his sins and found out the truth about his erst-while pals."

"Well, I suppose it was important to him," said Mendoza.

"I suppose. I don't expect we'll ever know just exactly what did happen, why they wanted to take him off. It doesn't look as if he meant to run to us with any secrets, he'd been here at least ten days and who knows how much longer? Maybe transferring from motel to motel for months. He'd grown a beard, by the way. And nothing, but nothing, to point to who did the job. Of course. Well, we'll go through the motions—but I don't anticipate catching up with X. I just thought you might like to join the party."

"What's the address? I would indeed," said Mendoza. He scribbled down the number and snatched up his hat.

In the anteroom, Sergeant Lake was on the phone. He said, "It's long distance, Lieutenant—they think—"

"*Vaya*, make a note, I'll see it later," said Mendoza, not pausing.

This morning there'd been an inquest on Valerie Ellis; Mendoza hadn't bothered to go because it would

195

be pure formality, police request for an open verdict. As Galeano's hit-and-run seemed to be dying a natural death on them, he'd sent Galeano over to watch it.

Palliser was still poking around on the Gertrude Dasher thing, and nobody but Hackett was in the office when a tired but triumphant Landers called in to say that he thought he'd caught up to Lover Boy.

"Don't tell me! Who and where? D'you want any help?"

"You're damn right," said Landers frankly. "He's about six-five and built in proportion. I don't want my name in the papers that bad."

"I'll be with you. Where?"

"Little drive," said Landers. "I'm about ten miles this side of Camarillo. Meet you at a place called Joe's Roadside Inn, on the highway."

"O.K.," said Hackett, and got going. He'd hear the whole story when he got there. It was a little drive indeed—sixty miles up the coast, once he got out of traffic. But past Malibu, he should make good time, on a weekday.

He made it in an hour and twenty-five minutes, good going, once out of the slow tangle downtown. As he approached the town he slowed a little, watching for Joe's . . . "So what's the story?" he asked Landers, sliding into the booth beside him.

It had, after all, been the dogged routine that had finally turned up Lover Boy, as Hackett had known it was bound to. The truck. Landers had come to this one on his list, from the new Ventura County list, and cursed at the necessity for the drive, got up here and had, he said, the hell of a time finding the address. Which wasn't an ad-

196

dress at all, just a farm back in the hills. Nobody around seemed to know much about it. But he finally found it, and one look at the farmer had been enough. "He's our boy for sure. Pockmarks and all. And he's about one degree above a gorilla, mentally speaking. Just as expected. You can hardly understand him, Deep South accent and maybe a cleft palate or something. It's a run-down old place, hardly big enough to call it a farm, off the highway back in there. Woman there too, about the same type."

"O.K., let's go," said Hackett. They took his car. "What's his name, by the way?"

"Henry Jackson. What beats me," said Landers, "is the truck. When you come to think. Well, these rural areas— But you'd think somebody at the local D.M.V. would take a second look at him, spot him for a moron. And I wonder how come he remembered to register it for this year. Maybe some cop stopped him and reminded him."

The farm, when they came to it, was hardly more than a vegetable garden. There was a ramshackle, unpainted one-room cabin built right on the ground. A couple of thin-looking pigs rooting in the yard, a raw-ribbed mongrel dog that shied away from the car. A baby about a year old sat on the ground near the pigs. The baby was dark brown and quite naked, a girl; she had the distended stomach of starvation, and dull eyes. The light-blue pickup truck, a battered eight-year-old Ford, was parked at the side of the shack.

"But there must be people around who know him, who've seen him," said Hackett. "There's been the hell of a lot of publicity on this. Why hasn't somebody called in?"

"I asked around, before and while I was waiting for

you," said Landers. "I said I had a hell of a time locating this place. Nobody does know him much. The fellow at the gas station back there, alongside Joe's, he's sold him gas. Knew vaguely that he had a little land back here in the hills, but he'd never paid much attention to him. Joe, about the same story. Jackson doesn't buy much in any store round here, evidently. Nobody could say how long he'd been here. Well, you see the setup—dirt poor."

"Yes," said Hackett. They got out of the car and went up to the door of the shack, knocked.

The man who opened to them was Jackson, obviously. He topped Hackett by a good two inches and outweighed him by fifty pounds. Hackett saw at once, irrelevantly, that the pockmarks were old scars of some skin disease.

"Who you?" asked Jackson. He took a step backward, his eyes rolling.

Hackett followed him into the shack. There were pallets on the floor, gray with filth. A woman, thin and black, sat on one nursing a very new baby. Terror leaped briefly in her eyes and she clutched the baby tighter.

She was wearing the diamond-and-platinum necklace valued at ten thousand dollars. A mink coat lay across one of the other pallets.

"Henry," said Hackett, "we've come to take you in for those women you killed." Jackson mumbled something and took another step back.

"Cops—you cops?" It was just possible to understand him.

"That's right, Henry. You did kill them, didn't you?"

The woman just sat, still as a frightened animal would be still, and her eyes were dull as the baby's eyes. Irrelevantly Hackett found a phrase running round his mind—

the Jukes and the Kallikaks, the Jukes and the Kallikaks.

"White wimmen," said Jackson. He sounded childishly pleased. He grinned amiably at Hackett, showing white teeth. "White wimmen. I show 'em, I do. Hang m' pa, they did—an' he nevah done nothin'— White wimmen! I show 'em. They take 'm to jail an' lynch 'm— I get back at 'm good—"

"All right, Henry," said Hackett, "you sure did." He took out the handcuffs and got them on before Jackson grasped what he was doing. "Let's go, Henry."

"You—you—you—take me to jail—" Jackson started to wrestle with the cuffs, looking scared. And then, just as Hackett was tensing himself to meet attack, ready to yank out the gun to use as a bludgeon, Jackson stopped struggling and asked earnestly, "You—you—you gi' me s'me nice po'k chop 'n jail? Ain't had no nice po'k chop long time—"

"I wouldn't be surprised," said Hackett. "We sure will, Henry." They didn't have any trouble getting him into the car; he was, for the moment, docile as a child. Hackett looked back at the open door of the cabin. The woman hadn't moved or spoken the whole time. The baby still sat, staring with dull eyes. There was, he saw, a heap of human manure on one side of the cabin. The dog sidled around sniffing at it.

Landers got in back with Jackson. Hackett thought he'd have to tell somebody official about the woman back there. County relief. Technically speaking, he should bring her in too; but at the moment Jackson was all he wanted to cope with. Better send a couple of boys right back here, bring her in, search the cabin, retrieve the loot there.

They didn't try to get anything out of him on the ride back. They just hoped he wouldn't suddenly decide he'd rather not go, and break loose. In fact, Hackett got so nervous about that, on the way back down to the highway, on the rutted dirt track, that when they got to Joe's he told Landers to drive and got in back with Jackson himself. Landers might be only thirty to his thirty-five, but Landers was only five-eleven and built thin. If Jackson went berserk, there was a good deal more of Hackett to grapple with him. And damn what the doctors said about the extra poundage.

But they got him back, and up to an interrogation room, with no trouble at all. Hackett, a little surprised and very relieved, set everybody present in the homicide office—only five men, as it chanced—to keep an eye on him, while he briefed Palliser, who had just come in. Everybody was feeling pretty happy about this.

"But, my God, that place," said Hackett. "That woman. And I don't want another ride like that soon. You got a picture of your Mrs. Dasher?"

"I have," said Palliser. "By the way, no record of any legacy."

"No," said Hackett. "We didn't expect it, did we?" He called Landers out to the hall. "Sorry to ask you, Tom, but you're the one knows the way. You and a couple of the boys had better get right back there, for the woman and the loot. And, incidentally, your car," he added, remembering that.

Landers, who had not forgotten it, grinned and said he didn't mind.

"Well, I doubt very much whether we'll get anything coherent out of Henry—not quite moron level, but close. But we'll try. And with these damn Black Muslims stirring up trouble, we're going to lean over backwards on this one, being very scrupulous. Nobody's going to ask him anything until somebody from the Public Defenders' office is here to hold his hand."

"Want me to call them?" asked Palliser.

Hackett said yes, please. He could have used a drink; he had a cardboard mug of black coffee instead, and defiantly he dropped three lumps of sugar in it . . .

The lawyer they sent over from the Public Defenders' office, to protect Jackson's legal rights, was very welcome to Hackett. The Public Defenders' office was as alive to certain situations as were the police, and they sent a young Negro lawyer, Marvin Fox, a thin dapper young man with alert eyes and an unexpected bass voice. He sat in on the questioning.

They didn't get much that was coherent, as Hackett had predicted. Henry didn't deny he'd killed the white women; showed 'em he had, for his dad getting lynched . . . "Nah tha' one," he said to the photograph of Gertrude Dasher. "Nev' seed tha' one—who she?"

Palliser looked pleased and worried at once, about that.

They'd try to trace Jackson back, find out more about him. There were a couple of papers on him; no driver's license, but a Social Security card—that would be a lot of help, tell them eventually what jobs he'd held where—and a hunting license, seven years out of date, issued in Clinch County, Georgia.

They took him out to the county jail, finally, and saw him booked in. Lingering on the steps outside, Hackett offered Fox a cigarette. "I can guess how you'll handle it," he said.

Fox made a small grimace, offering his lighter. "Played down," he said. "Oh, yes. There's been a little tension lately, some hot accusations of you boys, about the persecution bit."

"I hope you know that's damn nonsense," said Hackett. "We're spread out pretty thin in this town. We take surveys, we make up statistics, and we naturally find out the crime rate's higher in certain areas—so we concentrate men there. The Negro slum sections, the Mexican slum sections, the slum sections in general. It's not, for God's sake, higher because those people are Negro or Mexican. It's higher because—"

"You needn't tell me, Sergeant," said Fox sadly. "I know. It's because some of those people figure, what the hell, nine counts on us to start, why try? It's because a lot of people follow the course of least resistance. Most of all —but try to get the do-gooders to admit it—it's because, from the time Eve got Adam chased out of the Garden— if that ever happened—there've been smart people and dumb ones, good ones and bad. And you can't make the undesirables over, not all of 'em, by offering 'em a chance at free education and a flat in a nice clean new building. The louts like that one in there"—he jerked a shoulder at the jail behind them—"they come in all colors and they're walking around in every country. But there'll always be a certain number of people who misread the evidence."

"Isn't it the truth," said Hackett.

"And here," said Fox, looking up North Broadway, "come the press boys. So quick off the mark. I think we'll encourage them to take some pictures, Sergeant. Emphasizing the contrast, you know, between Henry and his smart, snappy young attorney."

Hackett laughed and left him to it, dodging the reporters with some difficulty. It was after six. He had to go back to headquarters to get his car, and he went up to the office to see if Mendoza was in, do a little boasting.

"Boss gone home, Jimmy?" Sergeant Lake was just leaving.

"Oh, Lord knows when we'll see our Luis again," said Lake. "He's on a little jaunt over to Blythe."

"Blythe?" said Hackett blankly. "You don't mean Blythe over by the Arizona border? Why the hell?"

"Well, it was like this—" said Lake.

Fifteen

There was nothing at all in the faintly shabby, neat motel unit to give them any clues as to how long Thorwald had been back, how he'd got in, who had caught up and killed him. There were a few groceries in the little kitchenette, and a bottle of bourbon three-quarters empty. There was one ancient cowhide suitcase and a newer aluminum one, both American-made, and a scattering of clothes, American suits and shirts, one ill-tailored topcoat that was probably Russian. No documents of any kind; maybe there had been and the killers had taken them.

No radio in the place. The killers had brought one along—a transistor, probably—to cover the sound of the shot. A single shot, and, said the doctor, probably a .38 or .45. See when they got the bullet out. No gun.

"So we go through the motions," said Waltham. "It's a waste of time but we have to do it."

"You think it was them? Well, of course—"

"Who else would it be? Sure. Maybe they were afraid he was going to run to us, and passed on orders to cool him off just in case. Anyway, at least we know where he is now. And it doesn't look as if this business ties up to your murder, does it? Or does it? If the Ellis girl knew where he was—"

"But they don't generally use sleeping-tablets," said Mendoza.

Waltham agreed. "Besides, what you've found out about her, she'd have told anything she knew for cash in hand. Only, it could be they got a little nervous about her knowing them, then?"

"No," said Mendoza. "Let's not reach. The murder is something else. Granted, it's a wild one—a funny one. That machine— But it wasn't the Communists slipped Valerie a spiked cocktail."

"What the hell *was* the connection?"

"I'm beyond guessing," said Mendoza. "I'm not up to standard lately, missing all this sleep," and he yawned. And at Waltham's inquiring look he added gloomily, "Twins. Five months old."

"Oh," said Waltham, and laughed. "I get you. Thank God our three are well past that stage. What disturbs my sleep these nights is Margaret out until midnight with the current boy friend, and Alan's grades in English. Not to mention Mike's grades in arithmetic."

"You're so encouraging," said Mendoza. "There's nothing for me here. Have fun."

All the same—you took it as it came, and after twenty-one years it didn't reach you as it once had—but, all the same, as he drove back downtown, he thought about Thorwald, who had repented his sins, singing "The Star-Spangled Banner" in a drunken frenzy, and felt an unaccustomed sting in his eyes. So the man was a traitor. Not the lowest kind of traitor: a traitor for ideals he'd believed in. So he'd been a fool to believe in them; few people hadn't been fools in this way or that at some time . . . *Through the perilous fight*, thought Mendoza; perilous indeed for people like Thorwald, all ideals and no common sense. But Thorwald had made it home, in more ways than one . . .

He went up to the office; Sergeant Lake said, "That long-distance call—" and was interrupted by the phone. "Bert," he said, handing it over.

"Lieutenant? I've just seen Manton back to his job. He and Cardenas ended up in a bar on Broadway to have a quiet drink together. Scarne and I managed to get the next booth, but it isn't the quietest place in town and we couldn't hear much. They seemed to be arguing at one point, couldn't say about what—it was confused—but, reason I thought you ought to hear this as soon as possible, Manton said that Dvorzhak name a couple of times, and Cardenas seemed to be hushing him up."

"*¿De veras—qué significa eso?* I'll be damned," said Mendoza.

"Yeah. Then they split. Manton went straight back to International. I guess Scarne'll be calling in on Cardenas."

"Yes, thanks, we'll set up reliefs for you." Mendoza put the phone down. The Dvorzhaks. If Bert had heard right. Looking so very much on the edge of the case—what connection could they possibly—?

"This phone call," began Sergeant Lake.

"Tell me later," said Mendoza absently, and went out again.

Ruminating, he drove up to Willoughby Drive and rang the bell of the Dvorzhak house. One of the lucky refugees, you could say. Those jewels—plenty of money. Very foresighted of Mr. Jan Dvorzhak . . .

Anya Dvorzhak, going to see Gloria? Maybe. Why the hell?

He yawned and pressed the bell again.

The girl Anya opened the door to him. As she recognized him, her liquid eyes flickered just once, and then met his straight. "Yes?" she said. "Oh—you are the police officer who came before. What is it, please?"

"I'd like to ask you a few more questions, Miss Dvorzhak."

The older woman, her mother, pattered down the hall asking agitated questions in their own tongue. The girl replied soothingly. "You must forgive my mother, sir, she is so fearful—of course, however I can help you, I will be happy." The other woman was half-sobbing, gazing at Mendoza with terror-stricken eyes. The girl sighed. "Please, sir, will you come in here—into my father's study, we can be private here—and excuse me one moment while I explain to her, reassure her?" She smiled at him, taking her mother's arm. "She has had—very bad experiences."

"I understand." Mendoza went into the room indicated. It was not a large room, but a pleasant one. Paneled, two of the walls were lined with bookcases; there was a large old desk, somewhat littered, and several comfortable chairs. He could hear the women talking, out in the hall, in their rapid incomprehensible language . . . What, he wondered suddenly, is Anya doing at home when she should be at her college classes?

The one large window was open; it was a warm day. From outside he heard the irregular patter of ping-pong

207

balls striking a table, a boy's triumphant shout: "That's game! I beat you!"

He strolled over to the window. Next door was the Farlow house. No, probably the property belonged technically to the boy, young Johnny Eininger. Odd to think, necessarily prying into private lives, what they knew about all these people, the people themselves unaware.

The window overlooked a very pleasant side patio belonging to the house next door. There was only a low clipped hedge between the properties. In the house next door, French windows gave onto a flagstoned rectangle at least forty feet long, with white-painted wrought-iron lawn furniture, a ping-pong table, a round table with a gay yellow umbrella over it. Toward the rear of the house, a widening driveway and a glimpse of a handrail told of a swimming-pool.

A big man and a boy had just finished a game. Farlow and Johnny; Farlow looked just about as you might expect from the reports on him. A big fellow in his late forties, starting to run to paunch a little but still good-looking. Wavy dark hair, regular features, mat of dark chest hair showing above his open-necked sports shirt.

The boy wore nothing but shorts, and his tanned, slim young body was smooth and muscled. "I *said* I could beat you! I've been practicing—let's play another!"

"O.K., kid, and this time I'll really take you—" Farlow was grinning happily.

Mendoza swung round as he heard Anya come in. "I am sorry," she said. "My mother is so fearful. She does not understand that here— Won't you sit down, sir?"

"I don't think this will take long," said Mendoza. "By

the way, why aren't you at your classes, Miss Dvorzhak? I understand you're attending U.C.L.A."

She hadn't expected that; a muscle twitched in her cheek. "If it is of interest," she said, "I had a bad headache this morning, and stayed home."

"I see. Do you know Gloria Litvak? Did you go to see her on Saturday?"

"I am sorry, no. No, I do not know that name," she said. She didn't ask why he wanted to know; just stood waiting for the next question.

"That's surprising. She was mentioned in several newspapers as one of Valerie Ellis's friends, and her address given. I thought I recognized you at her apartment house."

"No. That is impossible, I'm afraid. I do not know her." Her voice was steady. He offered her a cigarette. "Thank you, I do not smoke. But please do not hesitate."

Mendoza lit the cigarette and smiled at her. "I wonder," he said, "whether you can give me any idea why a Mr. Paul Manton and a Mr. Ricardo Cardenas should have been discussing you and your family this morning?"

The little muscle jumped again in her cheek, but she met his eyes unwaveringly. "I am so sorry, sir, you must be mistaken. I do not know these gentlemen you mention. None of us has ever met them—or anyone of these names."

"Oh, is that so?" said Mendoza. "Did you know that they were both friends of Valerie's?"

She considered. "I do not think so, sir. I recall hearing her mention a man named Paul, but not what his surname is."

"I see." No—one like this, with such experience behind

209

her, wouldn't shake easily; but he thought she was frightened.

What the hell about?

He didn't know. He didn't know anything more useful about this damned case than he'd known when the body got identified, that was the sum total.

His eyes held hers a moment longer. She was too calm, too co-operative, too incurious. "Thanks so much," he said, and started for the door. She saw him out politely.

He could hear, from next door, a new ping-pong game going. He wondered what the boy was doing out of school. He got into the Ferrari and started back downtown.

Odds and ends! And where the hell did they all fit in? And he'd missed lunch; it was nearly two o'clock.

The third time round, Sergeant Lake managed to fill him in on the long-distance call. "Fellow named Poynter. He's president of the California bank, branch down in Blythe. He says one of their girls has been off sick, with flu, and not taking much notice of the papers in consequence, but now she's back, and when she saw the papers—and Valerie's picture—she says she's pretty sure Valerie's been in quite a few times, has a lockbox there—she's the one looks after the lockboxes, this girl. Only Valerie was calling herself Carol Burns."

"How very interesting," said Mendoza. "Blythe? Quite a way from home. Quite a little drive to get at her lockbox. Yes, but Valerie was a canny one, wasn't she?" He ruminated. "I think—I just think—I'll take a run down there and have a look around. Sometimes the personal touch—" He looked at his watch. "God knows I'm not accomplishing much here. Yes, I think so. I'll probably be back sometime tomorrow—tell Art. It's what, around two hundred and thirty miles or so? With any luck, make it by seven. See this girl— I wonder if the Ellises have got a better picture of her than we have? I'd better ask . . . Yes, see you tomorrow then."

"Well, O.K.," said Lake. "Good luck."

Mendoza went home for a clean shirt and his razor, and was greeted in the driveway by El Señor—an El Señor somewhat the worse for wear, having a shaven patch down one flank showing a couple of stitches and violent purple medication painted on. "*¡Pobrecito!* What happened to you, boy?" Mendoza picked him up. "Alison!"

El Señor started telling him all about it, at loud length. Alison had heard the car, and came flying to meet him.

"What happened to—"

"Oh, he's all right," said Alison breathlessly. "The doctor said so, it's just a little cut—it was that stray tom— but, Luis, it was like *fate* or something! Wait until you meet her—we've *got* one! A simply wonderful one! Wait until I tell you—"

"I'm feeling sort of superstitious about it," Alison had said uneasily. "As if we aren't intended to find anybody."

"Well, now, that's silly, Mis' Mendoza," said Bertha in a forthright tone. "Acourse you'll find somebody, sooner or later. Bound to. They can't all be thieves, or like that Miss Freeman. There's different agencies, like, to try, aren't there? You go to another one, 'n' just see."

"Well, I suppose I'd better," said Alison. She trailed off to get dressed, still wondering if it was fate. But after all, she'd only tried two—maybe the saying was so, third time's the charm.

211

She put on the new green plaid cotton shirtmaker, the green alligator pumps; checked the matching bag, and looked in the yellow pages. There was an Acme Employment Agency on Wilshire, she hadn't tried that one. She started to copy down the address, and sprang up dropping everything as all hell broke loose in the back yard—*Cats*—

It was, as she'd known it would be, that big yellow stray tom, a battle-scarred veteran. If it had to be any of them he jumped, thank God it was El Señor, not one of the females who'd try to fight back. El Señor might lord it over his harem indoors, but in the presence of another tom he was remarkably unaggressive. This time he'd fled under the lantana bush by the kitchen door and was wailing like a siren; the yellow tom was burrowing after him grimly.

Alison and Bertha erupted out the kitchen door, Bertha with a saucepan of water to throw; the stray tom squalled bitterly and vanished in a long yellow streak; and Alison lay down prone beside the lantana bush and started to coax El Señor out.

After ten minutes of reassurance he crawled out sulkily. He had a long bloody gash down one flank, and the tip of one ear was bleeding. There was blood on his blond muzzle and one blond paw. "Oh, dear!" said Alison. "*Poor* Señor! That cat! The poor thing, it's not his fault—people just turning them out to wander—but all the same, I'll call the pound again. Poor boy, I know it hurts—have to take you to the doctor, heaven knows what infection—*Come* on, poor boy—" She heaved him up in her arms. "Get the carrier, will you, Bertha? In the garage—"

El Señor snarled at being thrust into the cat carrier, which he hated. Alison felt ready to snarl at that stray

212

tom. Not the tom's fault, no, but all the same— And the pound saying blandly, Well, you'll have to have the animal confined before we can send a man. Coax a wily old veteran like that yellow tom into a stout carton or something? And meanwhile he went around attacking defenseless pets. Mrs. Pettigrew up the hill was sure it had been that tom who'd slashed her silver Persian. On the other hand, the tom had made a big mistake (Alison thought in satisfaction) taking on the Hildebrands' Peke. That was where the tom had lost a slice out of one ear. He should have known better—a Peke . . .

"All right, be quiet," she said, sliding the Facel-Vega round the corner onto Los Feliz. "We're nearly there! You're not hurt that much."

"*Nyeouh!*" said El Señor. He knew perfectly well he was going to see Dr. Stocking, whom he hated. Alison reflected that it was another example of how unfair life was: that Dr. Stocking, like most other veterinary surgeons, who really liked cats, should be so bitterly hated by his patients.

She parked, and hauled the heavy cat carrier into the waiting room. There were several people ahead of her: a woman with an overfed dachshund, a man with a black-and-white mongrel, another man with a collie, and a woman just waiting. Alison announced herself to the receptionist, explained the circumstances, and sat down beside the lone woman, lowering the carrier to the floor between them.

"Ah, the poor boy," said the woman to El Señor, who wailed. "I do hope he's not badly hurt."

"I don't think so, by the way he's complaining," said Alison.

213

"Isn't he the pretty boy—*deas!*" She was gray-haired, with a round kind face, a pink-and-white complexion: a woman about fifty, in a clean starched cotton dress and sensible shoes.

"He's half Siamese and half Abyssinian," said Alison. You always got talking to people in a vet's waiting room.

"Now isn't that unusual!" She smiled at Alison. She had guilelessly childlike blue eyes and a soft Scots burr in her voice. "You do look worried— I don't think you need, *achara*, he's complaining so, the boy. When they're strong enough for that—"

"Oh, it's just that it's rather a nuisance," said Alison, and told her about the stray tom. "It's not that I'm not sorry for the poor thing, but you can see it's a nuisance. This is the third time he's jumped El Señor. And I was just going out—" Half the day wasted, she thought, so no new nursemaid tonight, and poor Luis— She added politely, "I hope yours isn't too—?"

"Ah, I'm only here to pick up my sister Janet's Jamie. Being as she doesn't drive." The woman had such a calm pleasant voice. The rough Scots burr reminded Alison nostalgically of her father. *Achara*, the woman said, friend. He had had a smattering of the Gaelic too, a Highland man, and said that sometimes. And *deas*, the pretty one. "We boarded the dear boy here while we went off on a little holiday, you see. But now I must be getting back to work."

The other three looked at them with the conscious superiority of dog-people to cat-people. The collie shook himself, rattling his chain collar.

El Señor wailed. "You be quiet," said Alison, "you'll be all right."

214

"Ah, now, let him get it out of his system," said the Scotswoman. "If it's any comfort to him. It's the same with babies—I always say, it's exercise for them to cry, you must just thole it. You hold them and comfort them, they settle down soon enough."

"You don't know my two," said Alison grimly. By the time she took El Señor home, it'd be afternoon, and the agency couldn't produce a nursemaid right away, you couldn't expect—

"Well, they're all different, that's so. It's interesting to see how different—they're themselves right from the start, true enough. Two, you have?" She smiled; she was interested. "How old are they?"

"Twins," said Alison above El Señor's complaints. "Five months. And they start howling at 2:30 A.M. *every* morning, and they're nearly driving us mad. My husband— And I'm at my wits' end trying to find a nurse for them. Someone to walk the floor instead of us, you know—"

"Mr. Gulbrandsen," said the receptionist, holding the little hinged door open. The man with the mongrel got up and went through. El Señor yelled. The collie shook himself again.

"Well, now, you have?" said the Scotswoman in her soft voice. "Isn't that a strange coincidence? For that's what I am, myself—at least what I've been at since I was left alone and came over to be with Janet, and she a widow herself." She smiled at Alison. "I don't know whether you think I'd suit you, my dear, but we could see. If you'd like. Not wanting to put myself forward . . . And here's our Jamie." She got up to take the cat carrier from the receptionist. Jamie was a fat black neuter with impressive jowls. "The poor Jamie, thinking we'd abandoned him! Home soon, my boy, *deas*—home to Janet." She opened her bag, paid the receptionist. Turning back to Alison, "If you'd care to try me, then."

Alison looked at her. Fate, she thought. The woman's steady blue eyes held all the calmness and serenity of a remote Highland loch; her slow voice with its Highland roughness was soothing.

"Not wanting to push myself onto you. I'm Mrs. Mac-Taggart, Máiri MacTaggart."

Alison heard herself say, "My father was born in Dunnett Bay. You remind me—excuse me, I mean the way you speak—"

"Ah, a Caithness man was he," said Mrs. MacTaggart. "And you'll have the red hair from some bold Viking back aways, then, if your mother wasna Glasga' Irish."

"A McCann," said Alison, smiling at her.

"Ah, now! And your twins with the red hair? No? What a pity!" Mrs. MacTaggart picked up the carrier with Jamie. "Would you like me to look after them, Mrs.—"

"Mendoza."

"Mrs. Mendoza," said the receptionist, "you may come in now."

"A gallant Spanish man you're wed to, so. I've never had twins to see to."

"Please do come and look after mine," said Alison. Fate, undoubtedly.

Sixteen

"I'm sorry," said Palliser for the sixth time that evening, interrupting himself. "You're not interested in all this. I can't seem to get my mind off this thing . . . Damn it, there's something I can't put a finger on, something—"

He should have been feeling happy about Jackson, and that his ideas about Gertrude Dasher seemed to be checking out. Instead, the last few weeks of round-the-clock work were catching up with him, and he just felt tired and irritable. The Dasher thing was as clueless and up in the air as the Valerie Ellis business. Damn it, who could have killed the woman and why?

Roberta Silverman gave him her slow, calm smile. "Just shows what a good detective you are. I ought to be apologizing to you, holding you to a date. I know how hard you've been at it. Where you ought to be, John David Palliser, is home in bed."

Palliser yawned. "And that's where I'm heading as soon as we've had that cup of coffee you promised me."

"I'll bet," said Roberta, going into the kitchen. "Sit up half the night meditating on your new case, if I know you."

217

"Damn it, who could have killed the woman? No place to look—nobody knew anything about her. Damn all secretive old ladies."

"I thought you'd figured out that she'd been blackmailing somebody."

"Yes," said Palliser absently. It was the only answer to where the money came from; provisionally, it was all but proved now. No legacy, no capital investments, just the nice green cash; and he had talked to the postman on that route, who remembered the letters . . .

("We get to know things about people on a route, you know," he'd said. "You can't help noticing—it's not prying, we haven't got the time for that, but you can't help noticing. One reason I remember those letters for Mrs. Dasher, they were the only personal mail she ever got. And always right at the first of the month. Depending what day the first was—if it was, like, a Sunday, the letter'd be postmarked next day. Like that. The envelopes were always typed . . . No, never any return address, but the postmark was always the central station—you know, the big main post office down by the Union Station.")

Well, all right, blackmail. The postman had gone on to say that he'd figured it was some relative, son or nephew or something, maybe sent her money in a letter every month. There wasn't anyone like that. If there had been, not only would Mrs. Powell have known, but whoever it was, living here (as witness the postmark) would have seen the news in the paper and come forward.

Oh, yes? Look at all the unlikely answers that were still possible. An illegitimate son or daughter, grown up, nobody who knew Dasher knowing about it. Voluntary contribution, but now mama is dead, no tie-up wanted, so keep still.

How wild could you get?

Roberta brought in the coffee on a tray. "You have exactly ten minutes to drink this and smoke another cigarette, and then you head for home. You look tired to death."

Palliser smiled at her. She had, paradoxically, a very restful effect on him, this tall dark girl with the still, unusual loveliness of a type not everybody would appreciate. And he hadn't asked her to marry him yet because he couldn't quite believe that Roberta would be interested in marrying a mere detective-sergeant (third grade) but maybe— "All right. Suits me. Even if we have caught up to Jackson"—he grimaced—"and what a type!—I've still got some work ahead of me, evidently. Damn it, Gertrude Dasher—I ask you—ordinary old woman living alone, pinching pennies . . . She liked money all right, but that's not—" Ever since this afternoon, through the abortive questioning of Jackson and through dinner with Roberta, something, some little idea, had been nagging at his mind, but he couldn't pin it down.

"Blackmail," she said. "A pretty good motive."

"Yes, but nothing to point to who she was— And then, you see, she'd been getting it without question, apparently, for six years. That's a long time for somebody being blackmailed to pay up so regular, before suddenly deciding to— My God!"

Roberta jumped. "What bit you?"

"My God," said Palliser blankly to himself. The little idea had suddenly got through to his conscious mind; but could there be anything in it? "Six years," he said. "Talk about wild ones—but I wonder—"

"Pull yourself together," said Roberta. "Five minutes to tell me about it before you start home."

219

Palliser took a deep breath. "Well, it sounds crazy—"

It was way out in left field, of course. But, depending on the times—he didn't know too many details about the Ellis case—there was a kind of logic in it.

"It's just a wild idea," he said to Hackett next morning. "There may not be anything in it at all. But all of a sudden it came to me—it's the same period of time."

"What is?" asked Hackett patiently. You always had to draw Palliser out, encourage him.

"That phone call, on the Ellis case. I heard something about it from Jimmy. I want to hear more details. But didn't whoever it was say something about Ellis getting killed 'because they killed that woman six years ago,' something like that?"

"That's right, why?"

"Well," said Palliser, "it was almost exactly six years ago that Mrs. Dasher retired, announced that she'd had a legacy, and started getting her five hundred per month all nice and regular."

"Oh," said Hackett. He considered, rubbing his jaw. He said he'd be damned.

"I mean, you could link it up—because she knew about the murder. The five hundred, that is. Whatever it was, whoever it was. And Valerie found out too. And put the bite on X, who didn't fancy the idea of paying out two sets of blackmail, so he handed her the spiked cocktail. And Mrs. Dasher, seeing the news in the paper, put two and two together and tried to get X to raise the ante. She did like the nice crisp cash, you know."

"It makes a story, in a way," said Hackett. He went out to the anteroom, Palliser following. "Jimmy—that anonymous call. What exactly did she say?"

Lake rummaged and found his scrawled memo. "What did she sound like?" asked Palliser, reading it. "Young, old? Any accent?"

"Lord," said Lake, "it was all so quick—only about thirty seconds, you know— Far's I remember, for what it's worth, I'd say not young. But then most anonymous calls and notes do come from the over-fifty group, don't they? No accent."

"Yes," said Hackett. "I do know that Luis thinks that call was made sole and simple to convince X she'd carry out her threat. It was bluff. So he says. If that's so, if there's anything to the call at all, she was telling a little piece of truth—there really was a woman murdered six years ago, and for some reason that had something to do with Valerie Ellis's murder a week ago . . . Of course he could be wrong. He sometimes is."

"What time did the call come through?" asked Palliser.

"I noted it down. Thirteen minutes to noon last Friday. I thought myself it could refer to the Overton case, only—"

"My God," said Palliser simply. "That convinces me. It convinces me good. The Overton case be damned. She died between eleven and one, so the surgeon said. By God, I can almost see it! She was asking for more hush-money, to keep quiet about Ellis—and X was arguing—and she made that call to let him see she meant business. So it was bluff—and he called it all right. She forgot that somebody who's killed once might not have any scruples about doing it again."

"There's not really an awful lot to back it up, John," said Hackett dubiously.

"I think there is," said Palliser stubbornly. "It'd be the

221

hell of a coincidence, if she wasn't somehow connected—
if she wasn't the one made that call—her getting murdered at just that time. The times are what sell me on it.
I think he was so mad and scared that he killed her right
after she'd made that phone call. And a few minutes later, maybe just as he was starting to leave, that
Fuller Brush man came by and scared him all over again.
And while he waited for him to go, he got the idea of setting it up to look like one of the rape-burglaries."

"You're going away out of sight of all the actual evidence," said Hackett. "I still say it's thin. You've got no
time pinpointed for her death. Nothing at all says it was
Dasher who made that call." He regarded Palliser disapprovingly. "Don't tell me you're growing into a detective
who goes on hunches too! One is enough for any homicide bureau."

"But it could be—"

"Sure it could be, but that's a long way from proving it
was. We'll bear it in mind, and when Luis gets back we'll
see what he says about it. But the one thing we always
come back to, on that phone call, is the thing that makes
me doubt there's anything in it at all. The phone call, or
your wild hunch."

"What's that?"

Hackett said, "You ought to see it for yourself. Six
years ago Valerie Ellis was only seventeen, in her second
year of high school. She hadn't gone on the bent yet, she
was an innocent—or reasonably innocent—teen-ager living at home with well-off parents who gave her anything
she wanted. Do you see a kid like that knowing anything
about a murder—maybe a murder not even spotted as one
by the police—and having any reason to keep still about
it?"

Palliser looked even more stubborn. "Maybe not, but it's something to keep in mind." He took up his hat and turned for the door.

"Wild-goose chasing?" asked Hackett.

"I'm going out to find that Fuller Brush man," said Palliser.

After a little silence, Lake said, "Well, it does fit in a kind of way, Art. About the times, I mean."

"It's way out," said Hackett. "I only hope Luis doesn't pick it up as an inspiration because it's a hunch. He's so damn' superstitious about these things—if you want my private opinion, it's compensation. Because he claims not to have any religion. It's a kind of substitute . . . He ought to be back sometime today."

"I suppose so," said Lake. "He only went down to check that lockbox and so on."

They were both wrong. At half-past twelve a telegram arrived, addressed to Hackett. Hackett read it, said, "Now what the hell?" and showed it to Lake.

"Why the hell does he want to go over there for?" asked Lake.

And then they both did a double take and said simultaneously, "So *that's* what she meant!"

What with hearing all about the stray tom and Mrs. MacTaggart—who was to come at once, a perfect dear, and only Thursdays and Sunday mornings off—and making a detour to stop by the Ellises' and borrow a better picture of Valerie than they had of the corpse, and another detour to the bank to cash a check, it was a quarter to four when Mendoza started for Blythe. There was a certain amount of home-going traffic even at that hour, and at no time is the traffic anywhere in L.A. County

223

light. It took him nearly two hours to make the sixty-odd miles to Riverside, even partly on freeways; but after that he was out of the big town and traffic thinned.

No choice: he had to climb through the San Bernardino mountains, and after he left Beaumont and Banning there wouldn't be much in the way of towns, excepting Palm Springs. He stopped in Banning for dinner, at a quarter to seven, and was on his way again at seven-thirty. He slid down the mountain road, in full dusk and then full dark, so early in the year, and then he was on the desert, and through Palm Springs, and even at night he could make time. But watch it, even on these lonely straight roads, because no man is infallible, and the Ferrari was insidious: before he realized, the big twelve-cylinder engine sliding up to eighty-five, ninety, ninety-five— *Look out!*

He stopped himself from swerving in a split second. Jack rabbit, bolting across the road. Thank God, hadn't hit it, but that was what caused accidents, swerving to avoid the animals; try to swerve at that speed, you'd be off the road in no time. These straight desert highways were always, sickeningly, littered with the little corpses— jack rabbits, prairie dogs, rattlers, the long-legged road runners, even occasionally a coyote. You couldn't help hitting them, traveling at the speeds such roads invited . . . He slowed to a meticulous seventy and kept it there, steady.

He was inside the borders of Joshua Tree National Monument, now. He crossed a short bridge over a nearly dry arroyo: the sign, picked out in reflected letters, said *Colorado River* . . . Come to think, the natives shouldn't be amused that visitors found California such

224

a surprising place. It *was* surprising. The mighty Colorado, its waters trapped up there at Boulder Dam two hundred odd miles northeast, to provide half the water for Southern California—and here barely a trickle . . . He passed through a dark sleeping village, Desert Center. Only the occasional highway markers winked at him from the dark roadside now: the state markers, shield-shaped, with the bear in profile: *California 60-70.*

Call it two hundred and forty miles or so. He passed the sign saying *Blythe, pop. 3,334* at a quarter to ten.

Obviously too late to contact the bank people tonight. At least, some compensations, he reflected: if no Alison, no twins either . . . He found a motel with a vacancy and went to bed.

But by a quarter to ten on Tuesday morning he had found the bank—one of two banks in town—and was waiting for its doors to open. At one minute past ten he was talking to Mr. Gerald Poynter.

Mr. Poynter was rather like a large egg—bald, round, and bland. When he learned who Mendoza was, the blandness fell from him. "Oh, my goodness, yes," he said. "You must see Greta—talk to Greta. A very nice, honest, truthful girl—did you say lieutenant? Yes—I could scarcely believe—a *murder* case—but when it was Greta, I— Absolutely reliable, you can believe me. German, you know, no imagination but ab-so-lute-ly reliable. Quite a sensation in our quiet little town—Communists—"

"I can imagine," said Mendoza. "If I could meet Greta?"

He was taken downstairs and introduced to Greta. The bank was a small separate building; in a town this small there wouldn't be much banking business. The vault was about an eighth the size of that in his L.A. bank, and there was only one attendant on duty: Miss Greta Krieger.

Looking at her, Mendoza believed Mr. Poynter. She was a large blond young woman, with slightly protruding blue eyes, a firm square jaw, and a no-nonsense air. She was obviously destined to marry a successful farmer and raise a brood of blond, square-jawed children like herself—honest hard-working citizens completely devoid of any imagination whatever.

He produced his picture. Mrs. Ellis had given it to him tearfully. The Ellises still blaming themselves, which was ridiculous but human . . . She said it had been taken just before Fred and Amy were killed, so it was four years old; but it was still a better picture of Valerie than the one the papers had run of the touched-up corpse.

Greta Krieger looked at it and said, "That's her. She was wearing her hair different here, though. I thought it was—you know I said so, Mr. Poynter, when I saw the picture in the paper."

"You're absolutely sure?" asked Mendoza.

"Sure I'm sure. Absolutely. Only she said her name was Carol Burns. Isn't that illegal or something, Mr. Poynter? I mean, renting a deposit box—"

"I think we'd better get that cleared up first," said Mendoza. A little flustered at being involved in a case that had made such headlines, Mr. Poynter agreed. He summoned a junior vice-president as an additional witness, and they opened the box assigned to Miss Carol Burns.

They found in it twelve thousand nine hundred and eighty dollars in cash, and that was all. It was, reflected Mendoza, quite enough. He wondered whether the Ellises would come in for it: a nice windfall. If he couldn't

226

fathom what the racket had been, who this crooked money might really belong to—

They got through the tiresome legal business, swearing out affidavits. No point in removing the money; he knew where it was, and left it there for the time being. He started questioning Greta, and after they'd been interrupted twice by people coming in to get at their boxes, Mr. Poynter summoned his own secretary to take temporary charge of the vault. Mendoza and Greta sat in two hard little chairs near the gate into the vault, with Mr. Poynter hovering excitedly nearby.

"Do you remember when she first came in? Was that when she rented the box?"

"Tell you by the record card," said Greta, and went back to the counter. After search, she came back with a six-by-eight card. "Here you are. Specimen signature and so on. I knew it was around then, couldn't have said the exact date. May seventh, 1962. About two years ago, little less. Yes, sure that was the first time she came in—that she rented the box, I mean. Why else'd she come in here? I remember, naturally, because, well, in a town this size most everybody knows everybody else. You know. And I'd never seen her before. And—" She hesitated, looking at him. Small towns apt to be insular: he read her mind. The big-city fellow, with his immaculate tailoring and narrow mustache and Latin name, something of an unknown quantity to Greta Krieger. "Well, you know, her clothes," she said. "She was a lot better dressed—I mean, what's the word, formal, kind of, than you usually see here—"

"Yes. Did she—if you remember—give any explanation of herself, Miss Krieger? She'd know that you knew she was a stranger, this small a town. Did she give any account of herself, why she—"

"Sure." Greta blinked her honest blue eyes at him. "She was kind of chatty. She said she was a saleswoman, wholesale like, for a big chain outfit that made cosmetics. And she was on the road a lot, going back and forth—she said she had the southwest territory. She said she'd come through here quite a lot, and figured it was a sort of handy base, you know, have a lockbox."

"I see. You believed her?"

Greta thought. "Well, gee, I didn't have a reason not to, mister. I don't guess I ever thought much about it. Except thinking it must be an interesting sort of job, traveling all around like that."

"How many times was she in, could you say?"

"Show you that by the records, too." She went up to the counter again . . . Valerie had visited her lockbox eighteen times in twenty-one months. Naturally, Greta wouldn't know whether she'd put something in or taken something out. Mendoza could have guessed. A very canny one, Valerie . . . He heard an echo of earnest James Ellis talking about how it was a good thing for young people, be on their own, learn the value of money. He thought, in a left-handed kind of way, Valerie had. He thought that every time she—or they, whoever they were—had taken a mark, on this caper, Valerie had socked some of it away. Had a ball with the rest, but some of it—maybe as much as half of it—tucked away under a false name. As security. So, even if she got caught up with, maybe got inside, she'd have something waiting.

("Often enough I told him—" James Ellis. Valerie more like her uncle than either of them suspected.)

"Were you here every time she came in?" he asked.

"I probably would be. Only times I'm off, for coffee

breaks in the morning 'n' afternoon, and at lunch, Georgia comes down from upstairs. But I guess I must've waited on her every time she came, or Georgia might have remembered her too."

"Did she ever say anything else to you, that you remember? Personal things, anything?"

Greta stared at him, bovine. "Gee, I don't remember much of anything. I'd notice her when she came, of course. Just on account she was—you know—a stranger. Not a regular like Mr. Mancini or Mrs. Pell or Judge Newhall. You know. And her clothes, and all. Well, I guess I'd say she was friendly." He almost saw her slow, precise mind working, casting back. "She—one time I remember, wasn't so long back, maybe in October, November—she came in, and said like she usually did, Here I am, just passing through again, what a life. And I said it must be a hard job, all the traveling, and she said she didn't mind when it paid so good. I mean, it was all just ordinary things, like that."

"It's quite astonishing, when you *think*," said Mr. Poynter raptly. "All the time, this girl mixed up with *Communists*—that Thorwald—"

Mendoza didn't enlighten him. And he didn't suppose that Valerie had said or done anything to give the smallest secret away to unimaginative Greta Krieger. This was interesting to know, it was another something they hadn't known, but it didn't take him much further toward finding out what Valerie's racket had been, who—if anybody —had been in it with her, or why she'd been slipped the spiked cocktail by whom.

"You could've knocked me down with a feather," Greta was saying. "Honest, when I saw the picture in the paper— Why, I said to Ma, That's that Miss Burns that's

229

got a box at the bank! I couldn't hardly believe it. A crook of some kind."

"And when Greta told me, and had convinced me she was absolutely positive, I thought it my duty—"

"Yes," said Mendoza. "Of course. We're very—"

"Oh, I guess maybe you'd want to hear about that," said Greta suddenly. "It just came back to me. About the first time she came in—the time she rented the box."

"Yes?"

"She told me this about her job and all," said Greta. "Like I said. She said it was a new territory for her, see, she'd been working back east. I just remembered this part. She was acting real friendly—I guess, looking back, and knowing now she was a real crook, like—I guess, she was trying to look natural, sort of convince me. You know?"

"Yes?"

"Well, she said that about her new sales territory, see? And she asked me what was the best road to take over to Vicksburg."

In the act of lighting a cigarette, Mendoza froze and stared at her. "Vicksburg—"

"Vicksburg over in Arizona," said Greta. "Tell the truth, I kinda wondered about it, because that's just a wide place in the road."

She had to be over at Vic's—Vicksburg, Arizona.

¡Qué demonio—! thought Mendoza. That Gloria knowing something indeed—knowing all about it—so, no wonder she'd nearly fainted when he heard that slip wrong.

She had to be over at Vic's. She had to be over at Vicksburg.

Why? Why the hell?

230

Seventeen

These great bare stretches of desolate country made Mendoza feel absurdly uneasy. At least there were mountains to be seen in the distance. He had never realized what part a man's familiar physical surroundings played in life until that time he'd been sent back to Chicago to escort a wanted man home. He had felt uneasy all the time he was there, with no mountains on any horizon: rather as if he might slip off the edge of that great flat plain. He had something of the same feeling now.

Blythe was only a few miles from the Arizona border: he was in Arizona within half an hour of leaving, after sending explanatory telegrams to Alison and Hackett. This was real desert—a howling wilderness. He'd driven on this secondary road up and down through what the map told him were the Chocolate Mountains, and found himself on the flat desert floor again. Miles and miles he had driven without passing so much as a ranch house, let alone a town. Once he thought he saw a man on a horse, a couple of miles off the road, but otherwise he'd seen only jack rabbits.

They had advised him at Blythe to take along some sandwiches and a gallon of water. Even in February, they said. Just in case. Even if it was only about seventy miles over there. He saw what they'd been talking about, now.

He passed two wooden buildings, so far away he couldn't identify what they were, and the lone rider, between the California border and Vicksburg.

If there had been more rural building, he might have passed Vicksburg without noticing it. It announced its population: *pop. 47*, the sign said. At first glance Mendoza couldn't see any of them. There was a street, and on it there was a drugstore, a general store, a bar, and a hay-and-feed store, and down at the end an enormous ice-dispensing machine. But Vicksburg could boast of the railroad running through: it had a station, at the end of the street. A ramshackle old clapboard station painted yellow, with a little platform.

Mendoza drove down there, thinking that there must at least be a stationmaster. What the hell had drawn Valerie Ellis to this godforsaken hole, he wondered.

There was one man sitting in the station, a man whose age it was impossible to guess, his face was so lined and seamed and tanned from the sun. He was crouched over the counter, his nose almost literally buried in a large book. He put it down as Mendoza came in, but not before Mendoza had read its title: *Metallurgical Science*.

"Well, and who might you be?" he asked.

Mendoza introduced himself, showed credentials. If he'd said he was the King of the Fairies, he thought, the other man wouldn't have shown any surprise. He merely remarked, "You don't say. Name of Ben Jenkins myself. Do for you?"

Mendoza produced Valerie's photograph. He remembered that her jaunts away from home had kept her out overnight, sometimes over two nights. Would there be a motel or hotel here? Doubtful. "I have information that this woman came here, probably a number of times." Or was that a valid deduction? No, of course not. It might have been only once. "Do you know anything about her, have you ever seen her?" In a place as small as this—

Ben Jenkins took the photograph and held it within three inches of his eyes. "Oh, *her!*" he said, enlightened. "Couldn't say her name, prob'ly Mike knows. You could ask him, acourse. Or Ellie. Damn funny thing," he added conversationally, "last couple of years, I got to get so close to things to see plain."

"Maybe you need glasses," suggested Mendoza only a trifle sarcastically. "Mike who?"

"Well, I don't know as I fancy the idea," said Jenkins. "Have to go clear into Phoenix to get any, I guess."

"Mike who?"

"Mike Cassidy, acourse. Though it could be, there might be a doctor in Peoria or Glendale."

"Where would I find him?" asked Mendoza.

"Find who?"

"Mike Cassidy!"

"Oh, you want Mike. Well, why the hell did you come to the station, y' damn fool? If he isn't out with Bessy, he'll be at home or to Hank's bar. White frame house next to Sam Hart's place on First Street."

First Street, thought Mendoza, my God. First and last street. "What's the address?"

"Hey? Oh, you can't miss it, Ellie's got new pink curtains up."

233

Mendoza gave up and went back to the Ferrari. There was actually another street, turning off at right angles from the ice machine. There was actually a sign: First Street. There were seven houses on this block of it, and another block ahead boasted six or seven more. He found the pink curtains at the front windows of a white-painted frame house about the middle of the block, parked, and climbed the rickety steps.

A woman came to answer his knock—there was no bell: a thin, gray-haired woman about fifty, with the same seamed, tanned face as Jenkins, but more attractive: she'd once been pretty. Her angular body was neatly clad in twill pants and shirt. She looked as taken aback to see him as if he *had* been the King of the Fairies. "Oh!" she said, a hand to her heart. And added, "Mike's out with Bessy."

She didn't seem unduly upset at the idea. Maybe Mike was her brother, not her husband? Mendoza said, "Mr. Jenkins at the station sent me. He thought Mr. Cassidy might know—" And he introduced himself again, produced Valerie's photograph.

"Well, just fancy!" said the woman, looking at it. "A policeman, are you? From Los Angeles? My. Well, I suppose you'd better step in out of the sun." Mendoza had been noticing the sun; even in February—

"Do you recognize her?"

"Why, yes. I ought to say, I'm Mrs. Cassidy. Fancy coming all this way just to ask that. You'll have a drop of Mike's whiskey? He'd be the first to offer it. He's only gone up into the Buckskins for a couple of weeks. You sit down."

Mendoza sat down on a Victorian-looking love seat upholstered in something that looked like burlap and was

234

extremely uncomfortable, and said, "No, thanks very much. You recognize the woman? How? Where did you meet her?"

"It wouldn't take a minute," said Mrs. Cassidy. "You're sure? Well, maybe a nice piece of blueberry pie then? They're canned blueberries, acourse."

"No, thank you. What I want to ask you—"

"Well, just as you like," said Mrs. Cassidy. "But it can't be said I ever welcomed a body under my roof and never so much as asked if they had a mouth on them. It's just out of the oven, the pie." She sat down at last, on a chair matching the love seat.

Mendoza felt rather as if he were wading through all that desert sand, taking one step back to two forward. "You *know* the woman?" he asked loudly.

"Oh, yes, I know her. Has something happened to her, poor thing? Not lost, is she? But there, I don't suppose she could be in a place like Los Angeles." She might have been saying The Fairy Isles. "And you wouldn't come here looking for her. It's a pity you missed Mike. Bessy wasn't over-mad to go, but he coaxed her along finally." Her faded eyes were placid on him.

Mendoza heard himself ask, "Who is Bessy?"

The eyes widened. "Why, the burro, to be sure."

The burro, of course. Presumably to carry the sleeping-bag and Geiger counter. "What do you know about this woman?"

"Why, it's Alice," said Mrs. Cassidy. "Alice Roberts, her name is. Didn't you know? What's happened to her?"

"Never mind, I just want to know everything you know about her, please."

"Oh. Well, that's soon told." Mrs. Cassidy settled her-

235

self for a comfortable chat. "She's a city girl, you could see that right off. There's some of these city folk, they like to come out 'n' poke around for the kind of thing they call gemstones. Call themselves rock-hounds, they do, maybe you know. Rough quartz, and fool's gold, and agate—that kind of thing. Foolishness. You heard of that?"

"Yes. She said— She was one of those?"

"That's right. A real greenhorn she was, at first. Didn't even know enough to carry water with her, fancy."

"When did she first come here?" He resisted the impulse to raise his voice as if she was deaf.

"When? Oh, it'd be a couple of years ago, about then," she said vaguely. "You see, she ended up here because I've the extra bedroom. Real surprised she was, find out there wasn't a motel or something around. Because sometimes she'd want to stay over, when she had a couple days off her job. She was a part-time secretary, she said. So finally, that first time, when she asked around, Bill at the drugstore sends her up here, knowing I could put her up. And I didn't overcharge, either. Two and a half dollars with breakfast and dinner, fair enough, don't you think?"

"Very fair," said Mendoza. "She was a rock-hound. She went out looking for quartz and so on? Where?"

"Oh, out east o' town, toward the Harquahala range, mostly, I guess. She wouldn't be going far off the road, acourse, not with just the car, and Mike told her all how to do, made her get a compass and all. Goodness, city girl like that'd get lost easy, fifty feet from the road. And he told her, get stout boots and all, for the rattlers."

Mendoza tried to visualize that good-time girl Valerie in boots and pants hunting for quartz and agate, and failed. Of course, probably no one in town took a news-

236

paper regularly; the Cassidys didn't know anything about the case. He started to ask another question, but Mrs. Cassidy was going on placidly. "She liked this part o' the desert, said she found a lot of things here. She'd come as often as she could get away from her job, after that first time. Sometimes she'd stay over, 'n' sometimes she'd just be out looking four-five hours, and come back and say she'd decided to get home, the sun played her out."

"How often did she come?"

"How often? Now that's hard to say," said Mrs. Cassidy. "There wasn't anything regular about it. After that first time, she knew she could land here any time and find accommodations. It made a bit o' change too, somebody new to talk to. Not that she'd be around much. Drive up in her big white car, and say here she was again, and change into her other gear—boots and so on—'n' be off. Depending what time it was she got here, acourse. She said it took her two or three hours, drive up from Phoenix."

"She told you she lived in Phoenix?"

"Why, yes, that's where she was from. Mike did laugh at her, he thought it was a cute trick, way she kept her car registered in California, with California plates and all— because, she said, a cop catches you doing something a little wrong, he makes allowances for a foreigner. What sort of surprised me, you turning up like this from Los Angeles asking about her. Why on earth?"

It would take her, thought Mendoza, around seven or eight hours from L.A. Less? Marion Keller said she liked to drive fast . . . Call it three hundred miles.

Deductions. This was how she'd piled up all the mileage on the Dodge. In the last twenty, twenty-one months— since May of 1962. Valerie, driving clear over to this god-

237

forsaken one-burro burg, to put on boots and venture among the rattlers hunting for the pretty rose quartz? *¡No hay tal!* That he couldn't see. But why the hell *had* she come?

"Maybe," he said, "about eighteen times since she first came—in May two years ago?"

Mrs. Cassidy thought. "It'd be about that," she agreed. "Funny what gets into city people. Worthless stuff like that. Instead of something you can stake a claim on. But she's a nice bright girl and pleasant company."

"She'd go out," said Mendoza, "daytimes? Not at night?"

She bent a surprised gaze on him that held indulgence for city people. "Well, naturally. You couldn't find anything like that in the dark."

"In her car. Yes. Do you know if she went far?"

"I suppose different places. I couldn't rightly say, I didn't pay notice. She'd mostly start out toward the Harquahalas, way I say."

"Did she ever show you and Mr. Cassidy any of her—er—finds?"

"We wouldn't be interested in anything like that," said Mrs. Cassidy. "Bits o' rubbish. Oh, some of the agate's pretty enough, but worth nothing. Mike used to laugh at her—she knows what he thinks o' that sort of thing. They polish them up and make jewelry, fancy. Pink quartz 'n' fool's gold. Foolishness."

"When was the last time she was here?"

Mrs. Cassidy reflected. "Let's see, do I recollect this is Tuesday? It'd be two weeks back tomorrow. Yes, because it was the same day that fool Mex Joe García got drunk at Hank's and made such a row. I remember. She

238

showed up here about four in the afternoon, Alice did—"

Caray, a fast driver, you could say: Mrs. Montague said she'd left about ten in the morning.

"—And said she'd have a little hunt round even if it was late. She changed, and went off, and I remember I was a bit worried because she didn't come back until after it was getting dark. She stayed over Wednesday night, and went out first thing Thursday morning—I made up a lunch for her—and she was gone all day. And Thursday night she said she'd be leaving first thing in the morning, and so she did."

"She started out east? Hunting her rocks, I mean?"

"That's right. Now, just why are you asking, anyways? A policeman—there's nothing *wrong*, is there? I just hired her my spare room—"

"Nothing wrong about that at all, no. Thanks very much." Mendoza made his escape. He drove up to the main street, conscious of her staring after him from the porch, and parked, and consulted a map.

There certainly wasn't much of anything around Vicksburg. There was another town about the same size called Salome some ten miles northeast; ten miles beyond that, Wenden. Both on the railroad: the Atchison, Topeka and Santa Fe railroad. The Harquahala Mountains, a thin trickle called the Bouse Wash. And empty desert.

What the hell had brought Valerie over here? The city-lights girl?

He started out on the road east—the only road out of town. In five minutes he might have been alone on the moon. Not quite: a few scattered head of white-faced Herefords on either side of the road.

Eighteen times (was that a valid deduction?) Valerie

239

had driven over here, passing through Blythe. No. She'd been in Blythe eighteen times, sure. But here, maybe the same number of times but not necessarily on the same occasions.

Work it out. She wasn't the genuine rock-hound; that he'd take a bet on. Valerie who'd done a little hustling, worked a tired old con game with Eddy Warren? City-lights Valerie? She had come here with that excuse on some crooked business connected with the racket she was working. How could it be connected, for God's sake? A God-forgotten spot like this? (The mountains were faint on the horizon and he felt uneasy again.)

All right. But the money was collected at home in L.A. Witness the address book. Before or after she came over here? For whatever reason?

And why the hell was he driving down this road? Presumably the way she'd come (or was that a blind?) but nothing to give him any clue. Empty country, rock formations, sand, and cows: nothing told him anything. Mendoza told himself bitterly that he was a fool.

She had to be over at Vicksburg. Why the hell?

That girl Gloria knew about it. She knew why. How? In the racket? What racket, for God's sake, necessitated irregular but periodic visits to the empty desert outside Vicksburg, Arizona? Gloria, a call girl—if the family was respectable. Valerie—liking money however it came . . .

He slowed. This was a very secondary road he was on, but just here another branched off—hardly more than a track across the desert to the right: it looked like an old road seldom used. Ahead, he could see that in places sage-brush had grown into the old ruts; but the brush had been crushed down by the passage of something larger

240

than a horse. On impulse he turned the Ferrari into it. A hundred yards up he stopped, got out of the car, and inspected the terrain more closely.

God knew he was no expert tracker, outside city limits: but anybody could see, here, that sage and other underbrush had started to grow across the old ruts, and been crushed down and killed by a car's passing.

A ranch back beyond those rolling hills? He stood with the sun beating fiercely down on him and thought, No. Because in that case, the track in constant use, the brush wouldn't have had a chance to grow into it in the first place.

He didn't really think this was any clue to where Valerie had gone or what she'd done here, but you automatically tried every direction indicated, even when the indication was slight.

He got back in the car and went on down the track, slowly, in deference to the Ferrari's springs.

Tall yuccas sprang up on each side. The track curved aimlessly and presently started to rise into the little rolling hills.

Gloria Litvak, thought Mendoza. The hour he got back to civilization, he'd have Gloria Litvak brought in and put her through the mill. Let her pass out on him a dozen times, he'd get out of her what she knew . . . There was Anya Dvorzhak too. She knew more than she was telling, damn it . . . And Waltham said (and the Feds should know) the family was absolutely clean, genuine refugees.

Manton and Cardenas—Cardenas the stuffed shirt— talking about the Dvorzhaks. For God's sake, why?

The track was definitely climbing now. The going was rougher, the track barely discernible in places. This was

241

senseless. Turn around right now before he broke a spring.

That address book . . . Quite suddenly it occurred to Mendoza that there was an aspect he hadn't considered. It was a funny little point that probably meant nothing at all, but there it was, and this was the first time it had occurred to him.

Vardas. Wilanowski. Dvorzhak. Names in the address book—fourteen names—Tronowsky, Klinger, Gsovskaya, Koltai, Imarosa.

Foreign names. What a lot of people would think of as foreign names.

What about it?

He hadn't turned around. The track led him up and over a little rise, and there was more flat empty desert below. Not quite empty. A building: a small building, about two hundred yards ahead. A little wooden shack of some sort, with what looked like the ruins of a corral at one side. He started down toward it.

Well, what the hell did that say? Nothing. Names Czechoslovakian, Polish, Hungarian, Russian, Japanese. So what?

But those were the names associated with the collections, the meeting-places marked with the dollar signs.

Root of all evil, he thought.

A plane roared over noisily.

He drew up by the shack and shut off the engine. The plane had died away in the distance; the silence was appalling. There was only the flat land stretching away, the remote line of hills, the smell of sage in the hot sun, and silence.

Mendoza got out of the car. The shack was derelict, all right. Somebody, a long while ago, had lived here briefly:

242

kept a horse, or horses, in the little corral: and had moved on (after establishing the track) elsewhere, abandoning the little thrown-together shack.

He walked toward it through rock-hard sand that yet drifted and got into his shoes; he felt gritty with sand. There were outcroppings of rock through the sand. The door sagged open on loosened hinges.

But it would be, he thought vaguely, a shelter of sorts from the merciless sun, while you waited— Waited for what?

Sometimes she'd stay over, and sometimes she'd just be out looking four-five hours—

He shoved the door wider and went in. Dirt floor. One window, without glass. Four walls and a roof: the whole place sagging, out of true.

But there in one corner a fairly new sleeping-bag, neatly rolled up. A squashy big plastic cushion propped against the wall.

He heard the plane again, in the distance.

Maybe, he thought, the first times she came, she'd taken care to carry everything away with her. But then she'd got careless—nobody ever came here—less of a bother, leave things here.

He walked across the packed dirt floor and looked at the corner of the one room. The sleeping-bag. (Not for Valerie, that.) The cushion. Plentiful scattered crumbs— sandwiches. Water she'd bring with her each time, fresh.

There was something else, lying on the sleeping-bag. A copy of *Vogue*, and it was the February issue, and they were just eleven days into February.

Two weeks ago tomorrow, the last time, Mrs. Cassidy said. Five days before Valerie died.

243

She must, thought Mendoza, have spent some damned boring hours here in this hut. Waiting. Waiting—

He went back to the sagging door and looked across the desert. The eminently flat desert.

And suddenly remembered just which Civil Service department Ricardo Cardenas' sister Maria worked in— The Department of Immigration. In the Americanization office. Dealing with recent immigrants.

"Oh, by God!" he said softly, suddenly. "By God, of course! ¡Con qué esas tenemos! Why didn't I see it before? So now we know—do we? By God, yes—it adds up, it's got to be that!"

The beautifully flat desert, where a light plane could sit down so anonymously, let out a single passenger—

Russian, Polish, Czechoslovakian names. Names from countries which hadn't a regular immigration quota for the United States. And people who—they'd tightened the rules the hell of a lot, who they let in these days—might not conform to regulations, so if they were determined to get in—

Thorwald. Oh, yes, of course. The stateless citizen.

Paul Manton and his little Cessna. The very good pilot. And Ricardo Cardenas, the civil servant, whose sister— Didn't it add up! And Valerie the go-between—

A dozen pieces of the jigsaw puzzle fitted themselves together magically, all in one moment.

Hell, and very probably not a Western Union office between here and Blythe— Mendoza wrenched the Ferrari around and headed back for the road, too fast. But he was smiling happily to himself.

At the same moment Hackett was staring at a telegram. "I just thought you'd like to see it," said Waltham. "We're sending a couple of men down, of course. I don't suppose it's got anything to do with the murder, but—"

"No," said Hackett. "I don't see how it could be. But thanks."

The telegram was from the *Jefe de Policía* of Mexico City. In excellent English it said succinctly that one corresponding to the description of Osgar Thorwald had been placed in that city, resident in a modest hotel for some two months, up to two weeks and three days ago, namely January 26th, when he had flown up to the city of Chihuahua. It had been ascertained that there he had hired a car and driver to take him to, of all unlikely places, a small village called Puerto Peñasca on the east coast of the Gulf of California, in the province of Sonora. If the FBI desired, further inquiries would be pursued.

"What the hell?" asked Hackett.

"Exactly," said Waltham. "We're sending a couple of men down. Just like to ferret out all the details, you know."

Eighteen

Palliser had identified the Fuller Brush man yesterday, but hadn't caught up with him in person until Wednesday morning. He had just come back to the office after a thought-provoking interview with him when Mendoza arrived. It was ten-thirty.

"I've had a couple of ideas I'd like to talk over—" began Palliser, as Mendoza came in almost on his heels.

"Later, later! *¡Ya está—Paso!*" said Mendoza briskly. He swept into the office in a hurry and glanced into the sergeants' room. "All of you lazing around here," he said disapprovingly to Hackett, Dwyer, Scarne, and Landers.

"Well, welcome home from the wilds," said Hackett. "Did you find the murderer lurking behind a Joshua tree?"

"No, but I found a few very interesting things," said Mendoza. He was looking rather raffish—for Mendoza: he had on the same suit he'd worn Monday and the same tie; but his shirt was reasonably clean and he had shaved.

He hadn't, on second thought, bothered about telegrams: the personal touch required here too. It had been about five o'clock yesterday afternoon when he stood in

246

that cabin doorway and had his inspiration about where the crooked money had come from. He'd driven straight back to Vicksburg and through it, and started home. Back through the desert to Blythe, and across the lonely empty country past Desert Center and the Joshua Tree Monument, the little trickle of the Colorado River. He'd stopped in Palm Springs for a late dinner at nine o'clock; but by the time he got to Beaumont the two days of long-distance driving had caught up with him (on top of the sleep he'd been losing lately) and he had to stop. He'd checked into the motel at midnight and left it at seven-thirty this morning to make the remaining seventy miles to L.A. as fast as possible. He hadn't been home at all.

"All right, boys, let's do a little work for a change," he said now. "*Pronto*, I want you to go out and bring in Gloria Litvak. I also want—how I want—Mr. Paul Manton and Ricardo Cardenas. And the Dvorzhaks—never mind the mother, the girl and her father will do. Wherever they are, whatever they're doing, haul them in. *Inmediatamente, por favor*."

"What's the excitement?" asked Hackett.

Mendoza sat down at his desk and reached for the outside phone. "We now know," he said, "what the racket was. Quite an offbeat caper, but— I want Mr. Waltham, please."

"Oh? He may not be there, they had a wire from Mexico City—" Hackett explained that.

"Oh, really? Another little piece of the jigsaw," said Mendoza pleasedly. "Waltham? Come to Papa, friend, with some blank warrants. I'm about to talk to a couple of people you'll want to charge—it's out of my jurisdiction, a Federal offense. We've found out what the caper is—let's be honest, I've found out . . . They were running their own special branch of the Immigration Department —with their own regulations. Cash down."

An hour later, he faced those five across his desk. The Dvorzhaks were resolutely wooden-faced. Gloria and Cardenas were frankly nervous. Manton sat easily with one leg crossed over the other, smoking.

"So maybe I was a little slow getting onto it," said Mendoza, "and there was also, of course, Greta Krieger's flu. If she'd seen the picture in the paper sooner— But we've figured it out now. I've just got back from Vicksburg, by the way." Gloria uttered a little whimper. "I wonder how many you'd brought in, in twenty-one months? Like to tell me, Manton?"

"How many what?" asked Manton in a bored voice. Cardenas went a curious gray color.

"Aliens," said Mendoza. "People who for this reason and that weren't eligible for legal admittance to this country. When you come to think about it, there must be a good many like that— I know they've tightened the rules about it. I'd be interested to hear the exact details of how you worked it, and I know Mr. Waltham here—of the FBI— would be even more interested." He looked at Cardenas, hoping the man wasn't going to have a fit; he was clutching at his collar and whispering, "No—no—no—" in a frantic undertone.

Manton said, "D'you have any real proof of that, Lieutenant?" He sounded merely interested: a very tough young man indeed.

"I can deduce a number of details, of course," said Mendoza. "After seeing the terrain. You'll be telling us how you got into the business, and how you made arrangements to meet the—mmh—clients. Mr. Cardenas' sister, working in the Immigration Department, would know what immigrants had relatives and friends anxious to get here. Could introduce prospective customers. But when that was done, Valerie would hie herself over to Vicksburg, as the rock-hound Alice Roberts from Phoenix, and establish herself in that dreary little shack. She must have been damn bored, but I expect she consoled herself with visions of all that nice cash to come. I can see that there'd be a little uncertainty as to times. You couldn't keep as regular schedules as the commercial airlines. You might have engine trouble, the weather might be unfavorable—head winds—and so on. But eventually, you'd sit down alongside that hut—such a useful landmark—with your grateful client, and Valerie would take over. Because naturally you couldn't land openly back at International with passengers like that."

Gloria had gone green-white and had her eyes shut. The Dvorzhaks were impassive; Anya's eyes were grave on him. Cardenas now seemed to be praying.

"You make up fancy stories," said Manton, putting out his cigarette.

"And sometimes," Mendoza went on, "such as in the latest job you pulled, a couple of weeks ago, you'd sit down so late in the afternoon that it wouldn't look natural for Valerie to leave the Cassidy house that night. Hence the sleeping-bag in the shack. I expect a few of your clients had slept in more uncomfortable places. She'd pick them up next morning and ferry them over to their destinations. To the loving friends and relatives waiting—conveniently introduced by Mr. Cardenas, who would have learned names from his sister."

Cardenas said faintly, "No—oh, my God—"

"I might add," said Mendoza, "that there are a couple of Federal men now down in Puerto Peñasca poking around."

Manton sat up and after a moment laughed. It was a genuine amused laugh; he looked at Mendoza, at Waltham, and his reckless brows seemed to tilt devilishly. "Well, that does it. *Finis. Terminar.* O.K., you got us. I'll tell you all about it—"

"*Please*—" wailed Gloria. "Please, Mr. Manton—"

"Don't be stupid," said Manton. "As soon as they get to that *zafio* Pedro Estéban he'll come apart in their hands. Or somebody—the whole place knows about it. It'll all have to come out now and they may as well get a straight version. We've had the hell of a good run, and"—he grinned at Mendoza—"I've got nothing on my conscience, *amigo.* If you know what I mean. Except Thorwald, of course," he added thoughtfully. "But how the hell were we to know who he was? And by what I've seen in a couple of press stories, I don't figure Thorwald had any nefarious plans. Just homesick."

"Paul—" moaned Cardenas. Gloria just leaned back in her chair and shut her eyes.

"How did the business get started?" asked Mendoza interestedly.

"Well—" Manton glanced at Gloria. "Sorry, honey, but they won't be fobbed off with a fib, and tell you the truth I can't think of a plausible one on the spur of the moment." He lit a new cigarette. "It wasn't Gloria's idea,

250

no, but it was her aunt. Older sister of her father's, got out of Poland into France and wanted to come here, but for some damn' fool technical reason she wasn't eligible."

"It wasn't fair," Gloria whispered miserably. "Honestly it wasn't fair— Daddy swore out an affidavit saying he'd be responsible and all, but it didn't make any difference, they said—"

"And she was moaning about it to Val, and Val thought of me." He laughed. "Said, suppose the woman got to Mexico somewhere, I could just fly down and pick her up, couldn't I? And probably the Litvaks would pay a lot—"

"Well, I don't suppose it was just as simple as that," said Mendoza. "Mr. Cardenas, would you like a doctor?"

"No—no," moaned Cardenas. "My job—I'll be *ruined* —and Maria—fired—go to jail—"

"Hell, you both knew what you were risking," said Manton contemptuously. "You ought to have enough socked away to make up for it . . . No, of course it wasn't that simple. I had to work it all out well in advance, sure —everything arranged for."

"I had an idea you masterminded it," said Mendoza.

"And I'd do it again tomorrow," said Manton. "I don't know if you know Mexico, Lieutenant . . . No? The little places—like Puerto Peñasca—miles from any kind of town. I happened to know that one because I'd been down that way fishing a lot of times. About two hundred people, in the village and scattered back in the hills—mostly full-blooded Indian—people, kids, and pigs all in one-room shacks—the little weedy gardens with corn planted and not much else—nobody in the place's ever seen electric light or more than one or two cars—don't quite

251

believe in 'em. Priest the only official authority within a couple of hundred miles—nearest city of any size, Chihuahua, three hundred-odd miles across wild country . . . You get the picture?" He drew strongly on his cigarette. "Well, I happened to know the place. A very handy spot to operate from, because it's only about a hundred miles below the Arizona border. I went down and—fixed things up. With Pete Estéban. He's a good-natured—"

"*Zafio*," said Mendoza with a smile as Manton hesitated.

"Lout," translated Manton, grinning. "Fishes a little for a living, lets his wife do all the work on the land, plays a mean guitar, and thinks all this talk about a village school is *muy absurdo*. Nine kids."

"*¡Qué hombre!*"

"So I said to Pete, listen, *hermano*— Well, it doesn't matter what I said, upshot is he agreed to look after the clients there—overnight usually—for a little cash in hand. Nobody'd take much notice, except of the hired car coming in. The whole place'd know about it, as I said, but nobody in Puerto Peñasca knows much about *norteamericano* laws—or cares. Priest's a fat old half-Indian going around in a dream, not often out of the church. Easy enough to keep him from knowing. When I landed, I was just flying around on a little scenic tour and had engine trouble. You know? And then I went down to Mexico and fixed things with a friend of mine there."

"Mexico City?" asked Waltham.

"That's what I said. He agreed to take charge of 'em there and get 'em up to Chihuahua—nearest taking-off spot for the Gulf country—and tell 'em where to hire the car and so on."

"Name, Mr. Manton?"

"Uh-uh," said Manton, smiling. "You know about Ricardo and his sister being in it, and I don't suppose you'll come down too heavy on Gloria. But I don't spill on pals, *amigo*. Leave him be."

"Well," said Mendoza mildly, lighting a cigarette, "I don't flatter myself that I'm better than the Communists at persuading you to talk. *Sigue*."

"After I set it up, we got going. It went smooth as cream, even the first time . . . For God's sake, Ricardo, can't you get it through your head they were bound to find out anyway? You came in with your eyes open, for the long green—"

"Which you didn't altogether," said Mendoza.

Manton looked at him thoughtfully. "Perspicacious," he said. "No, Lieutenant. You're perfectly right there. Val was only interested in the cash too . . . Even that first time, it went like silk. Val was the go-between, as you deduced. Nobody except Gloria ever knew about me—Val let that out to her. Never mind. I told her what to tell the Litvaks. Get the client to Mexico. They have the hell of a lot less strict laws about who gets in, see. Well, the Litvaks got the money together somehow—"

"Daddy m-mortgaged the house," murmured Gloria pallidly.

"And got her there. My boy saw her up to where I could pick her up, no questions asked. I'd made a reconnaissance tour over in Arizona, looking for a nice lonely rendezvous, and found that shack. It was a handy spot." He grinned reminiscently. "How damn bored Val got! She complained like hell—about the heat, about the boots and the rattlers and everything else—but she went. For the long green. You figured out that bit just fine, Lieutenant."

253

"Oh, God," said Cardenas. "My *reputation*—Maria—"

"It went so smooth, we got to thinking, maybe there's other people with friends and relatives like that—and Val had heard Gloria talk about Ricardo here, who was a cust— a friend of hers—"

"That's right!" said Cardenas bitterly. "Blacken my name every way possible! Really—"

"Oh, for God's sake," said Manton, "be your age, man! You can see—"

"Oh, yes, in an ideal position to give you names of possible clients," said Mendoza. "His sister would know of recent and not-so-recent immigrants who had the friends and relatives wanting to come here, barred for this reason or that. They'd be asking her advice—"

"That's the idea. Val sounded him out on it, and I may say," said Manton, looking amused, "that he jumped at it." Cardenas moaned some more. "You'll gather that I've known Val a good deal longer than I admitted, but I did meet her through Maureén, the way I told you. Just to get all the facts clear. I assure you, strictly business. She was built that way."

"So I gather. She was the go-between who made the actual contacts and collected the money. Mr. Cardenas, hearing that the Glessners or the Vardases had a cousin or sister or old mother panting to enter our portals and unable to, would pass the name on to Valerie. And she set up the bargain. Set rate?"

"What the traffic would bear at first. Since we're letting our hair down, we did a couple of cut-rate ones because I was sorry for the clients. Val and Ricardo set a minimum price—five G's. I argued them into doing a couple cheaper, by not taking a cut myself. We split even three ways

254

usually, and I paid my boy in Mexico out of my cut, and Pete—that was the agreement."

"How the hell did you come by Thorwald?" asked Waltham suddenly.

Manton laughed. "Pure accident," he said. "How could we know? I deduce he had ceased to be all palsy-walsy with his Red comrades, or he'd have been slipped across the border by the brotherhood. As it was, he ran across my agent in Mexico—said he'd been hunting for a deal like that for weeks, did my boy know where he could get fixed up? Well, naturally it looked like extra gravy. We set it up —that was the latest job. Two weeks ago today, Val and I both took off. I got down to Puerto Peñasca about dusk on Wednesday—call it four hundred miles from L.A. He was already there. He didn't say much about himself, put on an East European accent—obviously, looking back, to forestall any awkward questions about a hundred per cent American who had to sneak back home. I figured to take off next morning, but the damn ignition was acting up and I had to do some work on it. We didn't get airborne until three o'clock, and it was getting on for six when I landed by the shack. Too late for Val to start back with him that night, so he stayed in the shack and she picked him up on Friday morning, drove him up to L.A.—he said that was O.K. with him, anywhere."

"And he bought her that bottle of Madeira as a little thank-you present?"

"That's right. Insisted on coming in with her and drinking her health. Filthy stuff, she said. God, what a sweat we got into when that broke—Thorwald! My God, if I'd known who it was—! But of course that was our only connection with him. You can see—"

255

"Yes. And I'd make a guess that your meetings in Valerie's apartment were to discuss the fees, new jobs?"

"Hagglers," said Manton darkly. "Ricardo would know the financial circumstances, more or less, from his sister. Bloodsuckers. People having to raise the money by borrowing—taking the second mortgage—any way. Sure. We'd just lately been noticing how hawk-eyed the landlady was."

"There was one Wilanowski—"

Manton threw his head back and laughed. "By God, I admired that old boy! Canny old bastard. We'd been—or Val had been—all innocently collecting on delivery, so to speak. When she went to collect from that one, he just said calmly, Nothing doing. The—er—client was in the country, and we couldn't speak up without denouncing ourselves, so we could whistle for the money. God, Val was mad! Tossed a bottle of Four Roses at me because I laughed. Mercenary little bitch. After that she made a rule —cash in advance."

"Yes. Well, now, let's have some names," said Mendoza. "I'm sure Mr. Waltham's itching to hear some names. We start with Miss Litvak's aunt. And—?"

Manton sat back and lit a new cigarette from the stub of the old one. "*Terminar*, Lieutenant," he said. "No names. Not from me. You said I wasn't in this just for the long green—too right, as our Aussie friends say. Sure, we've got to have rules, but rules have a way of not allowing for human nature. I'll tell you this much. Six of those poor devils I ferried in were ineligible to come in the legit way because they'd served prison terms. Now that sounds reasonable enough, doesn't it?—keeping out the crooks. Only, what had they served terms for? Four of 'em for stealing food when they were starving, and the other two for inciting to riot against the Reds. Hardly pros, Lieutenant. But then I never was much of a man to go by the rules."

The girl Anya Dvorzhak broke her long silence. "You are a good man," she said quietly.

Manton looked more upset by that than anything that had been said before; he flushed, angrily embarrassed. "Well, hell," he said. "Those poor devils—"

"Did it ever occur to you," asked Waltham, looking very angry himself, "that you were maybe ferrying in secret agents? People actively dangerous to—"

Manton faced him, still flushed, and his heavy brows twisted to a frown. "No, it did not," he said coolly. "I've seen the comrades close to, sir. They've got their own routes and their own channels. Obviously. Any time they want to slip a man over the border, they don't leave it to chance he'll find a couple of amateurs running a ferry service."

Which was absolutely true, of course.

Manton turned on Cardenas savagely. "And you'll damn well keep quiet on any names too, you coward. Or you'll regret it, by God. I'm not going to give those poor bastards away now. Reasons!" he said to Mendoza. "Piddling little technical reasons. He's a stateless citizen, so he isn't eligible under any quota. She was once a member of the Nazi party. Who the hell in Germany didn't support the Nazis, if they wanted to go on living at home, running a business, keeping a job, Reasons! It was like—" He swung toward the Dvorzhaks, and shut up, and stabbed out his cigarette.

"Yes. I think Valerie was just setting up a job for you?" Mendoza looked at them.

They had listened to all this in silence, unexpressive. Now Jan Dvorzhak shrugged and spread his hands. "Since you know so much—" he said. His eyes were sad. "It was a last resort. We do not want to break the law. This country has been very kind to us. And I had foresight, I managed to bring away the jewels, so we are not poor. But—"

"I will tell him," said the girl gravely. "It is my cousin, Marya. She is in Austria, she has got there safe, and she wishes to come to us. But there is a history of—of the tubercular, you understand, and they say she is not allowed to come in. It is—" She swallowed nervously, and the pilot uttered a rude word.

"Excuse me, but it's— What the *hell?* So they send her money to go to a sanitarium in Switzerland—*and* get charged for converting the damn check into francs or whatever! Instead of—and not everybody's got the money to spare—"

"It is not of the contagious type," the girl went on. "And we only wish to bring her here, to have her in a hospital perhaps on the desert where they say she will recover. It is not certain, in Switzerland. It—it does not seem fair—"

"Fair!" said Manton contemptuously. "It's damn nonsense." He looked at Mendoza and Waltham. "Everybody I ferried in was like that. Technical reasons, my God. And there were a lot more I wanted to bring in, but Val and Ricardo quashed it—the loving relatives couldn't raise enough cash. And I couldn't do it alone."

"Mr. Cardenas put you in touch with Valerie Ellis?" asked Mendoza of Anya.

"Yes, that is so. I must tell you, I see. It was a lie that I met her at that shop. And I did not much like her. She was—hard. But she said she would make the arrange-

258

ments. We must send money for Marya to come to Mexico City, first. And then—"

"And then," said Mendoza gently, "Valerie was found dead, and you didn't know what to do. You went back to Mr. Cardenas, but I think he refused to help you—yes, he'd have been extremely nervous, especially when Thorwald entered the picture—"

Manton laughed. "Like hell!"

"—And so you went to see Gloria, who was mentioned in the papers as a close friend of Valerie's—"

"She told me of Mr. Manton, though she was frightened," said Anya. "I went to see him, and he said now it must be postponed for a while, because of the murder— he did not know anything about the murder, believe me, sir! None of us knew anything about that—but—" She stopped.

"And now postponed a while longer," said Manton. He smiled at Mendoza, and a teasing devil lurked in his eyes. "Damn it, when I think of that two hundred and fifty bucks I wasted on a phonograph and all those records, just to back up an artistic story—! How long d'you figure I'll get, Lieutenant?"

"I'm not up on Federal terms," said Mendoza. "I'd guess maybe a one-to-three."

Manton nodded. "Worth it," he said. "What the hell? Might be an interesting experience at that." He cast a glance at Cardenas, who had more or less collapsed, and grinned cheerfully at Anya. "Tell you what," he said. "You get Marya into Mexico—they've got some good sanitariums there, you know—and as soon as I get out we'll ferry her in past some other border. Texas or Louisiana, where they haven't got such smart-boy cops."

Two large tears started slowly down Anya's cheeks.

"You are a very good man. I am so sorry you must go to prison. You—"

"Hey, now," said Manton. "Not to make any fuss. I walked into it, and I'd walk into it again. Only next time," he added to Mendoza, "maybe with different accomplices. If you get me."

"I do. Miss Dvorzhak, I don't think the FBI's so vindictive they'll be prosecuting you for anything—you're both free to go."

Waltham nodded shortly; they got up hesitantly. She went to the pilot, touched his shoulder shyly.

"I will think of you often, Mr. Manton. I thank you for your kindness. I—I will pray for you."

"Good God, girl, it's not as bad as that," said Manton. "Way the deal came out, that's all. Don't worry about me . . . You might write me a nice sympathetic letter or two while I'm inside. Just to bolster my prestige, you know—let the other fellows know I've got friends. Nobody else to do it."

"I will write you letters," she said. "Yes, Mr. Manton."

"Anya, come away," and her father urged her out gently.

"Nice girl," said Manton to nobody in particular. "But where do you go from here, Lieutenant? O.K., you've caught us—you know about the extracurricular exercise. I assure you, neither Ricardo nor I murdered Val. That really caught us with our—well, came as a big surprise. Quite a little shock . . . Now listen to this. The last time I saw Val was about six o'clock that Thursday evening— two weeks ago tomorrow—when I landed Thorwald there. He paid off like a good boy, right there, and I took my cut then. He'd changed a wad into American currency in

260

Mexico. I wasn't expecting to hear from her on the Dvorzhak deal until they'd got the girl to Mexico, so I wasn't surprised at not hearing from her, after she called to say she'd dumped Thorwald—of course we didn't know who he was then. Outside the racket, we didn't pal around any. When I saw that item on Wednesday night, body identified as Valerie Ellis, *hermano*, I got butterflies. But that's the whole story . . . I understand Ricardo's got a nice watertight alibi. Well, I really was over at Vegas, way I told you, that Sunday and Monday. If you want to know the main reason, I'm a man believes in clichés, from experience—you have a close call, best thing you can do is get right back in the air again or maybe you'll get windy. That damn tank springing a leak, just after I'd handed Thorwald over and started home— So, I'd taken Wednesday to Friday off, my bosses get used to that. I had my regular days off coming—Sunday and Monday. I really did fly over to Vegas, and get in a couple of hot games. I guess if you really looked, you could prove it—some of the house attendants might remember me."

"I wouldn't be surprised," said Mendoza. He found he liked Paul Manton, and in private sympathized with him.

"Who in hell killed her? And why the hell? It wasn't anything to do with all this. You do believe that?" For once Manton was earnest. "I just can't figure it. I didn't believe it, at first. That it could be Val, I mean. So far as I know, she wasn't mixed up with any characters who'd— Hell, she was greedy, she was like a kid—immature, grabbing at life, but—any reason to *murder* her I can't see—"

"It's still a little problem," said Mendoza meditatively. "So it is."

Nineteen

"Mrs. Dasher?" he said to Palliser. "That's a new thought all right." Palliser had poured it all out to him as soon as they were alone. The hush-money sent in typewritten envelopes from the central station: the curious reticence of Gertrude Dasher: the Fuller Brush man who'd had no response to his ring at her door, at about noon that day.

"She *could* have been out, but the Flesches didn't see her go past and Mrs. Flesch had been in the living-room all morning where she would have seen her. And the times check—the time of that anonymous call, and then it was just six years ago that—"

"It's too far out," said Hackett. "We don't have one thing that says Dasher made that call."

"No," agreed Mendoza, "we haven't . . . So we start out on Valerie all over again, from scratch. Let's not miss any bets, however wild they may look. Damn it, now this little ride on the merry-go-round is over, we've got even fewer places to look than we had before! Cross out Manton, Cardenas, and her girl friends—no reason to want Valerie dead. Any of the people she knew, no apparent

262

reason. Yes, we've been led up the garden path in more ways than one, but none of that had anything to do with the murder . . . Mrs. Mandelbaum, for instance. She never knew her, Cardenas just wanted a back-up on a plausible tale of how he'd met Valerie. Probably Mrs. Mandelbaum once bought a job from them. Quite possibly the young Hausners ditto. Yes, well, leave all that to the Feds. Maybe Cardenas' records will give them some leads, where to look. I'm not wishing them luck on it—I'm with Manton, leave the poor devils alone. But we can cross all that out. I had a hunch from the start that the motive for the murder didn't tie up to the racket."

"That's for sure now," said Hackett. "I don't see anything that ties up at all."

"Well, there's one indicated place to look." Mendoza passed a hand across his face; he was tired. "But I can't see any possible reason there, either. It just doesn't make sense. And as for your time periods," he added to Palliser, "Mrs. Dasher starting to get her hush-money six years ago when the anonymous caller says 'they' murdered a woman — Well, my God, a lot of things happened six years ago, John. They don't all necessarily link up. It was six years ago they found out about Osgar Thorwald's treason. Quite a few people got themselves murdered that year. I forget who won the Kentucky Derby, but I do remember that a minor miracle happened and a pro football player took a blonde away from me. There was a summit meeting . . . There's nothing to say this is anything but a wild idea."

"I *know*," said Palliser, goaded. "But the times convince me of it. Damn it, if she hadn't been so secretive!

263

I don't even know who she was working for when she supposedly got the legacy—"

"You should be able to unearth that," said Mendoza, "from the banks. An employer would have paid her by check. Even if she didn't have a bank account somewhere then, those checks made out to her would duly wend their way homeward and get microfilmed."

"I know, I've got inquiries out to every bank in the county on it. But it'll take time. Either she never had a bank account before she opened this one—I haven't found one yet—or she closed it out and opened another at this bank with the first payment of blackmail money. That was on March third, 1958. She probably wasn't earning anything like five hundred a month before, she may never have bothered with an account. Husband didn't leave her anything but the house and enough insurance to bury him. And when we do turn up whoever she was working for then, well, whatever she was getting the blackmail money for might not have had one damn thing to do with them. Why should it? It might have been something she saw or heard somewhere else. But all the same, I'm looking— I've got a hunch—"

"Yes," said Mendoza. The more he looked at the Ellis case as it now stood, stripped bare of suspects or clues, the more irritated he felt. And this Dasher thing was just such another one. If she'd even kept one of the envelopes, so they had a sample from the typewriter! He said irrelevantly, "Valerie was a lot shrewder than her uncle thought. She was living in the cheap apartment so as not to attract the attention of the revenuers. Ditto the deposit box in a false name. All tax-free . . . What a mess *that's* going to be to untangle. Rather the Feds than me . . . Of course there is just one other small thing, John, that in a nebulous way could be a little link."

"What?"

"That postmark," said Mendoza through a yawn. "This is the twelfth of February. Valerie was murdered a week ago Sunday, the third. And somebody, being foiled by Mrs. Montague from staging a fake suicide in Valerie's apartment, instead stashed the body in that schoolyard, with the help of that mechanical monster. Whoever did that had to know the monster was there to be used. That men were working there along Garey Street. Well, they'd been there all that week, and whoever went down to the central post office, on Friday the first, to mail Mrs. Dasher's hush-money, might have noticed that. It's roughly the same neighborhood. Of course Garey isn't a main drag— it's two blocks up from the nearest main drag, Alameda— the street the post office is on. But they're short blocks. He could have noticed those big yellow machines up there at the corner. It's just a thought."

Hackett made a derisive sound. "Talk about reaching!"

"On a thing like this you've got to reach, in all directions," said Mendoza. "My God, I'm tired . . . Every little smell of a lead we thought we had just melting away. That visitor she was expecting on Tuesday, when Gloria and Mrs. Ellis came to call—of course it was Manton, telling her they'd start the newest job next day . . . At the moment, I don't see anything at all to do on Valerie. Nowhere to go and look. Except, of course— But what the hell could *they* have to do with it?"

"I kind of like that idea," said Palliser, still thinking of Mrs. Dasher. "Whoever mailed that letter could have done just that. And if he knew that school was there— Well,

265

in a way that rather cancels out my idea about whoever was employing her at the time being involved."

"Why?" asked Hackett.

"Neighborhoods," said Palliser. "Money. She was working for people, then, who could afford to hire baby nurses. That wouldn't be anybody who'd know Garey Street—not the best part of town, down there."

"Very nice deducing," said Mendoza somnolently. He reflected irrelevantly that nursemaids had been a recurring theme through both of these recent cases, the time they'd been working them . . . A tune started running aimlessly through his mind, Little Buttercup's song from *Pinafore* . . . They'd gone to see that British company on tour: a very good company . . . *A long concealéd crime I would confess* . . . "Because they murdered that woman six years ago—" Yes? Anything to do with it? Not a crank or a nut?

"Some bank will come through eventually," Palliser was saying. "But it isn't likely that whoever was employing her then—if they weren't involved in the blackmail—would know much more about her when even her closest friend—"

A-many years ago, When I was young and charming, As some of you may know, I practiced baby-farming . . .

"I still say—" said Hackett.

Two tender babes I nussed, One was of low condition—

"All right, I'll bet you," said Palliser excitedly. "I tell you, I've got a hunch—I'll lay you ten to one on it—" It must be the hell of a strong hunch; Palliser wasn't a gambling man as a rule.

"In dollars," said Hackett. "I'll take you. Of all the wild ideas—"

266

Oh, bitter is my cup! However could I do it? I mixed those children up—

Mendoza shook his head at himself and got up. "I'm getting old, boys," he said. "Ever since those twin monsters came home from the hospital, I've been aging rapidly. I won't be fit to do any thinking until I've had a nap. I'm going home for a while."

He heard the woman's voice as he came down the hall, having left the Ferrari in the drive. The Highland burr that was oddly soft and harsh at once, curiously attractive.

"But that's Caithness folk for you—or any of us Highland folk maybe—never like to be beholden to any. A Weir, you say you were? That'd be a sept to any of three clans—Buchanan, or MacFarlane, or MacNaughton. My grandda himself was a MacNaughton . . . Ah, no, *mo croidhe*, we mustn't be pulling the pretty cat's tail."

"So maybe we're related." Alison's voice sounded as if she were smiling.

"Very likely then. All the Scots and Irish are seventh cousins or around there, the countries being small."

Mendoza stopped on the threshold. The twins were having their exercise in the middle of the living-room floor, and Alison and Mrs. MacTaggart were sitting on the sectional with cups of coffee.

"Luis! You're back—" She scrambled up and came to him. "*Amado* . . . she's a dear, do like her." That in a whisper. "And the new chair's come, and— Did you have a nice trip over to the desert? You look—" She swung him around to be introduced.

"And you'll be the lieutenant I've been hearing about." Mrs. MacTaggart gave him a nice smile, holding out her

267

hand. "Now don't worrit the man with the new chair, *agradh*— Tired to death he looks, with catching murderers and all, and I never knew an honest man yet that was just so interested in the furniture. You look to me, sir, like a man needs to sit and relax maybe over a drop or two of good whiskey with not that much water to it."

"I see you're an addition to the household," said Mendoza, "a woman with so many of the right ideas! Barring the water. You heard what the woman said, *querida*—humor me. And not, Mrs. MacTaggart, catching murderers. Unfortunately. I'm stuck but very tight on this one, damn it." He sank down on the sectional and looked at the twins. "You really don't mind looking after these little devils?"

She twinkled at him. "You came to it late or you'd be boasting the roof down on them. Isn't young Johnny like you, now, barring his mother's eyes! I'll get you your drink, sir, that Bertha's busy over the stew." El Señor went out after her, hopefully.

"Isn't she a dear?"

"*Definido*—very nice woman . . . Either I'm losing my touch or this case is insoluble. All even higher up in the air than it was," and he brought her up to date on it. "Tell me where to go, what to look for!"

"Yes, I see," said Alison. "I'm sorry for Manton—I rather agree with him."

"So do I, but that's the Feds' headache. Damn it!" He got up and began to pace, automatically avoiding the squirming twins and the cats. "I'm thinking now about Eddy Warren. Funny little man, but he is a pro. If he's peddling reefers he may be tied up to somebody who's peddling H. And he was storing his stuff in her apart-

268

ment. If she found out a little too much— No, not Eddy, but one of his tougher pals. The only thing is, would anybody like that do it that way? Sleeping-pills—*¡pues no!*"

Mrs. MacTaggart came back with his two ounces of rye in a jigger glass. "That cat, for all what you call him, maybe some Irish ancestors he had, liking the rye too. Here you are, sir. For all of that, you're always reading about the Spaniards being wine drinkers."

Mendoza laughed. "If we looked back, without much doubt we'd find other blood in me—those crafty old Aztecs. As far as that goes, I'm told it's a Basque name, not Spanish, and nobody knows where they came from. Thanks." He swallowed the rye. "I needed that."

"Well, now," she said interestedly, "is that so? My father was a great student of history, as it happens. Maybe that's so, but the historians make some guesses as to where those Basque folk went, you know, sir. What else does research tell them but that those Danaan folk that went to Ireland to rule the place, all that time back, they came over the sea from the Iberian shore? Basque or Spanish they were, no doubt."

"You don't say," said Mendoza. "So there, my love, not so strange a combination at all. Some of my ancestors were probably your mother's too." He made Mrs. Mac-Taggart a bow and she laughed.

"*An Fhir!* And now it is time these two were in their beds and you two having a bit privacy and comfort." She picked up Master John and went off.

"You can see," said Mendoza, "just how damned up in the air it is. Aside from the people connected with that caper, who did she know? People like Maureen Mosko-

269

vitch, Eddy Warren. And also, everybody she knew might not have got into that address book. No way of telling. The snag I keep running into is the method—those sleeping-pills . . . Damn it, could it have been an accident, somehow? And somebody panicking when she passed out and—"

Mrs. MacTaggart came back and picked up Miss Teresa.

"No, by God!" said Mendoza. "It was a deliberate kill—I swear it was—a personal kill. It had to be. Bainbridge said at least ten capsules. Probably in a drink of some kind . . . It's natural enough nobody would have heard about it, I can see that—if she'd unexpectedly come across something that was—mmh—usable for blackmail, she wouldn't have confided in her erstwhile accomplices on the other thing. Not Valerie. She'd want all the profit for herself . . . Of course there's one obvious place to look, but I just don't see how they could tie up—"

"Where? I don't see."

"You disappoint me. That last notation in her address book. The Farlows. We said, before we knew what her racket was, maybe she'd seen the Farlows as new marks, and scribbled down those triumphant exclamation points for that reason. But now we know what the racket was, and it's unlikely that the Farlows have any anxious relatives abroad. Why was she so interested in the Farlows?"

"Oh, yes, I see," said Alison. "But, Luis—"

"I know, I don't see anything there either. The background looks very straightforward. Of course there's the money—all that Eininger money—and Valerie—"

"Excuse me," said Mrs. MacTaggart interestedly. She had come back for the blankets and toys, and straightened now with an armful of them. "I couldna help hearing the name. Would that be the Mr. Thomas Eininger that lived down in Bel-Air?"

"It would," said Mendoza, turning to look at her. "Why?"

"I was only interested because I looked after that baby when they were only just home from the hospital. A matter of a month I was with them, young Mrs. Eininger and the little boy. It was the first place I had after I came here, I was still that homesick, I remember. Not that I'm not that yet, whiles, for my own Kildonan and Ben Grian Mór on the horizon . . . But naturally I remember. And later on, I was reading about the terrible accident, with the boat he had, and both of them drowned dead. Nice folk they were—and the poor little baby."

"Why poor?" asked Alison. "I thought you said—"

"Well, of course in a way 'twas lucky it was a boy. A boy doesna think so much of such things. A fine healthy baby all other ways. The birthmark, it was."

"A birthmark," said Mendoza softly. "A—noticeable one?"

"Aye, you would say so. Lucky indeed, a boy, and so I said to Mrs. Eininger—a nice young thing she was, the husband older but a fine upstanding man for all that. A deal of foolish talk over what causes such things, marking and so on— I said, you just thank God the boy's strong and healthy. What they call a port-wine mark it was, spread all over his right shoulder and little back—and some marks they can do these grafts on, and take away, but not that kind—"

"¡Porvida!" said Mendoza in a near-whisper. "¡Qué casualidad—con qué esas tenemos! Talk about coincidence—if that stray tom hadn't jumped El Señor—if you

271

hadn't— For the love of God. I will be damned. I will be—"

"Luis, what on earth—"

But Mendoza was catching up on his jigsaw puzzle. "Mrs. Dasher," he said raptly. "Oh, yes, of course—of course. She must have been— Perfectly natural. And that woman—inexperienced with babies, maybe? Yes. He'd have been, what, two, three? Nearer three . . . Six years ago. Six years ago. And the will—all that nice money . . . But where did they—how could they—" He stood staring into space blankly, and then he said in a triumphant shout, "*Marion Keller!* But what the hell was the name she said?"

They were both staring at him as if he'd gone mad. He laughed. All his tiredness dropped away from him; there was work to do. He swung Mrs. MacTaggart off her feet and kissed her on both cheeks. "Up the MacTaggarts!" he said. "You've just solved both mysterious cases for us!" He ran for the phone.

"Well, indeed!" said Mrs. MacTaggart. "Isn't it the bold man then!"

"I beg your pardon?" said Marion Keller, sounding bewildered.

"The name you said—that woman Valerie had a crush on—"

"Oh. Yes. It was Pitman—Nan Pitman . . . Yes, on the same street. I don't remember the exact address, I'm sorry . . . Who? Oh, the— Yes, of course I remember them on account of the yachting accident . . . Yes, it was the house on the corner of Bellaggio Road and Copa de Oro. Why? I don't— What? . . . Why, yes, I seem to remember that Mrs. Ellis knew them fairly well."

"Thank you very much," said Mendoza fervently, hung up and immediately dialed again.

"Broken?" said Palliser. "What d'you mean, b— Who's this Pitman?"

"Try the *Times* morgue. Snap into it! All they've got on it. It was evidently put down to accident. I don't know the exact date, but it'll be early in 1958. Probably not long before Mrs. Dasher opened that bank account. Get a search warrant for the Farlow house, *pronto*. I'll be down to get it and go up there with a couple of the boys. I don't expect we'll find any incriminating evidence left lying around, but you never know—there was Valerie's handbag, and all that stuff from Mrs. Dasher's house— And I want to talk to that cook or maid or whatever she is— I'll bet if she does live in, she's off on Sundays . . . My God, offbeat you can say, but we've got there now— And, John!"

"Yes?"

"Before you do anything else, you collect that ten bucks from Art!" He hung up on Palliser's puzzled voice, did some more dialing.

"Waltham? Mendoza. I know you've quit looking into backgrounds, but while you were still looking, did you get any more on Jack Farlow?"

"Farlow?" said Waltham blankly. "Oh, that one. Well, let's see . . . That's kind of old stuff, with all this new line to work we've— Hang on a minute . . ." More than a minute, and a vast rustling of papers. Waltham came back on the line finally. "Hello? There's odds and ends

273

here, that's all. Not much. He played pro football a while. He's a native Californian. He's—"

"Where was he born, do you know? Parents?"

"L.A.," said Waltham. "May twelfth, 1916. Father was a carpenter—they lived down on Fourth Street then, if that means anything."

"Oh, very pretty," crooned Mendoza. Fourth Street was only a few blocks from Garey Street. "And?"

"Well, odds and ends . . . You sound a little excited."

"With reason," said Mendoza. "What kind of jobs did he hold before he married Grace Eininger, the millionaire's sister?"

"A good many, as far as we looked. Lifeguard, swimming teacher—he worked for the city a while—"

"He worked for the city a while," repeated Mendoza dreamily. "How nice. For the department of whatever they call it—street repairs, water-main repairs?"

"It just says here, the city," said Waltham. "Why?"

"He belongs," said Mendoza, "to an organization called Americans All. Do you know anything about it?"

Waltham made a disgusted noise. "That. Sure, we keep an eye on it. Just a casual eye, you know. Bunch of fanatic crackpots. They're agin a lot of things, but mostly it's on the religious basis. Mainly they're anti-Catholic. They don't like Jews either, or in fact anybody who isn't a hundred per cent white Protestant—they've put out some nasty brochures about Orientals and Negroes, as well as a lot more stuff about the proverbial Jewish conspiracy—but mainly they agitate about the Catholic Menace. Why? Have you—"

"That makes me very happy," said Mendoza. "I see. At

274

least I begin to see. A lot of things. Thanks very much." He put the phone down.

"Luis, what on earth— Do you know *who?*"

" 'A *long concealéd crime I would confess,'* " hummed Mendoza pleasedly. "And who would ever expect to find common-sense truth in Gilbert and Sullivan? Farce, in a way. My subconscious working overtime."

"Luis, if you don't tell me this minute—"

" '*Some day, no doubt, you'll rue it,'* " hummed Mendoza, " '*although no creature knew it, so many years ago!'* Always so satisfying to see things tidily cleared up . . ."

Twenty

Mendoza got back to the office just ahead of Palliser, who came in still looking puzzled. "Well, I think I've got what you wanted, but what possible connection— Here, I copied it down. No follow-up story. I chased Bert over to the coroners' office for the autopsy reports, I thought if you were interested—"

"Good boy." Mendoza took the folded sheet from him. From the *Times* of Friday morning, February 28, 1958.

"Mrs. Nancy Pitman, 29, and her two-and-a-half-year-old son Bobby both burned to death last night in an accidental fire which largely destroyed the guesthouse in which they were staying. The house was in the rear yard of a home on Cedarbrook Drive in Franklin Canyon, the property of Mr. and Mrs. Glen Hartfield, who are at present touring Europe. Mrs. Pitman, a friend of Mrs. Hartfield's, had been occupying the guesthouse since her recent divorce.

"Owing to the secluded position of the property, the fire was not seen and reported until it had nearly consumed the building. Sheriff's officers believe that Mrs. Pitman had been drinking heavily and started the fire accidentally, by dropping a cigarette or burning match.

"Her ex-husband, George Pitman, accountant, stated that he had called on her earlier in the evening and that she was then drinking. He had warned her to be careful.

"The bodies, all but destroyed by fire, were taken to the Hunter and Rose Funeral Home."

Mendoza sighed deeply and looked up. "I knew it," he said. "I knew it had to be that. And I don't suppose there'll ever be anything to say that that was murder—unless they come apart. The link—the missing link—was Bellaggio Road in Bel-Air."

"I don't get this," complained Hackett, taking the sheet from him.

"See if that search warrant's come through yet. I've got to call that lawyer, get details on that, and then let's get up to the house. I'll tell you about it on the way."

Grace and Jack Farlow came home at two-thirty, as Mendoza, Hackett, Palliser, and Landers were busy doing a thorough job on the house on Willoughby Drive. The maid, who had been dithering around asking agitated questions, flew to meet them.

"Oh, sir, oh, ma'am, I didn't know what to do—a warrant, they said, but I—"

"What the hell's all this?" asked Farlow. "What are you men doing here?"

Mendoza straightened from the contents of the top desk drawer in the living-room. "Welcome home," he said. "I'm glad to see you. I hoped you'd come in before the boy. So much better not to thrash all this out before him—though he'll have to know eventually."

277

"What do you want here?" Grace Farlow's voice went shrill with shock and alarm. "You get out of—" She stared at Palliser as he passed across the hall. "What right—"

"Search warrant, Mrs. Farlow. You thought you were so safe, didn't you? Everything taken care of—nobody suspecting anything." Mendoza smiled at her. "But murderers often get tripped up by the unexpected coincidence. The unforeseen witness."

"I don't know what you're talking about," she said furiously. He thought, looking at the vicious panic in her eyes, that she had been the brain and Farlow the brawn. The man's mind moved slower; he was panicky too, taken by surprise, but he just stood staring at them, waiting to take his cue from her. The maid began to cry nervously— a thin middle-aged woman.

"Let's not waste time," said Mendoza. "Come in and sit down. I can tell you the story almost without asking any questions."

"You've got the hell of a nerve," said Grace Farlow coldly, "walking in here like this." She came into the room. "Just what have you dreamed up, anyway?" Her long nose arched at him regally. Farlow followed her in.

"I think you're the one with the hell of a nerve," said Mendoza. "Sit down. It was quite a shock, wasn't it, when you found the boy was dead? One small thing I don't know is how, but maybe you'll tell me. You weren't very experienced at looking after small children—even when you'd been doing it for about nine months, since your brother and his wife had died. Were you? Died, leaving you and Mr. Harley Crawford, his attorney, co-trustees."

She went dead white, but said automatically, "I don't know what you—"

278

"How the hell did they find—" began Farlow in a rough bewildered tone.

"*Shut up!*" said the woman.

"Of course you only had to take care of Johnny Eininger on Mrs. Dasher's days off," said Mendoza. He could hear, they could all hear, the other men moving about the house. Landers came in and showed Mendoza a small plastic medicine bottle.

"Bathroom cabinet," he said laconically.

"Very nice. Without much doubt the same stuff found in Valerie. I see it's a prescription. Take it along."

"What the *hell?*" said Farlow. "What— I don't see—" He subsided, looking sullen, as she turned on him.

"It was disaster," said Mendoza, "for you. If the boy died while he was a minor, all that nice money went to various charities and you, as Thomas Eininger's sister, only got a lump sum of a hundred thousand. A nice piece of money, but nothing to live on the way you'd been living— the capital estate runs close to five million. As the boy's guardian, you—and Mr. Farlow—had been living very high indeed—Eininger's new house in Bel-Air, a car apiece, servants—the works. You were set for the rest of your lives, and with the boy looking on you as parents, naturally he'd go on seeing you had everything when he came into the money."

"You're just crazy! Where'd you get this lunatic idea, anyw—"

"I got it," said Mendoza gently, "from watching a ping-pong game, Mrs. Farlow. Last Monday afternoon. Incidentally, why was the boy out of school that day? Well?"

It was Farlow who said mechanically, "He had an appointment with the dent— Why the *hell?* I don't—"

"More coincidence," said Mendoza. "I got the idea, Mrs. Farlow, when I heard that the real Johnny Eininger had a rather noticeable birthmark. And the boy you're bringing up as Johnny Eininger hasn't."

"Crazy," she said contemptuously. "Don't you suppose, with all the money, we'd have had a thing like that rem—"

He laughed. "That particular kind of birthmark can't be removed, Mrs. Farlow . . . What happened? Did you let him drown in the bathtub while you answered the phone? Or maybe he got hold of some insect poison? Something like that. Anyway, it was disaster for you—the end of your high living." He looked at the man. "Mr. Farlow never earned much of a living, did he? You'd fallen into a soft place and now you were about to get tossed out of it.

"But only—when you came to think—for lack of a small boy between two and three. You think fast, and after finding he was definitely dead you thought about it before doing anything. It was Thursday, February twenty-seventh, 1958. Mrs. Dasher's day off. The maid's day off. You were alone in the house. You tried to think how you could conceal the death, get a substitute Johnny. It'd be a long gamble, but I think you're the kind prepared to take long gambles. And if any brawn was required, you had your husband handy."

The man was frightened—very frightened. He couldn't hide it. Alone, by now he'd be pouring out all sorts of self-incriminating statements, a tangle of silly lies; but her stronger will held him silent. But he couldn't hide the panic in his eyes.

"Well, you could conceal the body easily enough. A little boy not quite three years old isn't very big. The other problem was the tough one. You can't, these days, acquire a three-year-old child without leaving a lot of records behind. You can't steal one, to start a hue and cry—a three-year-old can talk, knows his own name. I don't know what wild ideas may have come to your mind before you thought of Nan Pitman. Who'd also lived on Bellaggio Road up to a while ago. Whom you knew—casually or quite well, Mrs. Farlow? I wonder. Nan Pitman and her little boy, not quite as old as Johnny but approximately that age. Nan Pitman was a gift from the gods, wasn't she? Living in that very secluded spot. Known lately to be hitting the bottle a little."

"Jesus," said Farlow. "Jesus, they know—" He looked around wildly.

"You set it up and your husband did the rough work. If she wasn't already passed out, gave her a little tap on the head. Passed the boy—Bobby Pitman—to you and put the body of Johnny Eininger in the house. Set the fire, carefully overturning an ash tray for the firemen to find. It was an easy job, wasn't it? A perfect setup for you. Sure enough, it was put down as accident, and I don't suppose there was enough left of the bodies to conduct autopsies on. And as for Bobby—well, a child that age might be difficult for a while, suddenly set down among strangers, called by a new name—but he'd be too young to know what had really happened, and he'd get used to being Johnny instead of Bobby. They say there's a block, don't they, at about the age of four, inhibiting the memory. There was, of course, the birthmark. But it was in a place normally covered by clothes, and no many people knew about it. It wasn't a thing Mrs. Eininger had boasted about. The nurse who'd come in when she was just back from the hospital knew—you didn't think of that, it was three years back and didn't matter. Mr. Crawford was merely your brother's attorney, not a personal friend, and didn't know about it. Of course, there was the baby's nurse, Mrs. Gertrude Dasher—"

"Oh, my *God*," said Farlow. "Grace—" He turned to her. She was staring remotely at the wall past Mendoza's shoulder, blank and white. She didn't move or speak.

"But you made a good plan about that too. Crawford tells me that you told him you'd decided to sell the Bel-Air house and move because the doctor said Johnny's sinus trouble would be better away from the sea breezes. The Einingers had lived in that house on Bellaggio Road for about four years—a few of the neighbors knew them. Maybe a few of the wives knew about that birthmark. Move away, among strangers, and be safe.

"And Gertrude Dasher, who knew about the birthmark —make an excuse to discharge her. Only that was easier said than done, wasn't it? She suspected something fishy, and she found out about the substitution. And she wasn't a fool—when she heard about the Pitman fire she added two and two quite easily. But she was willing to keep quiet for hush-money. You couldn't pay her a lump sum, but out of your very generous allowance from the estate you agreed to pay her five hundred a month."

Hackett came in with Palliser and showed Mendoza a wide old-fashioned gold bracelet. "John thinks that Mrs. Powell can identify it as Mrs. Dasher's."

"That's mine," said Grace Farlow. "You can't—"

Hackett looked at her. "Well, it was in Valerie Ellis's handbag," he said.

"*You can't prove—*"

"You overlooked a note that'd got pushed down in the

lining," said Hackett gently. "It starts out, Dear Val."

"Coincidence," said Mendoza, "played such a large part here. What a windfall. Isn't this nice. Awkward things to get rid of, that stuff from Mrs. Dasher's house. There's central heating, no convenient furnace. And they were so certain they'd never be remotely connected—and since they knew that Valerie had connected them by scribbling down the name and address, they'd be too scared we were keeping an eye out to try to dispose of it. Sit tight and take the gamble. Yes." He looked back at the Farlows.

"It worked out just fine for you—with the exception of Mrs. Dasher—for six years. You thought you were quite safe, it was all so long ago, nobody would ever suspect now. But there's a saying about the mills of the gods. There were still people around who knew about that birthmark. And Valerie Ellis happened to be one of them. Her mother had been friendly with Mrs. Eininger, had seen the birthmark and spoken of it—very likely Valerie had seen it too. It was just your bad luck that Valerie's latest unlawful occasions brought her to the house next door—that she saw you arriving home, and recognized you. And saw the pseudo Johnny with you—*without a shirt*. Isn't that so, Mrs. Farlow?"

It was the man who half whimpered, "Just been to his swimming lesson—oh, my God—Grace—"

"Valerie was no fool either. I don't suppose she'd thought about Johnny Eininger since she'd moved from Bel-Air, but when she recognized you she remembered that about him. She didn't know about the murder, but she did know this wasn't the real Johnny Eininger, and I think she tackled you about it right then. And you said, thinking fast, you'd have to discuss it with your hus-

283

band, and maybe made a date to meet the next day, Sunday. Didn't you? And the more you thought about it, the less you liked the idea of paying out more blackmail. I could guess how you set it up. You didn't want her seen coming to the house, so I think you met her somewhere else and drove her back here in your own car, straight down the drive to the kitchen door maybe . . . We needn't go into the details, they're obvious. No, Valerie didn't know you'd already done one murder, or she mightn't have accepted the offer of a drink so unsuspiciously."

Palliser reappeared, looking pleased. This time he had a plastic bag; he held it open for Mendoza to look. The real English silver set—teapot, sugar, and cream jug. "In an old trunk in the garage," he said. "Mrs. Powell can probably identify it for sure."

"Very nice," said Mendoza, and went on to the Farlows. "Only you forgot Mrs. Dasher. You forgot that Mrs. Dasher, who'd been—I think we'll find—taking care of Johnny Eininger since before the Einingers' fatal accident, knew who Mrs. Eininger's neighborhood friends were. Knew that one of them was Mrs. Ellis who had a daughter named Valerie . . . In a way, they both brought it on themselves—Valerie and Gertrude Dasher. If they hadn't been quite so fond of money— When Mrs. Dasher read in her paper that Valerie Ellis had been murdered, she wondered about it. She couldn't be sure, but I think she wondered. And I think she got you, Mr. Farlow, to come to see her on some pretext, and asked you a few questions. And— excuse me—not being very quick on the uptake, you gave it away somehow. That was on Friday morning about eleven-thirty, wasn't it? Yes. And she pressed you for more hush-money, and when you argued she called your bluff

284

by phoning us and started to tell the tale. She really should have known better. Because anyone who's already done two murders isn't going to worry much about a third one. You lost your temper, grabbed the phone away and hung it up, and hit her . . .

"And then, as you stood there with her body at your feet, the doorbell rang. Scared, weren't you? Grace not there to tell you what to do. But as you waited for whoever it was to go away, you got the idea—set it up to look like one of that series of rape-burglaries. You'd been prudent enough to leave your car down the street, come to the house on foot. With luck, you could slip off unnoticed— It wasn't a bad effort, Mr. Farlow. Only we're fairly bright these days . . . I'd take a private bet that Grace had told you off well and truly for being so clumsy about carrying out the bright notion for disposing of Valerie." He looked at the woman. "You should have gone with him," he said mockingly. "Mrs. Montague's sudden appearance wouldn't have rattled *you* into dropping the keys and running. You'd have thought of something. And you were quite bright in building that little plan—if Valerie had been found dead in bed, with an empty pill bottle beside her, we'd have written it off as suicide or accident. You show quite a talent for crime, Mrs. Farlow."

She didn't move or speak for a long moment, and then she began cursing him in a low voice, obscene and vicious.

"You lost the gamble in the end," said Mendoza, "as so often happens, because you had a stupid accomplice. We've got some nice solid evidence and we'll get more." He looked at Farlow. "I can even piece a little of that together. When the original plan was foiled, and you were left with the body still on your hands, for some reason—

285

just general hatred of Catholics, Farlow?—you decided to stash Valerie in that schoolyard. You'd noticed the machines there, on your way down to the central post office on the Friday before. And I think you'd once operated a machine like that and were familiar with—"

And Jack Farlow broke his silence to utter one fairly coherent remark. He sounded utterly bewildered and sincere.

He said, "Grace said I was a damn fool. But I thought sure it'd work. Why, hell, everybody knows how *they* do! All those priests and nuns carrying on, and they bury the babies all secret in the convent grounds—anybody knows anything about *them* knows— I thought they'd hush it up! Natural thing. Wouldn't want the church connected, so they'd get rid o' the body like they do and—"

The woman had started to hush him, and saw it was no use. She looked at Mendoza, and there was savage resignation, fear, and a kind of cynical humor in her eyes and her voice. "Aren't you right," she said flatly. "A real smart boy, the partner I picked. I asked him did he believe in fairies too. He just doesn't know from nothing. But it was too late then."

And in the little silence, the front door opened and the boy's clear voice called, "I'm home! Anybody here? Aunt Grace?"

"Mrs. MacTaggart was terribly shocked," said Alison, massaging cream from her face with Kleenex.

"And well she might be," said Mendoza.

"She thought about the little boy first, and I must say I do too. What'll happen to him?"

"Yes," said Mendoza, "a tragedy there. Hospital records

proved it, of course—he's the Pitman boy. Looks like a nice boy. His real father will get custody—a perfect stranger to him. But he's only nine, and maybe in time—"

Alison's tongue protruded pinkly as she rolled a few pin curls, sitting at the dressing-table. "Did you find out what happened to the real Johnny?"

"One of those unpreventable accidents. Farlow came apart, as I said. The real Johnny was trying to reach a plate of candy on the kitchen table, climbed up there, and fell off. Ordinarily, just a few bruises. But he evidently fell against the table leg at just the right angle to— Bainbridge said it was probably a skull fracture. He was dead when Grace picked him up."

"Poor little boy."

"The lawyer's having seven fits," said Mendoza. "Quite a legal mess to clear up."

"Yes. It's been a funny sort of case, hasn't it? Almost everything getting found out because of coincidences. It makes you think," said Alison, tying a gay blue scarf round the pin curls to match her blue waltz gown. "Like fate— or Nemesis, for the Farlows. All coming back to Mrs. MacTaggart in the end. Because you didn't have any idea where else to look, did you?"

"Certainly I did," said Mendoza. He was sitting up in bed smoking; El Señor sat on his lap and batted at the smoke as it rose, and Bast was established on the foot of the bed washing herself, while Nefertiti and Sheba wrestled with a catnip mouse on the floor. "I'd have looked at the Farlows—"

"But you mightn't have gone so far as to get a search warrant. There wasn't anything really suspicious about them. I still say it's like fate," said Alison. "Just think. If

287

I hadn't caught that obnoxious Miss Freeman kicking Bast, and tossed her out—if my second choice hadn't happened to be baby-sitting Betty—I wouldn't have still been looking for a nurse. And if that stray tom hadn't jumped El Señor—remind me to call the pound again tomorrow—I wouldn't have been at Dr. Stocking's at the same time as—"

"If you want to go all the way back to first causes," said Mendoza, "you could take it back to the Garden of Eden and the Tree of Knowledge. If we hadn't—mmh—collaborated to produce that pair of iron-lunged infants, we wouldn't have been in the market for Mrs. MacTaggart in the first place."

"Dear Mrs. MacTaggart," said Alison, recapping the jar of vanishing cream.

"And speaking of collaboration," said Mendoza, "are you coming to bed at all?"

"I'm coming, I'm coming," said Alison hastily, and came.

"Yes, I told you all along," said Mendoza, reaching for the lamp switch, "that all our problems would be solved by a nice knowledgeable nursemaid . . ."